'*Beginners* is infused with a smiling, Mozartean sensibility'

New York Times

'A modern-day myth of self-discovery . . . Family is redemptive and romance is not dead in this engaging story'

Guardian

By the same author

The Aerodynamics of Pork
Kansas in August
Ease
Facing the Tank
Little Bits of Baby
The Cat Sanctuary
Caesar's Wife
The Facts of Life
Dangerous Pleasures
Rough Music
A Sweet Obscurity
Friendly Fire
Notes from an Exhibition
The Whole Day Through
Gentleman's Relish

PATRICK GALE

Tree Surgery for Beginners

FOURTH ESTATE • *London*

Fourth Estate
An imprint of HarperCollins*Publishers*
77–85 Fulham Palace Road, Hammersmith, London W6 8JB

www.4thestate.co.uk
Visit our authors' blog at www.fifthestate.co.uk
Love this book? www.bookarmy.com

This Fourth Estate edition published 2009

3

First published by Flamingo in 1999

Copyright © Patrick Gale 1999, 2009

PS Section copyright © Rose Gaete 2009, except 'The Writing of *Tree Surgery for Beginners*' by Patrick Gale © Patrick Gale 2009

PS™ is a trademark of HarperCollins*Publishers* Ltd

Patrick Gale asserts the moral right
to be identified as the author of this work

A catalogue record for this book is available from the British Library

ISBN 978-0-00-730769-2

Set in Sabon by Palimpsest Book Production Limited, Grangemouth, Stirlingshire

Mixed Sources
Product group from well-managed
forests and other controlled sources
www.fsc.org Cert no. SW-COC-1806
© 1996 Forest Stewardship Council

FSC is a non-profit international organisation established to promote the
responsible management of the world's forests. Products carrying the FSC
label are independently certified to assure consumers that they come
from forests that are managed to meet the social, economic and
ecological needs of present and future generations.

Find out more about HarperCollins and the environment at
www.harpercollins.co.uk/green

For Barry Goodman

Where does the family start? It starts with a young man falling in love with a girl – no superior alternative has yet been found.

WINSTON CHURCHILL

The family you come from isn't as important as the family you're going to have.

RING LARDNER

The main cultural requirement is to form a sound branch system which will be capable of withstanding the gales, falls of wet snow and other natural calamities to which the tree will be subjected during its life.

KEITH RUSHFORTH
The Hillier Book of Tree Planting and Management

CHAPTER ONE

A noise woke Lawrence with a start. It was either the distant gunning of a car engine or a barking dog, he was too disorientated to tell which. Grimacing, he sat up and rubbed his neck. He was only thirty-two but, after a night curled on the hard seat of his pick-up truck with only a skimpy rug for cover, he felt twice that. The sun was barely up. Shivering, he slipped out of the cab and walked among the trees for a piss.

The official, tourist board view of the ancient cathedral city of Barrowcester (pronounced Brewster) was of a perfect medieval hill town rising in glorious isolation from wheaty plains and braceleted by the River Bross. From the best angle – and one only ever saw the best angle reproduced – it resembled an image of the New Jerusalem in an illuminated manuscript. In fact it was only one of a chain of interlinking hills, all of them lapped by the river, none so crowded as their famous sister but all of them inhabited. Aerial photographs and topographical maps showed the proud city as the head of a small serpent or cornering sperm. With a few exceptions, postal addresses grew less distinguished, property values less impressive, as one passed away from the principal hill. The final, least regarded hillock, the tail of the sperm, was mainly given over to Wumpett Woods, named, it was thought, after a corruption of worm-pit because the trees had sprung up on the site of an ancient plague grave and unconsecrated resting place for the city's outcasts.

It was here that Lawrence had begun his love affair with

trees. His boyhood home was two miles into the valley, on a village's edge, and he would regularly ride over to Wumpett on his bicycle, ostensibly to play with friends but actually to be alone. Perverse by nature, he liked to climb a tree which afforded a fine view *away* from the cathedral and its precincts. For him it was the carpet of wheat, winding river and vanishing motorway that suggested a future of possibilities, not the spiritual and commercial symbols of the city. A creature of habit, he always climbed the same tree and came to rest at the same point, where a forking branch provided a broad support on which he could relax without flinching at every gust of wind.

There was no great revelation. He was simply sitting up there one afternoon in spring, aged eight, when he noticed unclasping sticky buds a few inches from his nose. When he had done with examining them, he looked about him and saw, as for the first time, how the skeletal shapes rearing about him, barely touched with the year's first green, echoed the veiny patterns of the leaves they would soon unfurl. He became aware of the immense *strangeness* of organisms he had so far taken for granted; their height, their combination of hard and soft, new-born growth and ancient timber. He was not bookish, but this one afternoon fired his hunger for knowledge. With his next pocket money he bought the *Observer Book of Trees* and, in the spring and summer that followed, set about learning the names and natures of every tree that sprouted in Wumpett Woods or lay on the lane between them and his mother's house. He learned and delighted in their peculiarities, inevitably endowing them with human characteristics. The oak was sturdy, the cypress sad, the poplar pliant, the beech smooth and fresh. Yews in the graveyard were dark and secretive, harbourers of spells, absorbers of corpse juice. Planes in the cathedral close were urbane and – when he looked more closely – florid, with their pompoms of seeds and particoloured peeling bark. Horse-chestnuts were at once benign and exotic; the virtuosic variety of their display, from palmate leaves and creamy candelabra of blossom to the spike-shelled testicles of their autumn fruit, left him amazed they were not more celebrated. In time his studies took him further afield and taught him the precisions of scientific cataloguing, but Wumpett remained his primer and first catalogue of an abiding fascination.

The first walkers and joggers of the morning had arrived. As Lawrence climbed back into the cab, a dog was barking urgently. Yawning, a cavern in his belly where he had failed to eat the night before, he drove back along the road that formed the spine of the hills, then swung off onto the drive to his farmhouse. As always, the pleasure the building gave him on first sight was immediately undercut by its reminders of money he needed to spend. The paintwork on the windows was flaking. A piece of guttering over the bathroom window was coming adrift. He would soon have to get the entire north wall repointed. The Boston ivy was invading the roof and doubtless already loosening tiles.

He let himself in through the kitchen door and went directly to fill the kettle. Filling the kettle, like peering inside the fridge, checking the mail or taking a leak, was a settling, regular thing to do on returning to a house. He had only been away overnight but he felt such uncertainty in the familiar environment that he might have been gone far longer and become a stranger to the place. Its stillness seemed to challenge his right to be there. He froze, a hand on the cold tap.

There was a splash of blood, long since dried, in the sink and another, larger one on the floor below. Her head had struck the enamel rim when she fell and she had slid with a gasp to the floor and bled on the tiles down there. Shocked, he set down the kettle, snatched up a wet cloth and scrubbed. The tile stain came off easily – the tiles were relatively new and she kept them waxed. The sink was harder to clean. It was an old Belfast one, its creamy surface patterned with cracks and prone to staining by coffee-grounds or fruit juice. The surface coating of blood softened quickly and broke off swiftly as a ripened scab. Beneath it, however, blood had penetrated the cracks so that the sink appeared to have acquired veins.

He opened a cupboard, battling as usual with its toddler-proof catch, and found a bottle of thickened bleach. He poured a searing puddle of the stuff over the stain and ground it in with the vegetable brush. There was a cut on one of his fingers, where his knuckles had struck a metal button on her jacket. The bleach entered it and burned atrociously. A slender hank of her hair had snagged in the gap between sink and wooden draining-board. He teased it free and held it up in bleachy fingers. Where it had been pulled from her scalp there was a minute piece of bloodstained skin. He posted the hair into the overflow vent at the sink's side and washed his hands, leaving the bleach to soak into the porcelain.

He filled the kettle, as planned, slotted some bread into the toaster and began to lay a small tray for breakfast; a plate for toast, the big French cup she liked for her coffee. He used a small, sharp knife to peel her an orange the way she had taught him, slicing a disc through to the pith at each end then severing the remaining peel at four equal intervals, taking care not to puncture the flesh beneath, so that the four pieces could be torn off easily with his thumb.

It was seven-thirty. She was asleep still and there were no sounds of life from Lucy either. He would take Bonnie the tray, setting it on her bedside table, then retreat in humility to the armchair in the furthest corner to wait for the scents of breakfast to wake her. He would probably cry at the sight of her bruised body and the insufficiency of his apology. He could not remember when he had last wept for simple sorrow. He had shed no tears at an old school friend's death. This had maddened her, he recalled, and she had raged against his bottled-up emotions and his inability to express them.

He had parked his truck at the side of the house and had assumed her car was safely stowed in the barn beyond, but now he glanced from the window, alerted by a sudden cackle from the hutch where Lucy's bantams were stowed overnight. The barn door yawned wide and he could see that its gloomy interior was empty.

'Bonnie?' he called. 'Lucy?' and, still mopping his hands, he ran from the kitchen and into the hall. Lucy had a coat she wore incessantly at the moment, a thickly quilted thing with a curious, poppered pocket on its back where he jokingly hid a chocolate bar when they took walks together, making her laugh in her squirming effort to retrieve the treasure with the coat still on her. The coat was gone, as were the matching yellow boots and Bonnie's waxed jacket. He ran up the stairs now, calling their names again. At first he might have assumed they had merely got up early and gone out somewhere. There were clothes. There were possessions. Lucy's bed had been slept in, of course. He had tucked her in himself the previous night. The bed he shared with Bonnie, however, had not been slept in.

He saw then that certain crucial items had gone. Lucy's favourite bear. Bonnie's aviator jacket. Bonnie's jewellery box. Lucy's anti-asthma inhaler and the carton of drugs that went with it. He tugged open their bedroom wardrobe. Two suitcases had gone, one large, one small. And now that he looked again, he saw that there was a rectangular indentation on the bedspread, where she must have rested the larger case to pack it. Not all the clothes had gone, certainly, but she had taken anything of value or that she wore regularly. She had spread out what was left along the wardrobe rail, in an effort to cover her traces.

'Why?' he wondered. 'Why feel guilty?'

She had every reason to leave. Right was on her side. Then he realized that it was fear, not guilt, that made her take steps to delay his discovery of the truth.

He sat down, in shock, then stood up and checked the

sock drawer where she liked to hide a small stash of cash for emergencies. It was gone. As was her passport and their only painting of any worth – a small John Minton portrait of a young man with bare feet, bought with her down payment from McBugger. Lawrence laid a hand in disbelief on the small rectangle where the painting had prevented the yellow emulsion from fading in the scorching summer's light. Drawn inexorably back to the bedroom, the focus of loss, he tugged off his boots, crawled beneath the covers and lay there, breathing fast. After spending the night failing to sleep in the truck's harshly masculine cab, his body ached all over as though it were he, not Bonnie, who had suffered a beating.

The telephone woke him three hours later. He lay, immobilized by apprehension, watching it ring and then straining his ears to catch any message the caller might leave on the answering machine downstairs. It was John calling from the workshop to ask where the hell he was, his voice poised between peevishness and concern. There were a couple of estimates to make. One was for a felling job at the Deanery garden in Barrowcester, where a cedar planted too close to the house had cast all the garden rooms into sinister shade. Also a young widow towards Arkfield was keen to restore a nut walk now that her late husband's money was out of probate. John would go in his stead but did so with a bad grace as he had set aside the morning for updating their books and filing their VAT return. Lawrence rolled over to stare at the other wall. He was not especially fond of John and had long suspected that John did not entirely like him. This had never been a problem. On the contrary, it meant that they never socialized and so had the perfect business relationship.

The telephone rang again twice. Neither caller left a message and finally Lawrence slept. He dreamed he was being hunted through a moonlit wood by his father-in-law, who had two Dobermans and a rifle. He awoke to several more telephone calls. His mother rang, 'just for a chat darling,' John called again, angry now, and his father-in-law asked about their plans for Christmas, staking an early claim on his daughter's calendar.

From the rumbling in his stomach, Lawrence judged it to be mid-afternoon when a car drew up in the yard and someone gave the doorbell three long, insistent blasts. Then there were footsteps around the side of the house and back again, the sound of the letterbox clunking open and John's voice calling through it. Lawrence remained in silent hiding until John grew embarrassed at shouting into an apparently empty house and drove away.

As it grew dark, hunger pulled Lawrence back to the kitchen. He found bread and crushed some overripe Camembert between two slices. Eating proved a comfort – despite the unpleasant similarity between the lingering smell of bleach and the ammoniac tang of the cheese rind – and he felt able to drink a bottle of claret, which went down more easily than the cheese had done.

Fumbling in the gloom, he found the keys to the pick-up and decided to drive to the workshop to apologize to John for his absenteeism. Having omitted to turn on the lights, he backed into the flank of one of the outbuildings with a dull thud, followed by a wrenching tinkle as he cursed and pulled away. Jumping out to inspect the damage, he dropped the keys and was unable to find them in the dark. Groping in the wet gravel, he jarred a shoulder blade painfully on the corner of the open door. This sobered him up sufficiently to realize he was too drunk to drive, so he abandoned the hunt for the keys and returned to the house, where he opened a second bottle because the first had been such a comfort. Melancholy followed hard on the warmth this generated, however, and anxiety came close behind. Half-way through the second glass and the remains of the Camembert, eaten without bread, he telephoned his father-in-law, something he never did when sober.

'Charlie, it's Lawrence. How are you?'

'Lawrence? I'm fine. Are you okay? You sound a bit . . .'

'I'm fine. Fine.' Lawrence slurred the words in his effort not to. 'Charlie, I know this sounds stupid but is . . . Are Bonnie and Lucy with you?'

'No. I was just going to ask how they are. I rang earlier. Bonnie hasn't called me in weeks.'

'Oh. Well. I just wondered . . . Thanks, Charlie.'

'Lawrence? What's up?' Charlie's tone hardened.

'Nothing. We . . . We had a bit of a fight, that's all. I . . . I hurt her.'

Lawrence hung up rapidly, fumbling with the receiver and feeling slightly sick. Seconds later the telephone rang. He picked it up, heard Charlie shouting and hung up. It rang again. This time he let the answering machine take the call. Charlie ranted about what he would like to do to the man cowardly enough to hit his daughter, which portions of his anatomy he would like to sever, how he would then force-feed them to said coward before kicking his face to a pulp and breaking both his arms. He sounded unhinged. Channelled through the machine's tiny speaker in the darkened hall, his fury had nothing to feed off, however, and soon began to subside.

'Lawrence?' he called out. 'Lawrence, pick up the telephone.'

Lawrence obeyed.

'She's left me,' he said immediately. 'She took Lucy. I don't know where she's gone. I thought she might have come to you.'

'You're drunk.'

'Of course I'm drunk.'

'You're pathetic.'

'I know.'

'How *could* you, man?'

'I . . . I don't think that's why she left. She must have planned it. She went so fast. I spent the night out in the truck on Wumpett. I came back early this morning and they'd gone.'

'So why hasn't she rung me?'

'Well I dunno. Maybe she – '

'If Bonnie was in trouble, the first thing she'd do would be to ring me.'

'She's probably – '

Lawrence hung up as his father-in-law started to rant again. He lurched into the hall and tugged the answering machine cable from its socket. After a few seconds, the telephone by the bed began to ring. It rang so incessantly that Lawrence had to take refuge outside in the cab of the pick-up. He turned on the radio, curled himself in the rug and slowly passed out while a hushed stream of tearful ballads and dedications for the late-night lovelorn drained the truck's battery.

CHAPTER TWO

An uneducated, self-made man, ruler of a small, unhappy empire, Charlie Knights had always viewed his daughter with a dangerous lack of objectivity. She was his pearl without price, his princess. Swiftly eclipsed in his eyes by the child she had produced, her mother had died of cervical cancer when Bonnie was still an infant. The only woman in her father's life, at least officially, no suitor Bonnie chose could ever have pleased him, not a duke, not a film star, not a tycoon and certainly not a tree surgeon.

Bonnie was away at school when Lawrence first called on her father. There had been a gale the month before and Charlie had summoned him to see to an old oak. Perhaps a century earlier, the tree's trunk had been allowed to branch out in two directions far too early on. As a result the equivalent of two large trees now forked out, perilously flexible, from a point barely five feet from the ground. The wind had brought neither half down but had clearly weakened some central point in the great plant's structure for an ominous creaking now sounded at the slightest breath of wind.

Charlie had only bought the house a few years before. A four-square, Victorian structure, less handsome than it was imposing, the place had no family associations for him. Like many a rootless person whose money was as yet too fresh to have brought much faith in permanence, however, Charlie was obsessed with the preservation of every bush, brick and boot-scraper in his new domain. For safety's sake the oak should have been felled. It would free up a new area for planting, Lawrence pointed out, and provide valuable timber. Charlie was adamant, however, that he wanted the tree saved. Accordingly Lawrence shored up the weak fork with a steel rod, bolted at either end. A few feet higher, he braced one half of the tree to the other, using two more bolted rods held together by a short length of galvanized cable. One half now supported the other, much as though the tree had been properly trained with a single central trunk.

Charlie lacked a son, Lawrence a father, and the two men formed a watchful bond. Lawrence's interest fed Charlie's territorial pride, and Charlie asked Lawrence to tell him about the trees he owned. The previous owners had been collectors so there were some interesting exotics among the standard native varieties; a pagoda tree from Korea, a Wellingtonia already towering above the house, a smoky blue spruce, a Persian ironwood and, sheltered by the meeting of two old walls, a lovely, pure white *Magnolia campbellii*. Ever competitive, Charlie read up on the subject and, having run out of pruning for Lawrence to do, announced that he wanted to plant an arboretum. His daughter had lost interest in riding and her pony had been sold. The paddock below the house was therefore redundant space. Ordinary gardening did not interest him. He spent too much time away from home to maintain herbaceous borders. Trees appealed to him, representing, like a well-chosen unit trust, steady growth, a faith in the future and stability. A collection of trees would also shield the house from view.

Lawrence's work since he set up business after graduating from agriculture college had consisted largely of mundane pruning and felling. Like every forestry student, however, he had long nurtured a mental list of favourite trees. Charlie was the perfect client in that, having set his mind to do something, he would countenance no half-measures. No expense was too great, no specimen tree too rare. They drove to famous tree collections around the country, they pored over books and catalogues, they argued over plans.

They spent hours together. When they were away on tree hunting trips, they ate together and spent occasional nights in hotels. This was all at Charlie's expense. He also insisted that Lawrence continue to send him fortnightly invoices, charging him for his consultation and time by the hour. This began to feel awkward since they were almost friends, but when Lawrence demurred, Charlie grew quite angry and harangued him on the subject of 'good business practice'. He preferred the formal arrangement of client and consultant to the shapeless ambivalence of mere friendship. He preferred tabulated covenant to simple trust.

By the time Bonnie returned from her last term at school, the paddock was unrecognizable. Turf had been lifted and rolled up, and a large mass of earth had been moved to change the existing slope to the Bross into three distinct shelves of land, secured with stones from a collapsed dry-stone wall and the pony's demolished stable. Charlie hated to see his daughter idle and thought the other bored rich of the area a potential bad influence on her so he encouraged her to assist Lawrence. Used to obeying him, she donned old clothes and fell to with a spade, helping Lawrence dig holes, lugging buckets of water from the river, holding each sapling steady while he fastened it by straps to the double stakes he had malleted into the ground on either side.

The immediate impression Lawrence gained of her was one of good health and an intimidating cheerfulness. Still confident of being liked by all who met her, she seemed younger than her eighteen years. She wore her blonde hair long, straight down her back. When it threatened to bother her, she tied it tightly back into a ponytail, which made her seem younger still. She talked incessantly, asking him a stream of impertinent, intrusive questions about himself, his family, his boyhood. Did he have a girlfriend, she asked. Well why not? Was there something wrong with him? Never having had a sister, he did not know to win her respect by teasing her. Her being a valued client's daughter complicated their relationship further, so that he came to treat her as the master's irritating but precious spaniel that must be humoured however much one longed to kick it. She talked on regardless, even when his mind was clearly intent on his work. She talked, with the unabashed egotism of the very young, of herself, her friends, her enemies, her ambitions, all in peculiarly tedious detail, evidently impervious to the lengths of time in which he said nothing to break her flow. Her mind was so much faster than his, her tongue so much readier, that the verbal assault battered him into a numb submission and when Charlie asked, in her absence, if she was proving a pain in the arse, he heard himself say no, not at all, quite the contrary.

He was planting the final tree, a catalpa, already several years old so cruelly expensive. Digging down, he had found a mass of old stones, flags perhaps of some long forgotten building. Removing them to make a clear root run, he unearthed a layer of foundations. When Bonnie came back from watering the other saplings, she found him up to his ears in a moist pit, struggling to loosen the last stone. She jumped eagerly in to help him. They scrabbled until their fingers were sore and eventually rocked the piece of limestone free from the greedy clay. They heaved the lump clear of the pit mouth then slumped, laughing with exhaustion like a pair of sodden gravediggers. Then she kissed him, impulsively, grinding the back of his head into the earth. Giggling breathlessly at his astonished efforts to brush her off, she pulled his belt open and began tugging on his flies. It was nearly a year since he had last had sex and she was determined; inquisitive as a Brownie, insistent as a nurse. They made brisk, unpolished love on the floor of the pit. Her determination overpowered his nervousness about her father and he was shocked when she cried out and he saw, too late, that she had been a virgin. She hastily pulled her dungarees back on, kissed him once more, laughing in her throat as she smeared a muddy streak across his ear and cheek, then she used him as a ladder to clamber up out of the hole, and was gone as suddenly as she had arrived.

Labouring on in a daze, he managed to plant the catalpa on his own then washed his face and hands in the icy stream. He knocked at the back door, hoping to tell Charlie that the work was finished and to come to some arrangement about returning to make occasional inspections of the trees' growth rate and fastenings. There was no reply however and although dusk had fallen, the house was all in darkness. The next day, his telephone calls were rebuffed by an answering machine. The day after that he received a cheque and curt payment slip.

In full and final settlement, Charlie's secretary had typed. *Mr Knights thanks you for your services, which will no longer be required.*

In the five years that followed, Lawrence neither saw nor heard anything of the Knightses beyond his mother saying that the hairdresser in Barrowcester had told her that Charlie had almost lost his left hand in a nasty car crash, poor man, and that Bonnie had gone away to university in the south somewhere.

Helped, undoubtedly, by the contacts he had formed during his spell as Charlie's personal tree surgeon, Lawrence's business thrived and he went into partnership with John at the suggestion of their mutual accountant. He had a half-hearted affair with a girl called Lindy, who drank to excess, but neither was prepared to take responsibility for their lack of commitment. Over two sad years he returned fewer and fewer of her calls, and she was later and later for their every rendezvous until one day she failed to turn up altogether. He made enough money to buy a small cottage on an estate that was being broken up and sold off.

On returning from a short holiday he found that, in his absence, John had taken a call from Bonnie Knights and booked him in for some consultancy work with her. She had set up as a landscape gardener, apparently, and needed his expertise on a local project. Had he, not John, taken the call, he would have found some excuse to duck out of the booking or send John in his place. She was adamant that she wanted him, however, so he swallowed his embarrassment and drove over to the site, determined to do his job with concise professionalism then leave. After all, he told himself, she had as much cause for discomfort as he did, possibly more.

She had transformed herself from the gauche thing he remembered. She had cut her hair short and permed it into loose ringlets so that her face now looked as soft as her name. She had cast aside the jeans and dungarees of her teens for skirts, so that she appeared miraculously to have acquired hips and ankles. She pecked him on the cheek, which was unexpected, and introduced him to the client, one of the sons of the idle rich whose bad influence her father had feared and with whom she was, plainly, romantically involved. There was a good month's work. The old trees which lined the house's deceptive, winding approach had received no attention in decades and Bonnie wanted to reinstate an earlier coach drive whose avenue had been felled to provide floor timbers after a devastating fire. No mention was made of her father and she was either too well mannered or bashful to allude to the muddy encounter in their past. Relieved, Lawrence accepted the commission and set to work with ropes, harness and saws.

It became swiftly apparent that she believed she was reshaping the gardens of her future home. It also became cruelly plain that the rich and idle client took a less romantic view and, if his numerous trips to London without her were any proof, was using her landscaping commission as a heartless means of easing her out of his little black book. Whenever the client was away, which was more often than not, she would press Lawrence into joining her at the local pub for lunch. She was loquacious as ever, still hedging him round with words, but his slower perception had caught what her fleeter one had missed, so as she chatted of we this and we that, he sorrowed for her. Pity warmed to interest and he found himself slowly falling in love with her in a way he would never have done had she been paying him any more direct attention than using him as a sounding board.

When Lawrence was half-way through planting the new avenue, the client dropped her in the nastiest way possible, driving a new girlfriend down to stay with him and introducing Bonnie to her as though she were some quaint hired help.

'Well I'm not going back if you're not,' Lawrence told her over lunch.

'I can't afford to keep paying you if he doesn't pay me,' she warned.

'So? Buy you another drink?'

By the time her second, vengeful pint had been downed, Bonnie seemed actually to notice him for the first time since their reunion. Whereas before he had balked at her questioning, giving the shortest answers possible, now he found himself eager to tell her everything, about his mother, the dead father he had never known, his failure to shine at school and the revelation that he liked and could understand trees. He babbled about the tree he used to climb in Wumpett Woods, he explained bark to her and tried to convey the thrill of working high under the whispering canopy of an ancient beech or horse chestnut, with only a rope between exhilaration and a back-breaking fall. With hindsight, he guessed that she kissed him in the pub, where she and the client had been regulars, as an act of aggressive retribution, wanting to be seen and reported on. At the time, he believed his words had moved her and this lent him the courage to drive her back to the cottage where she spent the next three days.

Charlie Knights raged and blustered but there was nothing he could do short of disinheriting his only child and he doted on her too much for that. He tried to lure her away with an offer of work in Australia but she laughed at him. He tried to buy Lawrence off but Lawrence tore the cheque in two and hung it, framed, on his workshop wall. If Charlie had done nothing but indulge them, the affair might have run its short and shallow course. It was a liaison based on nothing stronger than sex on Lawrence's side and anger and frustrated ambition on Bonnie's and, unfuelled, would have devoured itself in time. Charlie's strenuous efforts to abort it, however, caused the lovers to entrench. In particular, his rejection of Lawrence caused Bonnie defiantly to seek out every ounce of her lover's worth. Defending him, she came to love him, believing that his unsophisticated devotion was a finer thing than the temporary shelter for which she had first commandeered it.

Once she became pregnant, Charlie abandoned all faith in severing them and set out instead on a pragmatic accommodation with his disappointed hopes and unsatisfactory son-in-law. Broking a grumbling peace, he discovered he had underestimated Lawrence's background. Lawrence's uncle was a wealthy if effete businessman and his mother a still glamorous widow of some means with all the brittle poise of a frustrated actress. Charlie was charmed by her and slightly awed. He made a pass at her on their third meeting, which she graciously overlooked. She had already welcomed Bonnie with open arms and, as the marriage approached, shamed Charlie into an approximation of the same for her cherished only son.

What neither parent knew was that the pregnancy was not a crude cause of obligation. When Bonnie first announced it to Lawrence, his initial, secret reaction was panic. Their defiant idyll, already losing its charm, seemed suddenly a disguised trap. His reaction was less than ecstatic and, when this prompted her to say that of course she 'would not go through with it', his heart leaped with a sense of reprieve and he guiltily agreed. He would break with her, he decided, as soon as a decent interval had passed; one month, six weeks at the most. She was the enthusiastic type. She loved easily. She would mend and live to love again and more appropriately. He would escape.

That night, however, he woke to find her crying in the dark and she confessed that it would be the second child of his she had aborted. Their very first encounter had left her pregnant and her father had insisted on an abortion.

'It's like – It's like a second chance,' she stammered. Despairing, he proposed marriage several times in the course of the night, growing bolder with her every, tearfully heroic, refusal. Astonished at how easy it was going to be to play a noble role and still duck his responsibilities with something approaching honour, he proposed once too often however. Just when he thought she had sighed herself to tearful sleep, she accepted. Dawn was colouring the room about them and Bonnie wept as he made horrified love to her.

As a boy he had no intimate acquaintance with married life. His mother was a widow, his uncle, Darius, an apparently loveless bachelor. He was aware that Darius could fill the public aspects, at least, of the fatherly and husbandly roles. When the two of them hosted a birthday party for him or attended, with world-weary picnic or too-elegant clothes, a sports day or a school play, he was aware that they were play-acting. Marriage, it seemed, was a light thing one could assume with soft mockery and discard at will, a simple matter of form and observance. His mother had been married – was still married in a sense, in that the mere word *widow* would instantly summon up the dead husband, as if she carried him, reduced, about her person like a discreet piece of jewellery or a love token. And yet beyond this, the condition seemed to have left her unmarked by grief or regret. Her marriage was a memory of which Lawrence was the sole significance. Both mother and uncle unconsciously spoke of couples with a tone of teasing patronage, as of children. She regularly entertained married men without their wives and his social life tended to revolve around married women without their husbands. It was not surprising, therefore, if Lawrence approached marriage with little respect for the institution, or real understanding of the burden of commitment he was about to shoulder. Marriage, he felt, was less an activity than something which merely happened to one, like the automatically happy ending of a fairy tale.

Indeed, in the weeks after he proposed to Bonnie, it did seem to be something that had happened to him, as external as a birthday celebration or a burst water pipe. He had merely asked the question and received the answer and was suddenly, irreversibly, on the other side of an invisible barrier. It was as if he had been thrust through a looking-glass; his life looked much the same but everything in it had changed, its values, its purpose, its future. He could no longer drift, no longer do only as he liked. For the first time since leaving home, he was subject to the padded rule of domestic democracy. He sold the cottage and together they purchased a larger farmhouse.

Everyone, even Charlie Knights, once Lawrence's mother had corrected his initial reaction, conspired to celebrate the young couple's love.

'You must be so happy,' people told Lawrence. 'She's quite a catch.'

Even worse, they would stand back to talk about him in the third person.

'Ah, you can tell he's walking in the clouds. Just look at him!'

And he would realize with a sudden dread that his impending nuptials had people talking of him in the same infantilizing fashion his uncle and mother reserved for married couples.

Of course, to announce that he was *not* happy was impossible. To declare to the fatuously smiling faces that he did *not* love Bonnie, that now that he was to be bound to her by law and public recognition, the mere proximity of her would cause a kind of panic in him, would be an outrage to the cult of love, still more to propriety. Borne with him to visit her relatives and college friends, her favourite shops for baby clothes and kitchenware, his secret felt as reprehensible as murder. Always so cool in matters of the heart, so pragmatic when discussing other people's domestic arrangements, his mother could have saved him with a few sharp questions, but she swiftly became chief celebrant of the match, designer of floral tributes, chooser of bridesmaids. She welcomed her daughter-in-law and sloughed off her son in a single complex psychological manoeuvre which left him feeling betrayed, as if all the years of tender motherhood had been a mere show or, worse, a kind of warm-up act for the star turn played by the first candidate to meet with her voracious approval.

Only his Uncle Darius appeared not to be fooled. At least, only Darius voiced his doubts. Sadly he left this far too late. Sensing Lawrence's horror of stag nights, he spirited him up to London for one last evening *à deux* two nights before the wedding. He bought Lawrence a set of six botanical engravings to hang on his dining room walls.

'These are not a wedding present,' he said. 'You know I abhor the practice of confounding the individual within the mere domestic unit. These are a present for *you*.'

He took him to the theatre, to see a cruel French farce, then on to dinner. Cracking the claw of a steaming half-lobster, he fixed Lawrence with his most searching stare and said,

'You do know nothing in life is fixed. No arrangement short of disability or death, need be final. Marriage is an economic convenience and a shelter for children, nothing more. If you're only doing this because she's pregnant, think again. I can see that the child is provided for. Everyone would understand, even your mother.'

Lawrence felt his cheeks burn so hot that tears of intimidation welled in the corners of his eyes.

'No,' he stammered, and tried to laugh. 'I . . . I do understand. And thanks, Darius. But I love her. I really love her.'

Darius searched his face once more then apologized briskly and plunged a skewer into the lobster claw. By rights, a cockerel should have crowed but there was merely a gasp and a small rush of flame at a nearby table where someone had ordered a nostalgic steak *Diane*. For a few pitiful seconds, Lawrence felt a child's naive assumption that his pain could be divined and cured without his saying a thing. Then he perceived that Darius had retreated from him, twitching spiritual skirts clear of such palpable cowardice as he left him to his fate.

CHAPTER THREE

Lawrence woke in the small hours, bitterly cold, and returned to his bed for the rest of the night. In the morning he was surprisingly clear-headed. Appalled at having lost a day, he dressed, snatched breakfast, fed the ravenous bantams and set them loose in the garden, jump-started the pick-up and drove into work. John's understandable indignation was swiftly stifled.

'Look, I'm sorry I messed you around, but Bonnie left me yesterday and she took Lucy and I was in a bit of a state.'

At once John was all concern. Where had she gone? Had she telephoned? Had he got enough to eat? Did he want to move out to his place for a few nights? This was just what Lawrence needed because it enabled him to sweep aside all enquiries and re-establish his authority. There was work to be done and he would do it. Work had sustained him before he had met her, it would bear him up now that she had gone.

He rang his mother on the mobile telephone during his lunch break.

'I know,' she said. 'Her father told me. He rang to ask if I was hiding her. Darling, are you alright? Well of course you're not but – Oh. Oh darling how could you be so *stupid*!' She started to cry then so he hung up. She did not call back but his Uncle Darius rang an hour later. Lawrence was half-way up a cedar of Lebanon when he took the call.

'I won't say I'm sorry,' Darius said, 'because that's pointless. I just thought you should know, Charlie Knights has been ringing all sorts of people. I think he's trying to stir up trouble. I thought you should know, that's all. Call me if I can do anything.'

Working helped. Lawrence had always found reassurance in the application of specific knowledge. When he drove the pick-up home in late afternoon, his limbs were pleasantly weary from the juddering of the chain saw and shredder, his hands sore from scraping on bark, his cheeks tight from cold air. His thick hair was peppered with wood chips. The cab and his work clothes were permeated with the resinous tang of sawdust, a scent Bonnie had once claimed to find intensely arousing. They would often make love when each had just returned from work, when their hair smelled of outdoors, their nails were grimy and their bodies exhausted before they began.

There was a car in the yard. As he drew near, its doors opened and a stocky woman and a younger man emerged, scattering the scavenging bantams. She was not in uniform and did not flash her police identity card until he came closer, but her confident, world-weary bearing betrayed her.

'Mr Lawrence Frost?'

'Yes?'

'Detective Inspector Faithe.'

Confused, he offered her his dusty hand. Hers was cold, ringless and dry, its grasp assertively firm. Standing back, her colleague stared at him in silent impudence.

'Could we come in for a minute?'

'Er. Of course.'

'It won't take long. Just something we wanted cleared up.'

She was not local. Her accent was Cockney. Although she could not have been more than forty-something, her face was craggy with tension lines. He wondered if she had transferred to a rural division because of stress. He led them into the kitchen and saw her glance at the neglected washing-up, the vase of wilting roses, the empty wine bottles, the savaged, rapidly staling, loaf of bread. As they sat down at the table and he reached to pull out a chair as well, he found that his hands were shaking. Authority figures, even nurses and traffic wardens, always made him nervous; he had often been in trouble as a boy.

'Mind if I smoke?'

'Be my guest.'

Faithe produced a cigarette which her colleague hastily lit for her. Lawrence noticed that she had a scar on one cheek, puckered from where a wound had been too tightly stitched. She dragged deep on the cigarette and exhaled slowly then reached into her pocket for a small portable ashtray whose black enamelled lid she flipped open with casual expertise. Lawrence warmed to her. He liked people who relished their pleasures.

'We had a visit from your father-in-law this morning,' she said. 'He was in quite a state. He wanted us to register your wife and daughter as missing persons. Nothing wrong with that, only it's rather strange to hear from the father and not the husband. When did you last see her?'

'The night before last.'

The colleague took notes while Faithe tapped her cigarette on the ashtray brim.

'Did she announce any intention of going away?'

'No.'

'Do you know where she is?'

'No. We . . .'

'Yes?'

'We had an argument. A bad argument. And I left her here, with Lucy – that's our daughter. I was angry and thought I should make myself scarce. I drove for a bit and spent the night in my truck.'

'Where?' she asked, apparently without interest.

'In Wumpett Woods. I often take Lucy there for walks at weekends. There's a car park. I spent the night in the car park.'

Faithe minutely raised an eyebrow. She stubbed out her cigarette half-smoked.

'Trying to give up and failing miserably,' she muttered then suddenly turned her candid grey eyes on him.

'How bad an argument was it?'

'Bad. I . . . accused her of having an affair. With a client of hers. She's a landscape gardener.'

'I know.'

'She denied it. She was very angry.'

'Was Lucy with you?'

'No. She was in bed.'

'Did you hit your wife, Mr Frost?'

'No.'

There was a pause.

'Did you hit her, Mr Frost?' Faithe asked again. 'Mr Knights seemed to think you had, but maybe he's prone to exaggeration.'

'Yes,' he sighed, avoiding her stare. 'Well, I *pushed* her. Just once. I sort of shoved her and she fell back against the sink. Then I was frightened of what I might do. I was still angry. It scared me. That was why I left.'

'And presumably why she did . . . ?'

'Yes. I came back the next morning at about seven. She had gone and taken Lucy with her. Her car was gone and some clothes and things. She didn't leave a note.'

'I see. And you've no idea where she might have gone?'

Lawrence paused.

'She'd hate me for saying this . . . I mean, it's why we had the fight . . .'

'Why you hit her, you mean.'

'Yes . . . Can I get you a drink?' Lawrence was gasping for a glass of wine. He could see the unopened bottles in their box beside the fridge.

'Not when we're on duty, thanks. You were saying where you thought she'd gone.'

'Oh. Yes.' He wished he had never begun to tell them.

He knew now that Bonnie had been entirely innocent. The policeman paused in his scribbling and looked up from his pad accusingly. 'She has a client, an American architect. He designed a hall of residence for the university and hired her to do the garden. He's been staying off and on at the Gladstone.'

'And she's having an affair with him?'

'No. Christ. Maybe. It's what I thought.'

'But she may be with him in any case?'

'She might. She might just have gone to ground some-where. She might be with old friends. Isn't it a bit early to go putting her on a missing persons list?'

'Mr Knights seemed to think there was a special urgency. Don't you want to know where she is?'

'Well of course I do!' he shouted so that Detective Inspector Faithe jumped slightly. 'Sorry,' he said. 'Of course I want to know, but I don't think I'm likely to hear from her for some time. A week. Maybe longer.'

'Has she walked out on you before, then?'

'Never.'

'So how do you know?'

'She's my wife. I know how she is.'

'This architect – '

'McBugger.'

'Sorry?'

'He's called McBride. Craig McBride.'

'You got his number?'

'No but you can ask at the Gladstone. He's the kind of man who leaves contact numbers with everyone he meets. He assumes the world and his wife are just aching to call him.'

Hearing the anger that was boiling up unbidden, Faithe rose and her partner followed suit.

'Yes, well, that's all for now. Thanks for your time, Mr Frost. You going to be around, then, for a few days?'

'Sure.' Lawrence nodded, puzzled, watching them go. 'I'm going nowhere.'

As they drove off, he opened a bottle of claret.

Craig McBride. Drinking, Lawrence pictured the man, his mature poise, his easy plausibility. He looked like a film star, too old to play romantic leads yet strong enough a presence to carry a Western on his own rugged merits. He walked with his feet slightly turned out and his thighs splayed, as though a horse had just spent some hours between them.

'He's ridiculously good-looking,' Bonnie had exclaimed after their first meeting. 'He looks as if he's carved from granite. That chin!'

The chin did indeed have a Kirk Douglas cleft in it, not a feature one often saw in England luckily. The bugger, the McBugger, had contacted her through a former client. She returned from meeting him full of enthusiasm, not just because the commission meant good money and probably some magazine coverage, but because, Lawrence guessed, she had begun to feel herself mired in a provincial rut and this new client represented contact with a wider, more exciting sphere.

He strove to be happy for her. He *was* happy. Things had been almost good between them recently. He had learned that he was threatened by her assertiveness and her ambition and the knowledge was protecting him. He was able to see the absurd posturing his fear represented. In turn she had learned to move at his slower pace sometimes, not to badger him with slippery speeches.

Lucy too had lived up to her name, illuminating their relationship by her mere presence and changing them both irreversibly. When she was a baby he had felt helpless with her, unable to satisfy her, maddened by her crying jags. As soon as she began to stagger about the house, however, as soon as she began to laugh, he was captivated by her. She had a bewilderingly developed character for so immature a creature. At times she was less child than goblin. She would mimic him and laugh. She imitated her mother, her grand-mother, the telephone. Her round face, with her mother's piercing blue eyes, was remarkably flexible. Meeting a dog, a cat, a pony, a cow, she stood in heavy breathing silence then worked up a passable imitation of their expression before startling them away with her mischievous laugh. The first time she fell asleep on his lap and he felt the trusting weightiness of her as she subsided against him, he knew himself her abject slave and arrived at a fresh sympathy with his similarly besotted father-in-law. He had only heard how infants deprived husbands of their wives, not how gratitude for the joy of them could rekindle a husband's waning affection.

McBugger took the two of them out to dinner in Barrowcester to 'welcome Bonnie on board' as he put it. He was, indeed, charm itself, with such hackneyed good-guy looks that it would have been perverse not to trust him on sight. Lawrence was used to clients of Bonnie's dismissing him as just a tree surgeon, a mere technician, with no creative spirit. If McBride neglected anyone that evening, however, it was Bonnie. He wanted to know all about Lawrence. Why, given every opportunity, had he chosen this particular field? He wanted to know about trees, why they were shaped the way they were, why they lived so long, where they had come from, and whether they had evolved much over the millennia. Lawrence found himself digging up knowledge he had not needed since his last bout of exams. He was uncomfortable at having to talk so much and grateful when Bonnie at last swung the conversation back to herself and her plans for the university project. Resuming his usual bystander's role, he watched her enthusiasm and was able to see that McBride heralded a new stage in their relationship. She would travel further afield for work. She might rely on him increasingly to care for Lucy. It was likely that she would use him professionally less and less. He saw all this and astonished himself by accepting it with equanimity. As her eyes shone with wine and chatter, he found he could be glad for her success. He did not need to control her, to bring her down. He could even bc grateful to McBride, not for taking her off his hands exactly, but for taking up the slack in his own attentions to her.

As the weeks passed however, and she spent hours hunched over the telephone and plant lists at her drawing board, his trust curdled. Her every other word was Craig. Craig says this. Craig says that. Craig thinks. Craig believes.

'Be calm,' he told himself, taking Lucy for a long walk around Wumpett Woods. 'He's old enough to be her father. He's clever in a way her father isn't. He's a match for Charlie. This is a necessary stage. This is good for her. And the downgrading of the father-in-law can only be good for the husband.'

But then McBride began to come to their house – which of course he admired but began immediately to replan – for suppers, lunches, long afternoons while Lawrence was out at work, long weekends at which he was all too present. He wooed Lucy with presents and his big, rangy charm. During one of the weekends when McBride had invaded the spare room and taken over the bathroom with his razor, his contact lens paraphernalia, his alien smells, his high design clutter, Charlie invited them all to his house for Sunday lunch. Inevitably this led to a stroll around the maturing arboretum. Walking behind with Lucy, who insisted on keeping slow company with Megan, Charlie's old, scent-obsessed Doberman, he watched the other three striding on ahead, pointing and talking, always talking. Charlie slapped McBride on the back to emphasize some point he was making, Bonnie smiled and Lawrence saw that this was the man she should have married, the man who could match her father and wrest her fairly from him.

He began to watch her. He counted her smiles obsessively, mentally tabulating how many she gave him, how many McBride. He watched for physical contact like a hawk. He did not need to watch long. McBride was freely tactile, with men as with women. Lawrence's jealousy built up like a store of festering matter behind a stretching skin, until he had to speak or be utterly poisoned. A stranger to diplomacy, he blurted out his suspicions one evening. She responded with a torrent of outraged mockery. He slapped the table top to silence her and sent a plate flying. The plate was a wedding present, one of her favourites, one he had always disliked, which did not help matters greatly. He apologized, of course, made profuse, even tearful amends, but a part of her withdrew from him and would not be appeased. The next time he saw McBride, the American eyed him warily and Lawrence knew she had told him. This only made matters worse since it confirmed at least some level of collusion between the two of them.

He was powerless. He was not her jailer. He had to go out to work each day. Lucy went to nursery in the morning and was picked up by a childminder in the afternoon. Bonnie was at liberty from nine till five, to go where she chose, speak to whoever she pleased. As part of her job, she certainly spoke to, or saw McBride every day. In his quieter moments, Lawrence could understand the American's psychological appeal for her – his confidence, his maturity, his flattering attention. The man had never seen her in awkward youth and accepted unreservedly the adult professional and capable mother she had become.

What Lawrence could not understand or abide was the thought of them in a sexual context. For all the fluctuations in his emotional investment, sex was the one area in which his marriage had rarely wavered. Conscious of the age gap between them, he kept himself in good shape. He refused to let his stamina slide even when parenthood threatened to take its toll on them both. He made her satisfaction a point of pride, determined to respond to her every whim, never to have a headache or be too tired. He would spend half an hour with his face between her legs even as she whimpered to be allowed to sleep. All this care sprang naturally from desire, but also from watchfulness against the appeal of rivals her own age. The six years between them had seemed at times such a terrible threat, and yet here she was involved with a man more than two decades her senior. Scalded by his curiosity, he became as obsessed with McBride as she and determined he must be hung like a donkey, have the stamina of an eighteen-year-old, or both. He had powerfully erotic dreams in which he stood with a small crowd to watch Bonnie and the American overpowered by desire, rutting in a public space. The extent of her duplicity astonished him. She continued to make love with him at night as though McBride had not been servicing her all afternoon, still mounting a pretty show of desire. Sometimes he played along, treating her body as the arena where he and the American could blatantly compete for her favour. He would will her to prefer him, love her into submission. At others it was more than he could bear, especially if he had been drinking. He fancied he smelled the other man's traces on her skin.

The thought of another man desiring and possessing her cruelly reawakened the desire he had been fabricating for so long that even he had begun to be taken in. He grew hard merely at the sound of her voice on the telephone. When she leaned over his shoulders as he sat at the kitchen table or when he sat beside her as she drove, he felt an immoderate desire to paw and kiss her. He returned to the warm shores of love but she was stranded on the ice floes of disenchanted marriage and finding his handling and touching her offensively possessive, would shrug off his touch in irritation. A part of her welcomed his renewed attentions, perhaps, but she was angered at his lousy timing, then angered further at her inability to respond to them in kind.

On the night of their last disastrous confrontation, he had brought her home an extravagant bouquet of pink roses and the ingredients for dinner. It was the anniversary not of their wedding, which he mentally discounted as inherently unromantic, but of their first, spontaneous lovemaking in the pit in her father's garden. He had planned it all like a lovesick swain, knowing she was on a site visit at the new university and not due back until seven. He picked up Lucy from Sian, the childminder, and encouraged her to draw Mummy a waxy happy anniversary picture with crayons while he arranged the flowers in a vase and prepared dinner. He gave Lucy her supper, bathed her, put her to bed, read her a story. He bathed himself and dressed up – or as up as his basic wardrobe allowed – then waited. Seven came and went, as did eight then nine. While dinner slowly dried out, he drank the wine he had left to breathe and blew out the candles before they burned down entirely.

By the time the telephone rang, he was taut with nerves and had convinced himself her car had crashed and it was the police or casualty department calling. It was McBride, ruggedly charming as ever but perhaps less plausible than usual.

'Oh hi, Lawrence. It's Craig.'

'Hello.'

'Hi. Just to let you know Bonnie's on her way home finally. We ended up working so late I insisted she let me buy her dinner and she clean forgot to ring you to say don't wait. She asked me to give you a call in case you were worried. I said I was sure you'd have eaten hours ago and be watching TV with a beer by now but, well, you know how she gets. Always convinced she's putting people out. You have eaten haven't you?'

'Oh yes,' Lawrence assured him, his mouth dry from the wine. 'Hours ago.'

He hung up and tried to eat but anger made it hard to swallow and the meat seemed to dry out and expand in his mouth as he chewed it. He pushed the food aside and brooded. It had been dark for hours. The site visit could not have gone on so very late. She had already arranged for him to collect Lucy but it was entirely out of character for her to come home past the child's bedtime without calling, less to speak to him than to say goodnight to her. Even if they had been in a restaurant, she would have slipped away from the table after placing her order, to make the quick duty call. But she had not been in a restaurant. McBride might have lured her to the hotel with the suggestion of a meal but they had gone directly to his bed and stayed there. He pictured her efficiently combing her hair and brushing out the wrinkles in her dress as he dialled the number, then hissing to him.

'No. *You* speak to him. Say I'm already on my way home,' pictured McBride wincing as she riskily nuzzled his shoulder as he spoke the agreed lie to her husband. He splashed the last of the wine into his glass and imagined her daintily crouching over the hotel bidet, dabbing at herself with one hand, clutching a small, white towel in the other.

She was charmed by the roses, aghast at his romantic gesture, appalled by her forgetfulness.

'Eat it anyway,' he said, uncorking a second bottle. 'You must be hungry.'

'Didn't Craig ring?'

'Yes. But still . . .'

'I'm stuffed,' she said ruefully.

'What did you eat?'

'Oh . . . Little smoked salmon parcels with mousse inside,' she improvised expertly. 'Veal cordon bleu. Lots of creamy potatoes. You know. Hotel food.' He watched her eyes flick, uncontrollably, to the roast chicken, however. He knew she was ravenous, worn out by lovemaking. He saw her swallow and imagined the guilty spittle on her tongue. 'Oh but it smells so *good*!' she sighed. 'Maybe just a bit of skin. I can't resist.' And she tore off a large hank of skin. It left a trickle of fat on her chin, which she dabbed away with one of the napkins he had laid out in honour of the occasion.

'Have a potato with it,' he had said. 'Or a drumstick.'

Padding into the downstairs loo on his way up to bed, he

trod on something hard. He flicked on the light and was disgusted to see there was more dried blood in here which he had not cleaned up. It was splashed across the small washbasin. There was some on the floor and more on the rim of the lavatory pan. Whatever he had trodden on had snagged in the wool of his sock. He picked it out and held it up to the light. Assuming it to be a chip of gravel that had worked its way inside his boot, he was disturbed to see that it was a chunk of tooth, a canine with a slightly ragged point. He stuffed it in the pocket of his cords and fought off the urge to whimper as he scrubbed at the blood with a sponge.

CHAPTER FOUR

In the post the following morning there was still no word from Bonnie. As was her wont occasionally, his mother had sent a postcard for Lucy. It was a reproduction of a naïve nineteenth-century painting of a greyhound asleep by a fire.

> *Dear Lucy*, it said. *I think this dog is dreaming about rabbits, don't you? It's your birthday soon so let Mummy know what you want and I'll see what I can do! Lots and lots of love, darling. Granny.*

He read the card through twice. His mother had taken care to write large and round, even though the child was still too young to read much. He missed Lucy unspeakably. It came over him in a great, grey wave of melancholy. The house was so quiet without her subversive laughter, her galumphing shouts of triumph, her fearless mockery.

Snatching at a possibility, he ran to the telephone and called the nursery. There was a slim chance Bonnie had called them with an explanation of her absence or even a new telephone number. The teacher said only how much the silence had worried her, however. Was Lucy ill? He told her no, but Lucy and her mother had gone away on a trip. He was sorry not to have called earlier, he said, but he forgot. He then rang the childminder in the neighbouring village, with less hope in his heart and received much the same reaction. Sian was a great talker and was just settling in for a gossip when he cut her short.

'Sorry, Sian,' he said 'I've got visitors.'

He watched through the hall window as two police cars drove up from the lane and parked in front of the house.

Detective Inspector Faithe had returned with a small team of subordinates this time. She produced a slip of official paper as Lawrence stepped out to meet her.

'I've a warrant to search your house, Mr Frost. Sorry. Were you just leaving?'

'I've got to go to work. What the – ?'

Her subordinates, all in plain clothes, filed past him into the house.

'As I say, I have a warrant.'

'You can't do this.'

'Oh but we can. Have you heard from Mrs Frost at all?'

'No. What *is* this?'

He followed her into the hall. A woman was crouching in the downstairs lavatory taking flash photographs. A young man, not more than nineteen, had slipped the kitchen floor-cloth into a plastic evidence bag. A woman in latex gloves was picking through the contents of the cutlery drawer. A man emerged from outside clutching the chain saw from the back of the pick-up. There were heavy footsteps overhead. In seconds, it seemed, the house was being methodically and evenly ransacked. Lawrence slumped into a kitchen chair. He felt sick. It was one of those rare occasions when his mother's presence might have been a comfort.

'I'll call my solicitors,' he said weakly. 'This is . . . This is . . .' He realized that, although in theory it was an outrage, it actually felt as though supernatural justice were being meted out, as though a man with a loft full of stolen jewels were accused of stealing a necklace he had never seen before.

'We're just eliminating you from our enquiries,' Faithe assured him. 'It's very bad luck, of course, but a lot of the circumstantial evidence points to you.'

'What evidence?'

'Apart from the fact that you called your daughter's nursery this morning and told them she and your wife had "gone on a trip"? Well you were there, Mr Frost.'

'Where?'

'Wumpett Woods.'

'I often go there.'

'You were there for several hours on the night she was killed.'

'Who?'

Faithe looked away at her colleagues filling boxes with their small plastic bags of household miscellany as one of them typed out an inventory on a laptop computer. She smiled minutely.

'That's what we're trying to establish.'

'Ma'am,' a woman called. 'Come and look at this.'

Faithe stood to confer with a detective who had come downstairs clutching the piece of tooth Lawrence had slipped into his cords pocket last night, sealed in a bag. He had left the trousers on a bedroom chair and this morning put on jeans.

'Mr Frost, I must ask you to come with me to the station,' she said and turned to him, her worn face still a laconic mask, her eyes seeming more wintry than ever. 'You need to answer some questions.'

The strangest thing about Faithe was the way she could proceed in her interrogation without once implying that she thought he had done anything wrong. He had broken the law, of course, by murdering his wife, and possibly his child, but she implied not one ounce of personal opprobrium.

'It's a free world,' she seemed to be saying. 'You do your thing. I do mine. It's just bad luck that we've caught you at it.'

As the gruelling day progressed, marked out in cups of coffee and extremely frightening interludes when she muttered into the tape recorder, 'DI Faithe left the room,' leaving her male subordinate to shout and snarl and hurl abuse, Lawrence gained the unmistakable impression that she actually liked him.

A violently dismembered female body had been found in Wumpett Woods. Even as he scrubbed Bonnie's blood off the floor and laid her breakfast tray, a jogger's collie was excitedly digging up layers of leaf mould and newly turned earth, only returning to its horrified owner once it had secured the charred remains of a human hand. Cause of death was hard to ascertain but, judging from tissue and bone damage, the pathologist thought the woman had died from two blows to the head; one to the front, one to the side. The teeth had been smashed in with some blunt instrument and the clothes removed and hidden elsewhere. The body had been laid in a grave in a clearing in the wood, then set on fire with paraffin until all distinguishing external features had been obliterated. Corruption had barely set in.

As well as Bonnie's tooth the house search had revealed traces of her blood around the kitchen sink and downstairs lavatory. Her blood type – not a rare one – matched that of the body. The hank of hair was retrieved from the sink overflow. All these Lawrence could explain, through his tears, as evidence not of murder but of an accidental fall at the height of a vicious argument.

'I didn't kill her.'

'Where'd you put Lucy? Is she in the wood too? We've got dogs out there and we're digging and there are local families helping to search, but you could save us all a lot of time and heartache.'

'What do you take me for?' he wailed. 'She's my daughter, my little girl. I *love* her.'

'Like you loved Bonnie.'

'Love. I still love her.'

'Funny way of showing it, breaking her teeth.'

'She must have broken her tooth when her face hit the

floor,' he protested but Faithe continued, relentless, 'There was a car registered in your wife's name. A dark green Saab. Where'd you hide that, then? You were in the woods all night. You came back at seven. Your partner John says he called round repeatedly during the day and you weren't in. Your truck was there but there was no sign of the car or you. You were off dumping her car somewhere, weren't you? Maybe you were dumping Lucy too.'

'You've got this all wrong. All wrong. I was upstairs in bed. I heard the telephone ring. I heard John come to the door and shout through the letterbox. I was there.'

'So why didn't you answer?'

'I – I was too upset at her leaving me. I love her, fuck it. I love them both!'

In his frustration, Lawrence's temper rose with dangerous speed. He smacked his fist down furiously on the table. Coffee slopped from their mugs and two butts rolled from the heavily laden ashtray. Faithe's expression froze over. She took a fresh cigarette then promptly quit the room and her colleague proceeded to hurl abuse at Lawrence and accuse him of brutalizing and murdering Lucy. Coward, he called him, and scum and pervert.

McBride had apparently left his Barrowcester hotel the night before Bonnie walked out. He had then taken the train through the Chunnel to Paris, beyond where he could not be traced. Lawrence's solicitor advised him to sit tight and not be bullied into confessing anything.

'Remember,' he insisted, 'in the eyes of the law you assaulted her, but that's no offence unless she presses charges, which she hasn't. However guilty you feel, whatever they insinuate, you've no previous history.' He pointed out that wherever she was, she had to live, she needed money. However much cash she had squirrelled away, she had to make a credit card purchase or withdraw cash from a bank machine sooner or later.

The Saab was traced to a police pound in London. It had

been illegally parked on a back street parking lot in South-wark, had accumulated two tickets then a clamp then been towed away. Ever since a loss of grip had caused a near crash, Bonnie religiously used driving gloves, which she kept tucked in the door, so the only prints on the wheel, brake and gear stick were Lawrence's and the thief's. Two days passed and still there were no sightings and no financial trace of Bonnie's continued existence. Lawrence was finally charged with murder and held in the cells pending a remand hearing.

He tried to tell himself he was not a violent man. He knew the stories. He knew there were men who beat the same woman week after week, year after incomprehensible year. The series of little digs and pokes they had given each other as they argued had escalated until suddenly, without knowing the force of his own strength, he had shoved her too hard and she had slipped to the floor, knocking her head on the sink as she fell and then on the floor tiles. This did not make him a wife-beater in the same league, perhaps, as the men who branded their wives with steam irons, broke their noses, slammed their hands in drawers. Read purely in physical terms, it was no more horrific than the kind of violence witnessed daily between brawling schoolboys or over-fuelled drinking partners. And yet, his conscience told him there was no degree in this. A spouse was not a school bully or a pool-hall rival. One could argue with her, shout at her, even break her property – these were all clichés of healthily tempestuous domesticity, traditionally reconciled in bed – but one did not touch her in anger. He had only hurt Bonnie the once but on the instant he passed through a one-way turnstile into the company of bad men, men who had to be restrained by court orders or bars. He was now among men whose wives might stab them in self-defence in confidence of a broad measure of public support. With each passing hour, his ability to see himself self-righteously apart from, or above them grew feebler.

At last he was allowed visitors. His mother and John Docherty had been trying to see him ever since his arrest. Lacking any precedent as to the proper form of behaviour in such circumstances, she treated the occasion like a hospital visit. She brought grapes and a bag of treats from Hart's, a fashionable delicatessen. She brought walnut cake, a Camembert, a bar of bitter chocolate and, with blithe insensitivity, two crime novels from the library. She tried and failed to find anything nice to say about his cell. Then she hugged him and said she didn't believe a word of it and would stand by him whatever happened. She told him to get a haircut and eat properly then cried so much she had to leave.

John Docherty's visit was even shorter. He had dressed up as if for a special occasion. Watching him pace nervously about the cell, Lawrence sensed he had worn a suit in case he was seen arriving and photographed. John announced that he had acquired his own solicitor – as business partners they had previously shared the one – and had instructed her to dissolve the partnership.

'It's Carol,' he said and Lawrence pictured his tight-lipped wife. She had seen through him on their first meeting, but misread his covert dislike of her husband as snobbery. 'She says if even half the things they're saying are true, she'd leave me if I carried on working with you.'

'What things . . . ?' Lawrence began.

'The papers have got hold of it,' John told him. 'The way you beat her, the teeth, the hair, your chainsaw, everything. Goodbye, Lawrence.'

And he left.

Curiously, the dissolution of the partnership came as a relief since it freed Lawrence at least from worrying that he was letting John down by neglecting his work. He was left with the twelve square feet of his windowless cell, daily visits from his mother, his now very own solicitor, whose bill, he feared, must be mounting spectacularly, and the torture of worry. Remorse chewed him from within, relentlessly working over the cold suspicion that he had misjudged his wife, until it was left sourly indigestible, weakening his system ever further, like a kidney stone.

Then he began to dwell on the thought of the body in the wood, the body burned and buried even as he tried to sleep in the cab of his pick-up ten minutes' walk away, and who the murderer might be and who they might kill next and where else their victims might lie hidden. It occurred to him that Bonnie and Lucy might well be dead, their bodies hidden elsewhere, and once the thought took root in his mind it would not be dislodged by reason. If they were dead then his innocence of their murder would never be proved. He would be condemned and probably found mad as well as murderous.

Faithe let him read copies of day-old newspapers from the staff room. He had become notorious overnight, already tried and condemned in the minds of the reading public. He saw his photograph reproduced repeatedly and Bonnie's and Lucy's.

Article after article homed in on Lucy. Was she dead? Abducted? Hiding? Sian the childminder was wheeled out, as was a shattered and vengeful Charlie Knights, full of how 'Frost' had wickedly seduced his innocent, mother-less daughter when she was barely out of college and he a rough-handed gardener, little more than a caveman in his appetites. Lawrence's mother was being doorstepped, evidently, as there were shots of her, pinched and harassed, scurrying in dark glasses from car to front door or angrily attempting to shoo photographers out of her gates. Bewil-deringly, they had even established that he was *illegitimate*. After all these years, his mother's gracious cover had been blown and her son was the last to know. The suspect was portrayed as having a background of privileged hypocrisy. He had learning difficulties, they said. They even tracked down boys he had fought at school. He tried to avoid the articles about him and read of other things but the case appeared to permeate entire newspapers in one form or another. It proved an occasion for leaders on domestic violence, discussions of the purported ill effects of fatherless childhoods and the emotional inarticulacy of the male. It even crept, like a grey mould, into gardening columns.

Inept at remembering the simplest dates and telephone numbers, Lawrence had an almost autistic skill at memorizing the names of trees and shrubs. At agricultural college this had proved a kind of party piece in which he would rattle off name after name to a disbelieving, encyclopaedia-clutching audience. Confined to a cell, with not a green leaf in sight, this proved his salvation, as he found he could empty his mind into readiness for sleep by mentally reciting the names in alphabetical order, from *abies* to *zelcova*, forcing himself to stop and begin again from the beginning if he summoned one out of sequence.

The freshly demonized Wumpett Woods were dug over and over again, as was the land around the farmhouse, with no sign of Lucy's body being unearthed. The local environmentalist lobby was up in arms. A chapter of local Pagans set up camp on the wood's edge, offering prayers for the deaths of trees and oblations for the dishonouring of the ancient dead. Then, after ten days, a young woman presented herself at Barrowcester police station, announced who she was, and gave ample proof of identity and explanation of absence. There remained the chain saw from the back of the pick-up truck, clearly of the type used to dismember the body. This was covered in the suspect's fingerprints and bore a small trace of blood which could be his or his wife's. However he had used it so thoroughly in the interim that any significant forensic traces had been scoured off or overpowered by sawdust and juice from a cedar of Lebanon, so that alone was scarcely proof enough to sustain a faltering charge. There were now no women on Faithe's brief list of missing persons whose descriptions bore even a tenuous resemblance to the physical type of the corpse in the wood.

On Lawrence's release, his solicitor immediately began pressing for him to sue for damages against both the police for wrongful arrest and Charlie Knights and various tabloid newspapers for defamation of character. Lawrence might not be a murderer but he had admitted to hurting his wife, however, so he was reluctant to pursue the matter. The apologies he received were less than profound and the station was mobbed by hostile journalist crews and interested bystanders as soon as news broke of his cleared name. It was now Faithe's blood they bayed for but their attitude towards him remained prurient and ugly. His farmhouse was vulnerable to invasion. His mother's place at least had a wall and gates so, while a dummy van lured the mob away, an unmarked car was laid on to whisk him there until the fuss subsided. He sat in the very middle of the back seat, with both doors locked, horribly aware of how smelly his clothes had become and dazzled by the sudden profusion of green flashing past on either side.

CHAPTER FIVE

Long before the tabloids locked teeth on her pampered flesh, Dora Frost had been touched by controversy, having been an unmarried mother at a time when the adjectives most commonly applied to such women were *loose* or *fallen*, not independent. Her father had taken work with an oil company in Southern California uprooting his wife and teenage twins in the process. Dora and Darius had graduated from a Los Angeles high school and been enrolled at university in Berkeley. Dora was to study English and Drama, for she was determined to become an actress, Darius settled for Economics, set only on being spectacularly rich so as to avoid the puritanical ways of their parents. When Dora became pregnant, her father's first reaction was that she must name the man and marry him. When she named him and he was found to be already married, his second reaction was to banish her back to England where she was to begin a new, quieter life, posing as a young widow.

She and her mother were sent to hide out in the Ahwahnee, a remote, stately hotel deep in the mountain forests of Yosemite for the remainder of the pregnancy, their suite being converted to a private clinic for the actual birth. As a smoke screen, her mother had fostered rumours of a *woman's operation* and the need for a long recuperation. Dora, it was to be supposed, was merely keeping her suffering parent company. The imaginary invalid read her way through the hotel library and took long, punitive hikes, leaving Dora and her shame concealed from gossip's view. Dora played game upon game of patience, spied on hotel guests, counted trees and danced by herself to the radio, hugging her swollen belly with love and rebellious joy as she circled the room. Her only reading was a guide to the trees of North America which she used to identify every tree she could see from the suite's windows. Since these were mainly redwoods, this was swiftly done, but she liked to think this burst of study had affected her son's later choice of expertise.

There was a trauma concerning the birth, to which only her mother, the midwife and the doctor were party. Dora never saw either parent again, crossing America by train with Lawrence, and sailing from New York as soon as she was strong enough to travel. From what she inferred from her mother's few, dry letters and Darius's later conversation, Dora had no reason to believe that the trauma and its cancerous pain spread any further. To this day she had never spoken of it and intended to take it with her to her grave. There were whole weeks when it failed to cross her mind, then something in Lawrence's behaviour or the sight of a young mother with a pram would bring it sharply back to her and she would feel briefly nauseous with guilt and uncertainty. She was resolved that this trouble should never curse Lawrence and that it should only influence his childhood for the good. The more it overshadowed her thoughts, the greater her determination to have him live only in the light.

She was attractive and lively so the assumption all round was that she would swiftly find a British husband. She took the name Mrs Robert Frost in honour of the poet she had a crush on at the time. Motherhood absorbed her more than thoughts of matrimony ever had and she soon found that she enjoyed more freedom as a merry widow than any dwindled wives of her acquaintance. When Lawrence was older, she threw herself into the Barrowcester amateur dramatic society, of which, with her looks, legs and facility at jumping accents, she soon became unofficial queen. She caused a stir as Norah, as Blanche Dubois, as Hedda, as a languid Tracey in *The Philadelphia Story*. She was popular but, because she was at once guarded, mischievous and attractive, close to few and trusted by fewer.

Having enjoyed her brief liaison with an athletic executive met at a country club, for all that it caused her disgrace and trouble, she continued to have affairs with married men. Unlike bachelors, they seemed to appreciate her independence and have no desire to circumscribe it. She was a light sleeper, habitually waking in the small hours to listen to the radio, and it amazed her that married acquaintances could sleep night after night with someone breathing and stirring and mouthing alongside them. Her afternoons might be taken up by the occasional man but she trusted she would pass the nights of her life in luxurious solitude.

Her mother died soon after becoming so unexpectedly a grandparent – died of disappointment, it was said. Her father married a younger woman and died within a year, apparently of exhaustion. Dora cursed both their memories. Darius graduated with honours and followed his sister back to England where he duly became a businessman and Dora's principal financial support. As the boy grew and a father figure was occasionally required, Darius was happy to fulfil the role. It amused him how often, when brother and sister appeared with the child, they were taken for husband and wife. Darius was a confirmed bachelor and kept whatever private life he enjoyed impenetrably private.

Lawrence was a beautiful child, with unruly blond hair, huge brown eyes and a frequent pink flush to his cheeks – an old-fashioned, even archaic image of innocence. As a baby he never crawled. He spent a worrying extra two months sitting and moonily gazing, then lurched directly into an unsteady walk. He proved similarly slow in learning to talk and tardier still at mastering written language. This was not a problem. Dora was no great reader herself since graduating from high school and was unflagging in her adoration. She would have found a precociously bookish child far more alarming. He turned out to be anti-social, however, a far worse problem in her eyes. Chatty enough at home, he became sullen, wordless and even truculent when left among other children. After repeated, profoundly embarrassing enquiries as to the happiness of what the head teacher called his 'home situation', he was asked to leave Barrowcester's only satisfactory primary school because his withdrawn attitude was thought to be depressing his classmates. Dora's bustling home tuition in *how to be nice* and *how to make conversation* made matters worse for, after a promising start once she had won his connivance with a bribe, he was actually expelled from the cathedral choir school after less than a term for reacting with a storm of tears and what the matron called *language* when that redoubtable lady had mocked his refusal to answer her simple questions at the lunch table.

Dora was aghast. At home he appeared no less angelic. Questioned, he only cried or froze up in stammering confusion and she abhorred stammerers. She had carved a discreet niche for herself in Barrowcester society and had no desire to jeopardize her position with anything so glaring as a 'problem child'. For a while she tried teaching Lawrence at home but the effort soon exhausted her slender resources and, anti-social or no, he plainly now missed the company of other children. He became fractious and began to speak to Dora in monosyllables, and then only when spoken to.

'Perhaps I should tell him?' she suggested to Darius. 'Perhaps this is all to do with having no father?'

After much thought they had decided early on that the boy should be raised in the belief that his mother was indeed a widow, that she had married foolishly young, for love, and that his father, a soldier, had been shot down in Vietnam.

'Tosh,' Darius snapped when she suggested the infant knew it was being lied to and was obscurely punishing her into truth. 'He needs a psychiatrist.'

A child psychiatrist was duly procured and Lawrence went to see her twice a week. She discerned dyslexia and saw that the withdrawal and truculence represented frustration at a failure to match his peers in communication skills.

'If they tease him, he can't find the words to answer back,' she said, 'so he turns in on himself.'

This was no great surprise, but she also unearthed Lawrence's dexterity.

'It's a cliché, I know,' she said, 'but he *is* very good with his hands and we need to focus on that as a way of boosting his self-esteem.'

Dora swallowed her maternal pride and, with the psychiatrist's intervention, a place was found at a preparatory school for 'special' children. The problem apparently had been solved. The boy thrived and, at nine, had caught up sufficiently with his peers to enjoy an ordinary education. His hair remained untameable but there were no more bad reports. He was no high-flier but he enjoyed biology and shone at carpentry to the point of his teacher suggesting he try for national qualifications in the skill. Lawrence made Dora a string box, a letter rack, a bookcase, a garden table, even a piano stool with a music compartment under the seat.

He seemed to develop a sixth sense for preserving his own equilibrium. Far from falling prey to hero worship, he instinctively shunned the company of high achievers, the brilliant, the chatterers, so that as he progressed into the sullen teen years, the only boys he spent silent time with were similarly wordless; sportsmen, plodders, occasionally an uncommunicative ponderer. Dora did not entirely mind this. These were not boys, but premature men, taciturn models of taciturn fathers, and their slouching company made her feel flattered into vivacious ultra-femininity by comparison. It was only a shock when the other plodders acquired girl-friends and moved away to independence and places on surprisingly academic university courses leaving Lawrence still single, still living at home and studying forestry at Arkfield Agricultural College with a bunch of farmers' sons.

Forestry, Darius gloomily assured her, was notoriously a

'thicko's' subject but the field seemed truly to absorb the boy. For the first time she found her son not just poring over books but eagerly finishing them and acquiring others. He began to train the hedges and trees in her garden and, as an end-of-year project, created a pretty line of espaliered fruit trees along one side of her lawn. He acquired the occasional sullen girlfriend, nothing serious, but persevered in his studies and graduated with a commendation. Dora found that all things to do with gardening and landscape had become deeply fashionable, so that far from snobbishly lamenting his acquiring a trade, she was able to boast of his setting up as a qualified tree surgeon and openly to pity her friends whose children languished on the dole with useless arts degrees and unrealized ambitions.

As to his lack of wanderlust, she was ultimately glad of it. No longer a *young* widow, and finding her supply of admirers growing shorter with maturity, she was content to have a son close to hand as her prop and comfort. When his business began to take off and he set up home on his own, he moved barely three miles uphill from the village. The admirers that remained were grateful of the liberty this granted her and she allowed herself a certain pleasure in losing her 'great cuckoo' as she fondly called him.

The advent of Bonnie in Lawrence's life was an unlooked-for delight. Dora had long felt keenly her lack of a daughter and Bonnie was entirely the kind of daughter for which she would have wished. She warmed to her instantly – with her liveliness, independence and early pregnancy, the girl was an echo of her own younger self – and loved her not least for the final vindication Bonnie's love seemed to grant her undervalued son. Dora was no great advocate of marriage, regarding it as the obstacle to be overcome in most people's lives rather than the happy goal towards which their faltering steps should tend. She made an exception for Lawrence, however. Without a wife, she feared, there would always be something unfinished about him. Prettier and brighter (and wealthier) than any of her murky predecessors, Bonnie should not only finish his education but prove his indefinite visa to what Dora thought of as The World – a world where people loved, bred, paid visits, issued invitations, achieved social consequence. For the sake of form, she felt she must register at least some disapproval at their carelessness over the pregnancy but she confided in Darius that in such cases one could be sure that, whatever problems might beset the couple, their sex life would be regular. When the baby proved to be a girl, she was thrilled. She had always observed the love between fathers and daughters to be far less problematic than the competitive, ambivalent bond between fathers and their sons. In her heart, she hoped that Lucy would ensnare her father as she had never sufficiently succeeded in ensnaring her own. The girl would settle Dora's oldest score and thereby legitimize both bastard father and outcast grandmother.

Dora had no inkling that anything was awry in her son's marriage until Bonnie's disappearance. They did not always present her with a falsely smiling front. She knew they argued. Lucy had recently mentioned that they shouted at each other sometimes. Bonnie often came round, ostensibly to drop Lucy off for a few hours, and over a drink or coffee would enjoy a daughterly moan, but it was all ordinary stuff about how uncommunicative he could be, about how maddeningly unambitious she found him, about how pent-up his emotions had been. Nothing about violence. Not a murmur. Not a bruise. God knew, Dora was no believer in wifely stoicism, but she had observed enough poisoned partnerships in her time to know that it took more than a single slap to drive a wife to break silence and run. Bitter though the idea was, she found herself pressured to assume, like everybody else, that Bonnie had been beaten repeatedly.

The revelation was a betrayal of friendship. Dora had plenty of women she thoughtlessly referred to as friends but in fact these were merely women she saw, women who rang up, women who included her in their plans, people dismissed by Darius as 'diary-fillers'. Although Bonnie was so much younger than she, they swiftly became true intimates, calling each other every day, if only to speak about nothing in particular. Lacking a mother or sisters, Bonnie needed an older woman's solidarity through her pregnancy and the early months of motherhood. Each was lively in company because they felt that was expected of them but alone together they allowed themselves the luxury of gravity. They lay on chairs in Dora's garden or curled up on her sofa and discussed death, love and their parents with an openness and lack of protective irony Dora had not experienced since she was at high school. She knew how close their friendship had become when she perceived that neither of them had let on to Lawrence how much they saw of one another; a friendship which excluded a husband was close indeed. And yet, for Bonnie, Lawrence had continued to come first all the while since she had kept entirely silent about the state of their marriage. Or perhaps it was Dora she had been protecting, aware how profoundly the truth concerning her son's inadequacy would wound her?

When the butch woman detective turned up on her doorstep asking questions, Dora was angry with Charlie Knights for taking such an hysterical step as registering Bonnie as a missing person, when the girl had probably locked herself and her daughter away on a health farm for a few quiet, feminine days to think over her situation. When Detective Inspector Faithe began asking questions about Lawrence's violence, Dora became furious. As she could tell the detective in all honesty, she had seen no signs of domestic violence and it struck her that perhaps it was all a jealous father's sick fantasy. The odious man had manipulated Faithe and was blackening her poor boy's name groundlessly!

'I'm afraid not,' Faithe told her, and with disarming gentleness explained that they had *physical evidence*.

When Lawrence was arrested for Bonnie's murder, Dora attempted, purely as an experiment, to believe him guilty. The very thought induced an almost physical revulsion in her. It was as unnatural as trying to breathe underwater. She knew Lawrence too intimately. She had suckled him, nursed him through fevers, bandaged his cuts, washed his clothes. It was axiomatic that most murders were among friends, yet to believe someone a murderer, they must be made an alien or an enemy or at least no more than a passing acquaintance. Granted, she could just, and guiltily, believe him capable of pushing Bonnie around a bit, but murder ... Besides, she knew he adored Lucy, sensed he would do nothing to frighten or harm her so it followed that he would not harm her mother. Surely it did!

Suddenly Dora found herself in the position of murderer's mum, besieged by journalists who, when she deigned to speak to them, garbled her words into a grotesquely inappropriate Cockney so that she was reported as defending 'my boy' and 'my brave lad, Larry' and portrayed, on the strength of one, routine visit to the parish church to buy cheap postcards, as a religious maniac.

She had not taken a newspaper for years, preferring to glean whatever news might come her way through the calmer medium of the kitchen and bedside radios. The village newsagent now began to deliver her a daily tabloid, however, either from sanctimonious spite or from a faintly charming reverence for neighbourhood notoriety. After the initial shock, Dora took to reading them calmly at the kitchen table with coffee and biscuits. She cut out any mentions of herself or Lawrence and pasted them tidily into a scrapbook she kept hidden in a drawer of her desk.

The gleeful revelation that she had been posing as a widow all these years and had, in fact, never been married, caused her comparatively little grief. None of her neighbours was speaking to her by now in any case. A year, even six months ago, she would have predicted such disgrace would bring her measured rural life to an end but in this context it was almost welcome, a sign that she was merely flesh and blood, human, not a monster after all. The journalist who had gone to so much trouble had even, God knew how, found a charming Californian snapshot of her with some high school pals, aged seventeen, all legs and laughter and puffed-out skirt. She was appalled and saddened at how young and vulnerable she looked back then and felt a fresh stab of loathing for her dead mother.

Were he still a husband rather than a widower, Charlie Knights would surely have been a suitable specimen for Dora's collection. He was no Adonis, but she did not require beauty in a male. With his thick-set build, receding, iron-grey hair cropped close to bristle, broken nose, hands like clutches of sausage and a fondness for double-breasted suits, he resembled a retired boxer, rugger coach or American general and made her feel small and delicate although she was neither. She knew him by sight long before their children met, and they had finally been introduced at a wedding, ironically enough, by her married man of the moment. He was sexy in the forceful, who-gives-a-damn manner of ugly men with money and he was plainly keen on her. She could tell from the way he held her hand a second longer than was necessary and from his posture as he stood foursquare before her in the stifling marquee. She knew from local gossip that he was said to visit prostitutes, even to have one on permanent retainer, and that excited her interest in return. It implied an anti-romantic approach to passion akin to her own. She also took the stories as a warning, however, that he was the kind of man who liked to annexe a woman. Dora was not wee wifey material. She moved on, grateful for the narrow escape, only to be brought face to face with him again when Lawrence displayed such uncharacteristic romantic brio in taking up with his daughter.

Ostensibly doing her bit to oil troubled waters, she let Charlie buy her dinner. He sat and talked about himself. She sat and imagined him red-faced and naked. As he made a show of ordering a cognac then rejecting the few the restaurant had to offer, she was tempted afresh. Happily she maintained old-fashioned values in allowing no more than a peck on a first date, and Darius was on hand to prevent her venturing on a second. He made unkind jokes about a Shakespearean double wedding and emphasized the hideousness of being forced to continue socializing with Charlie for years after the relationship reached its conclusion, as her affairs tended to, in a matter of months.

'If you wanted to *marry* him,' he went on, 'that would be another thing entirely. You know I'd like nothing better than to see you settled well.'

'But I don't,' she protested. 'I couldn't! Mrs Charlie Knights? And leave my pretty house to live in that great, sad barn of a place?'

'Quite. So you wouldn't even consider it? If he asked you, that is.'

'Darius, no!'

She had dined with Charlie several times since and had used the occasions to introduce him to other eligible spinsters of the parish. To the best of her knowledge, none of these aroused his interest as she had, but he read her signals and ceased paying court. Just occasionally, when his possessiveness had irritated her or his apparent solitude had caused her a filial pang, Bonnie might murmur how she wished he would marry again. Dora would entertain an immediate rear-view image of him with some woman decked out in sacrificial cream lace and experience a twinge of jealous panic.

The journalists faded away as suddenly as they had come. Doubtless they would be back for the trial but there was no one, therefore, to photograph Dora as she sped her car out of the drive. Leaving the village behind her as she drove towards Barrowcester, she tweaked off her silk scarf and dark glasses, feeling as foolish and obscurely wounded as any temporary celebrity whose fleeting star has just lost its ascendancy.

Charlie's house lay in the lee of a hill. Gloomy to the rear, it still commanded a fine view across the fields to the city, had the River Bross babbling at the garden's edge and might have proved quite charming in understanding hands. A mason at heart, however, he had stripped the house of the Virginia creeper that had once lent a bronzy softness to its edges and so repointed and retiled and repainted the place that he had pared a century off its appearance leaving it bald amid the surrounding green. The weedless lawn had been extended to swallow the spaces where flower beds had once been. The gravel on the drive was an inorganic shade of orange and the terrace, where Dora would have placed some pretty Edwardian benches in fanciful wrought iron, sported generic patio furniture in ageless white plastic. The cliché repelled her but it was, she reflected afresh, a house in urgent need of a woman's touch. It lacked any trace of the unnecessary or the playful. It might have been a conference centre or the rural head office of a building society.

Pulling up in her car, Dora found the place fed her right-eous anger so that by the time she was knocking on the front door she was ready for a fight and jumpy as a lover before a second assignation. She paused then knocked again furiously, glowering up at the blank windows. Dogs bayed deep within the building, then their voices grew louder as an inner door opened and she heard the skittering of claws on tiles as the barking drew nearer the porch.

'Shut up,' she heard him groan. 'Rex. Megan. Get down. Will you shut up you silly bitch!'

When he opened the door, the Dobermans were hunched obediently on the floor but they jumped up as soon as they sensed his recognition and pushed forwards past him to sniff Dora's skirt and lick her offered hands.

'Dora!' he exclaimed and held out his arms as if to embrace her. 'I'm so very sorry.'

But she pushed angrily past him into the cavernous, under-furnished hall.

'The hell you are. This entire nightmare's of your making. You called the police. You spoke to the papers.'

'I didn't.'

'Well who else was it? You were *quoted*. You said he's been beating her for months.'

'I never said that.'

'One bad spat and he's locked up and as good as found guilty of *murder*. When this is over, you'll look ridiculous and he'll have to move. I hope he sues you. As for Bonnie, wherever she's gone, you've stirred up such a stink she's probably afraid of coming back now.'

'You assume she's alive.'

'Well of course she is. You don't honestly think that poor creature they found in the woods . . . ?'

Without thinking, she had led the way into the sitting room and claimed a deep leather armchair. The dogs promptly sat on either side of her so the three of them now faced him. Megan, the bitch, leaned heavily against her knees and Dora stroked her ears abstractedly. Now that she was looking at him properly, she was shocked at the alteration in him. His jaw was silvered with stubble. His eyes were bloodshot and shadowed from lack of sleep. As he sat heavily on a sofa, he was so hunched, so shrunk into himself, that her pity was immediate.

'Oh my God,' she exclaimed, deeply regretting her anger, 'You really *do* think it's her!' Looking even more the hopeless convict than Lawrence, he raised a big hand to shade his eyes and let out a harsh sob. 'Charlie?' she asked. 'Charlie, stop it!'

She hurried over to sit on the sofa beside him. As she drew near, he was slapping out blindly with his free hand, desperate in his shame, as though her mere concern were an unmanning touch he must fight off. The moment he felt her arm across his shoulder, however, he abandoned all show of strength and surrendered to her sympathy, slumping into her embrace and sobbing, his stubble rough against her neck.

Twisted unnaturally, she held him close, resisting the impulse to hang the consequences, slip down to the rug and pull him on top of her. She ran a hand repeatedly across his hair and solid back, aware that her guilty fingers felt the body not the clothes that hid it.

'She's fine,' she murmured. 'You'll see. They'll run tests and prove it's not her. She'll come back. And Lucy. Of course they will. Ssh. Don't. She'll be back.'

His anguish was contagious. She remained convinced that Lawrence was blameless but her certainty that Bonnie was alive and merely in hiding was weakening by the second, even as she sought to reassure him. Imperceptibly her assurances turned to prayer and it may well have been because she was saying, 'Please let them be alive,' aloud as she rocked him in her arms that she missed the sound of the approaching car. All she knew was that suddenly the dogs had rushed into the hall and returned with Lucy who stood for a moment staring at the tableau of her embracing grandparents while the animals licked ecstatically at her face.

Dora stared too for a moment, unable to believe the small, stolid vision before her, then she sprang away from Charlie, lurched awkwardly to her feet and ran to sweep the astonished child into her arms. She felt the tears wet on her face as she laughed and squeezed and drew the familiar soapy-sweet smell of her into her nostrils as if crazed with hunger. She was dimly aware of Charlie coming up to hug her and Lucy in one, then pulled away to set Lucy down and hurry, with the barking dogs, back to the hall.

Bonnie entered her father's house slowly, wearing dark glasses and charcoal wool, like a principal mourner. She had lost weight. Dora had never seen her so gravely composed. One cheek still bore the yellow marks of a fading bruise.

'Lucy, dear, go back to the car. Granny and Grandpa and I need to talk.'

'But – ' Lucy started to protest.

'Now, Lucy.'

Dora received the child's fulsome, sticky kiss on her cheek and let her go. Bonnie staggered slightly as she drew near. Dora held her close, feeling the bones beneath the wool, imagining bruises.

'Dad,' she heard her say over her shoulder. 'Hello. You look terrible. I went to Paris,' she muttered on. 'I had the tooth fixed there. They made a porcelain one and had to sort of screw it into my jaw bone. Hurt like hell. There was nothing in any of the papers there. Not a thing. Craig paid for everything. I left my wallet on the train like an idiot.'

'Craig?'

'You remember. My client on the university job. From Chicago.'

'Oh yes. Thank God. Thank *God*!' Dora began to laugh, clasping Bonnie afresh. 'I knew it wasn't you in the wood. I knew it. Because of Lucy, as much as anything. I told your Pa just now. I even prayed!'

Dora felt Charlie standing by them. She pulled back, feeling she must let him have a share of Bonnie, but he only stared and, rather than touch him, Bonnie chattered on as though the sight of him so ruined, in such obvious emotional need, unnerved her.

'It wasn't in any of the papers. Not the French ones. I only found out when we came back this morning and it was all over the place. Craig drove me straight down.'

'He's here?'

'He's out in the car. I wanted to see you on my own. Oh Dora, what am I going to do?'

'You must go to the police. Tell them you're still alive.'

Bonnie laughed at her simplicity.

'Not that. Well of course I'll do that. I'll go in a bit. No. I meant generally. Do generally. I miss him, Dora. I miss him in spite of everything. I could walk into those cells and drive home with him tonight.'

'You're joking. He broke your tooth, for Christ's sake. He bruised your cheek.'

'Knocked me out cold, you mean. He gave me a bloody great egg on the back of my head on the edge of the sink.' Bonnie laughed dryly, touching the spot with her fingertips. 'He nearly fractured my bloody skull.'

'He *could* have killed you, then!'

'He didn't mean to. He needs help, Dora. He needs therapy, that's all.'

Dora took her friend firmly by the shoulders. For all the lost weight, Bonnie's body felt young still, resilient. Dora was briefly inhibited by Charlie standing beside them like a halted sleepwalker.

'You're to get away,' she said at last. 'Right away. You have to leave him.' She sensed she was referring as much to the father as the husband.

'But you're his mother.'

'So I know. You *have* to leave him.'

'I still love him, Dora. It's so stupid.'

'You're not listening to me.'

'I am. I am. Oh. Oh what about Lucy? She adores him. She keeps saying where is he, and why can't Daddy come too and when are we going to see him. She cried for hours last night. I very nearly hit *her*,' she added, grimly humorous. 'God I need to pee. It's all the excitement and this cold wind. Hang on. I won't be a sec.'

She ran along the hall and through a door beneath the stairs. Dora watched her go, amazed, horrified even, at the bizarre inappropriateness of her young friend's mood.

'She's in shock,' she told Charlie, masking incomprehension with certainty. 'She's not herself.' His bizarre lack of reaction was no easier to comprehend. All those tears, all that need and yet now, far from shouting with surprise and relief and running out to see his granddaughter again, he had merely slumped onto a hall chair and was staring down the corridor after Bonnie. Dora thought a moment then hurried out to the drive and the waiting car. As she drew near, the driver's door opened and a man got out. He had crinkled, greying hair and wore a wedding ring. He held out his hand. As she took it, Dora wanted to laugh because he was so good-looking.

'Isn't it a heavenly day?' she blurted like a fool. 'Sorry.' She coughed. 'You must think Bonnie awfully rude leaving you outside.'

He merely smiled, crinkling blue eyes and revealing reassuringly un-American teeth.

'You must be the famous Dora,' he said. 'I'm Craig. Craig McBride.'

She took back her hand, needing to regain control, reminding herself she had long since ceased to be the age she could feel. She cast a glance back to the house, to Bonnie.

'Can you take her away?' she asked quickly. Lucy had clambered into the driver's seat and was playing with the steering wheel. 'She mustn't stay here.'

'You read my mind,' he said. 'It's like she's taken this big step into the unknown and now she hasn't the faintest idea which way to turn. I was thinking that if I help her put some distance between her and Lawrence it might help her see things more clearly. I mean,' he added hastily, 'it's not that I – Well. I wouldn't want you to think that I – '

'Take her away,' Dora assured him. 'You must. Whatever she says, it's her only hope. She's still in love with him and it's hopeless. It's not fair to either of them. This is the only chance they've got. Please?'

He touched her elbow and indicated that Bonnie and her father were drawing near. She turned. Bonnie laughed. She took Charlie's hand but dropped it again swiftly as though she had found it cold.

'Dora don't look so *worried*, darling,' she called out. 'Everything's been vile but it's all going to be just fine now. We'll drive straight into Barrowcester to the police station and I'll swear I'm Mrs Lawrence Frost and still alive and show them my driving licence and passport or whatever and Lucy and they'll let him out and everything'll be fine.' She kissed Dora's cheek. 'I do love you when you worry. Don't *look* like that. Honestly. We'll all be laughing about this in a few months' time.'

'Bye darling,' Dora said to her. She wanted to hug her so much but was afraid of betraying any emotions that might seem suspiciously final. She shook the American's huge hand.

'Lovely to have met you,' she said.

'Sure,' he replied and nodded. 'We'll sort something out,' he added quietly. He looked like a man who could dig ditches and build walls. Dora trusted him.

'Take care of them,' she thought and waved to Lucy who was waving through the back window and continued to wave as the car pulled out with a small spurt of gravel.

Watching them go, she knew a part of herself was being torn out forever. She felt breathless. She resisted the urge to cry.

'I must go,' she said to Charlie. 'Lawrence will need me now. They'll be sending him home. Are you – Are you going to be okay?'

He said nothing for a few seconds then seemed to click back into his old, ebullient self as abruptly and unconvincingly as an automaton.

'Oh fine. Fine. Thanks so much for coming over,' he added, apparently forgetting that she had come to rage not to comfort.

'Yes,' she said clumsily. 'I'm sure she'll be back in an hour or so. She'll sort things out with the police then she'll want to come back and talk things over with her Dad and . . . I'll be off then.'

He had slipped away and only his body was standing there. Sensing his master was not as reliable as he had been, the younger of the dogs, Rex, jumped into her car when she opened the door and showed a disloyal reluctance to be left behind. As she drove away, he ran alongside making unnerving, darting movements towards its tyres. She was torn between watching out for the dog and looking at Charlie's immobile figure, shrinking in the rear-view mirror. Half-way home she was overcome with sick dizziness as though she were about to faint and had to pull over into the entrance to a field, open the door and sit hunched forward with her head between her knees.

CHAPTER SIX

During a long, tense wait in the Channel Tunnel, Craig, who prided himself on being good with children, had made the error of teaching Lucy to sing *Ay Yi Yippee*. Excited at returning to familiar ground and doubtless picking up on her mother's tension, the child had been singing the song over and over in the back of the hired car ever since Craig had pointed to a motorway sign with some relief and said,

'Look, Lucy. Barrowcester forty-five miles.'

Now, as they left her father's house and pulled up to the ancient city, the mindless repetition was threatening to make Bonnie lash out.

'Lucy?'

'What?'

'Could you maybe sing something else? Maybe?'

'Why? *She'll be wearing pink pyjamas when she* – '

'Look, Lucy. There's the cathedral! See the two towers?'

'Oh yes. Are we going to see Daddy now?'

'Maybe. Soon. Maybe.'

Craig parked across the road from the police station.

'Is that it?' he asked gently. 'Do I drop you both here?'

'Are you mad? Oh. God. Sorry. I dunno.'

'Do you want me to come in with you?' he asked, patiently smiling.

'No!' she gasped. 'You saw those papers. The place is probably crawling with journalists.'

'I'll stay with the munchkin.'

'Yes. Teach her a new song.'

*   *   *

On the night when he tried to celebrate, with so character-istically warped sensitivity, the anniversary of their first, abortion-haunted sex, Lawrence picked a fight with her. His name-calling and jealous accusations incensed her to the point where she felt the urge to lash out at him. The last thing she remembered was his hand flying up and her losing her balance. She came to with a sick headache worse than any hangover. Her cheek was pressed against the icy floor in a small pool of congealing blood, which had matted her hair on one side. Staring at the floor, she became aware of Lucy's weeping. Then her tongue sought the hole where one of her teeth had been and a white bolt of pain startled her into com-plete awareness. Checking the damage in the looking-glass in the downstairs loo, she found the broken tooth digging into the cut it had made inside her cheek and spat it out.

When Lucy asked where her father was, she realized they had the house to themselves and told Lucy he had gone away for a while. For fun.

'What happened? Why were you bleeding?'

'I fell over.'

'Silly Mummy.'

'Yes. Very silly Mummy. Shall we go away too? Would that be fun? Just you and me?'

Breathlessly enthusing, she hurried Lucy upstairs as fast as her throbbing head would let her, downed a handful of painkillers, packed, seized money, passport and the painting that was her only possession of value then dressed her daughter and drove south as fast as she dared.

Addicted to romance and to animals as a child, she had always, in her fantasies, cast herself in the role of the plucky but helpless princess and her father in that of the dragon. Her relationship with the dragon was ambivalent. It was now her pet and guardian, now her tormentor and worst fate. The man who could vanquish the dragon, killing what she loved, would win her as a matter of course. Looking with some envy from her friends' mothers to her widowed father, she entertained too the possibility of a stepmother, wicked, quite possibly, but usefully worldly too and infinitely glamorous. When she was sent away to school, the fairy tales gave way to more adult fantasies, often less well written, but her father remained the dragon in her dreams, her bed the rich treasure at the heart of a forest of briars.

She fell in unquestioning love with Lawrence the moment she saw him, with his thick, unruly hair, sinewy limbs and brown eyes. With his lack of fine speeches and his array of axes and saws, he was short on traditional princely charm but he had the stuff of heroism about him. A giant-killer perhaps, or an unexpectedly victorious third son. She could hardly believe her luck when her father told her to work with him on the arboretum or how nervous and gabbling this labourer made her. He seemed impervious to her teenage charm, however much she sought to impress him, and she marked out the hopelessness of her case in trees, calculating the days until the end of his commission. At last, when she saw there were no saplings left to plant but the catalpa, desperation and a complete lack of self-consciousness lent her strength. She seduced him as if by natural magic.

The moment it was done however it was she who was disenchanted. She was still of an age when to kiss someone with one's tongue was to embark on a steady relationship and to go *all the way* was to entertain serious thoughts of marriage. With the rude loss of her virginity, all the judicious snobbery her education had inculcated in her came to the fore. She was a princess. He was her father's tree surgeon. She could never marry him. She had to leave home still. She had to make a life elsewhere. She had to leave her mark. She discovered later that Lawrence assumed her father knew what had happened and, furious, cut him off for that reason. In fact her father knew nothing, but she had engineered the breach by complaining that the tree surgeon had made passes at her.

She realized she was pregnant a fortnight later and dealt with it herself with some money from her newly matured trust fund, tearfully drunk on cheap vodka and pineapple juice. It was unpleasant and shameful but she was young enough for regrets to pass easily. Nothing was to interfere with her ideals. She left home and went to university as planned. No princes materialized, only frauds, and she found herself working and independent and beginning to enjoy it. She avoided Barrowcester until, amused at the coincidence of their shared birthplace, she became involved with Alexander, the debonair heir to a local estate and the next Lord Barrow. When he repeatedly invited her home, declared he loved her to distraction and set her to redesign his garden, it seemed more than likely she would become his wife. Blind to his veiled sneers at her father's background, she was triumphantly happy and hired Lawrence to work for her partly to lay an old ghost but also from a mischievous desire to compare the man she might have settled for with the one that was control's reward.

She should never have done it. Looking back with fatalism, she saw that malicious impulse as her downfall. Lawrence seemed no more interested in her than before but, regarding him with wiser, adult eyes, she found that, compared with Alexander, he won hands down. Alexander was conventionally handsome, rich and better educated but Lawrence was more grounded. He had the calm, untrumpeting self-assurance of an expert. He had no need of human props to justify his importance. He looked even better in jeans than she remembered. In a way that disarmed her utterly, he also seemed *good*. She thought, with a pang, of their lost child and knew him for a kind and responsible father. Too late she saw herself trapped in a gilded compromise and the bitter tears she shed when Alexander revealed his perfidy drew as deeply on relief as on humiliation. Even if Lawrence had not taken her hand in the crowded snug of the Tracer's Arms and let her kiss him, he would still have proved her unconscious rescuer.

For all that she was spoiled, for all her fantasies and childish, worldly ambition, Bonnie was not a fool. She saw he did not love her as she loved him. If she had not become pregnant a second time, she might have let him go. She could not face a second abortion, however. She felt sure her love was strong enough for two and she was wise enough to have observed that some of the firmest marriages were founded on imperfect grounds and inequality of feeling. She was not, however, experienced and had no mother to advise her that any problems writ small in courtship loomed large in matrimony.

At first her faith seemed justified. He was a good father and she felt the adoration he shone on Lucy spill over onto her as loving gratitude. His lack of ambition began to madden her, however, and his inarticulacy and, more than either of these, the way his emotions, which fatherhood and domestic intimacy should have released, seemed as inaccessible to him as ever. As time passed and, ironically, as she found a dear friend in his mother, she came to be indignant that she should ever have been *grateful* for whatever love he could offer. She came instead to see his love or rather the demonstration of his love and of *his* gratitude, as her contractual right. She was not the kind of woman who flirts to recapture her husband's interest but when Craig entered her professional life and began to spend time with the two of them, she did hope that an element of jealousy might prick Lawrence's conscience. Craig, who was so naturally courteous, so overtly warm, might lead him to cherish her by example. Nothing could have prepared her for the demonic reaction she unleashed. They had argued before, like any couple. They had said hateful things. But they had always spoken, she believed, out of simple frustration or anger, never from actual hatred.

She had maintained a front for Craig, as she had for

Dora, but the work on the new university site was so time-consuming and threw her into his company for so long, that it was perhaps a foregone conclusion that the handsome American should come to perceive the truth about her marriage.

From the moment she unburdened herself, his sympathy was persuasive. In spite of Lawrence's shortcomings, she persisted in reaffirming her love for him. For she did love him. Deeply. When she secretly read a marital self-help book, it was with small shocks of guilty self-recognition. And yet something in her love must have died or at least lost its potency or she would have taken the simple solution of handing over her designs to Craig and asking, with apologies, that he find someone else to oversee the work. She did not desire Craig. Handsome or no, he was not at all what she thought of as her type. Yet it was surely more than professional assiduity that made her stick by his side even as her marriage spiralled down in flames. Had her only confidante not been Dora, with whom she could never be entirely honest for obvious reasons, she might have been brought to admit that Craig was proving the chiselled, upstanding means to a matrimonial end.

Had she had him in mind for a lover, she would have fled directly to his side. Instead, woozy from painkillers, envious of Lucy's sound backseat slumbers, she drove to London. She headed towards Parson's Green, the haunt of her student days, where several girlfriends still lived, then realized abruptly that she was no longer close enough to any of them to materialize on their doorstep so late with two suitcases, a sleeping child and a face like a prize-fighter's. Hating herself for sounding tearful and pathetic, she rang Craig's Barrowcester hotel from a kiosk. He asked no questions and was with her in less than two hours, tapping on the window to wake her. He made her leave her car in a side street – from where it was later stolen – then gave her his dark glasses and swept her and Lucy in a taxi to

Waterloo International. Unprepared, cashless, anxious not to be traced, she accepted his protection, his tickets to Paris, his payment of a dentistry bill, but when she locked herself in her bathroom at the Bristol for a silent weep, it was for the physical loss of Lawrence. Her hotel bed felt empty without him and, for all Craig's chaste chivalry and her staunch independence, she felt ridiculously vulnerable and alone without her husband beside her.

Bonnie entered Barrowcester police station alone and unrecognized. When she had made herself known to a stunned duty officer and he asked if she wanted to wait to see her husband, she panicked.

'Er. No,' she told him foolishly. 'I can't. The car's on a double yellow line and my little girl's in it. Tell him. Oh. God. Er. Tell him anything. Tell him I've been found, that's all.'

He protested, but she hurried out and made Craig drive her swiftly to the farmhouse. Lucy was overjoyed, of course, thinking she was coming home at last and about to see her father. Leaving her with capable Craig, Bonnie walked distractedly around the house, packing another case with a jumble of things she had forgotten before. Packing in broad daylight felt more real than on her first, bloodstained flit. She became suddenly, painfully tearful at the sense that she was leaving the house she loved. She lay on their bed for a few perilously seductive minutes and even began to write Lawrence a letter, then she thought better of it, imagined the ugly scene if he returned any minute to find Craig playing with his daughter, and she hurried out.

Lucy began to play up when she found they were on the move again, producing a repetitive whine like a wounded animal.

'Where now?' Craig asked over the noise.

'Back to *Dad's*, I thought. There's plenty of room.'

'Won't he come after you there?'

'Dad would probably shoot him,' she laughed, desperately unhappy. Lucy's misery was infectious, brain-scraping.

'I think you need to get right away,' Craig said, driving back to the main road.

'But where?' she asked. When he suggested a few weeks in Chicago, he had to raise his voice over Lucy's continuing complaint. Her future was uncertain, she could not face Lawrence just yet and the offer of a temporary haven proved irresistible. She allowed him to swing the car away from Barrowcester and onto the motorway to Birmingham and the airport.

When they stopped for petrol, she climbed into the back to comfort Lucy and was overcome with sudden, stressed-out exhaustion. She fell fast asleep with the child sprawled across her lap. She had always been active, a doer not a thinker, a seizer of opportunity, but there was a certain luxury in allowing Craig to become her destiny, an irresistible force, sweeping her away from old world, old life, old troubles to the new. There she would still be beset with doubts and guilt, but she felt as entirely safe, as entirely cared for as a small child being fed soup in an enormous bed. As Craig hummed along to the radio and sped them nearer and nearer safety, she drifted in and out of sleep and dreamed of being forced to leave limbs behind, an arm caught in a closing door, a foot snatched by unseen hands as she tried to climb out from a sunless cave.

CHAPTER SEVEN

It was always blithely assumed that a mother wanted nothing more than to have her son at home with her; as if all the years of dealing with cut knees, projectile vomit, tedious homework and boyish mess were an investment in the remote future possibility of having him back as a useful adult, a younger, fitter version perhaps of one's depressingly aged husband. Certainly Lawrence had not been a planned child, but there had still been times when, like any mother, Dora had watched her growing boy and wondered what on earth the point of motherhood could be if one was only to lose the object of so much love and labour if not to another woman then to the World. With no husband to fall back on, she had dreaded empty nest syndrome more than most. He was not her entire life, but he was its largest part.

Happy that he chose to settle nearby, happier still that his wife proved so easy to love, she had nonetheless striven to fill the vacancy his departure created. Amateur dramatics had lost its charm since she could not abide to play the comic aunts of the heroines she had once embodied. Encouraged by Darius, who was a demon of the game, she took up bridge instead. She enrolled for evening classes in Italian and upholstery. She discovered the mindless pleasure of working up tapestry cushions from expensive kits. She was also diverted, one afternoon a week, by prison visiting, becoming one of a small troop of carefully vetted volunteers at HMP Barrowcester. This was a stelliform Victorian structure in red brick and white stone, now lost in the hinterland of railway sidings and industrial estates on the city's 'wrong' side. There she spent two hours in a large room rank with desperation and cigarette smoke, visiting those who had no one to visit them. She had grown fond of one particular lifer, a sad wife-killer old enough to be her father. He could not read or write and refused to learn but with her encouragement, found a pen pal in Parkhurst and dictated his letters to Dora who in turn read the replies back to him. She thus became an expert in prison argot and convict politics, more startling than upholstery if less practically useful.

Bonnie's disappearance and the public interpretation cast upon it were all the more disturbing for having coincided with one of Dora's occasional morbid fantasies. She was always a fretter and could not help wondering what would happen if Bonnie died and Lawrence were crippled. She had never ever wanted Bonnie dead but she had entertained the possibility if only to satisfy the fantasy of having her son about the place again with the added bonus of her granddaughter. In her secret dreams, he had sometimes lost the use of his legs – his hands, she cynically told herself, were still free for odd jobs about the house and garden and spared him the ultimate degradation of going back to being spoon-fed.

As fate would have it, Lawrence was not chair-bound, but he was a kind of cripple. She said nothing to him of her brief encounter with Bonnie and Craig at Charlie's house and he had no reason to guess at it. As far as he was concerned his wife had gone straight to a London police station on returning to the country, he was released, all charges dropped and that was that. Dora had worried that he would fight against his fate, certainly against the period of retreat at her house that renewed journalistic interest enforced. The entire traumatic episode, however, his interrogation, imprisonment, exposure and trial by press seemed to have sapped his will. He had a horror of being seen by people. It was all she could do to persuade him into the garden. The police ruse of eluding the press failed and within a day of his return a clutch of reporters and photographers returned to besiege the village.

'I think we should go out and talk to them,' she said, 'or they'll never go.'

She helped him write a careful statement to read out and led him down the drive to face them at the gates, her hand shaking as much as his. He departed from the statement however.

'The police made an erroneous arrest,' he said, 'but I was treated well at all times. I was feeling bad about my treatment of Bonnie and in a way I started to feel being locked up was a punishment I deserved. I can't expect her to forgive me but I still love her wherever she is and – '

'She's in America,' a small woman muttered from the front of the crowd. There was a ripple of interest as Lawrence froze. 'She's in the States,' the woman went on flatly. 'She's with Craig McBride. We got a photo of them boarding their flight.'

Dora took a more protective hold on Lawrence's arm, hating the beady eyes and ill-mannered microphones ranged about them. Now that he was not a murderer, they were determined to make him an unpaid soap opera star instead.

'We had a letter from her this morning,' she told them, willing Lawrence not to interrupt her. 'Lawrence hasn't had time to read it. He's had so many letters of support. People have been so kind. Just amazing.'

'What do you plan to do now, Larry?' a man called out but Lawrence had broken away from Dora's support and was walking back to the house.

'I think Lawrence plans to take things gently for a while,' Dora told them. 'As you can imagine, he's been under a terrible strain lately. As . . . As has Bonnie. The best thing would be for you to just leave them alone to rebuild their lives.'

They took pictures as she closed the gates against them. One photograph of her rejoining Lawrence and placing her arm through his won a photojournalism prize later that year and was widely reproduced, long after its sad context had been forgotten.

He rounded on her savagely when they were back indoors. 'What was that crap about letters?' he asked. 'We haven't had any letters, least of all from her.'

Then he retreated into his room and a forbidding silence.

They had received letters however. Hate mail arrived every day, ludicrous and corrosive, but Dora took care to intercept and burn it. Before he came home she had been torn between shame and pity but now that he was sleeping in his boyhood room again, she found herself protective as a she-bear. Her lie became truth two days later when a slim airmail letter arrived from Bonnie. There was a covering letter to Dora wrapped around a folded envelope addressed to Lawrence. Dora unfolded the single, onionskin sheet and read it, trembling, on the porch.

Dearest Dora,

You'll be pleased to hear, I know, that Craig has effectively kidnapped us for a few weeks. I wanted to see Lawrence but Craig was adamant. In a strange way it's a huge relief being able to relinquish all control. I have never felt so passive in my life. I miss him – Lawrence, I mean – miss him so much I can't sleep but I know it's like a drug and I must break my habit. You were so right. But I miss you too!! As does Lucy. She adores Craig but I think she finds him a bit grown up and serious sometimes. You've been like a mother and a sister to me and suddenly I feel orphaned. I thought it better to send L's letter via you in case people were messing with his post or he wasn't at home. Don't let him see this. I'll write again soon. Maybe even ring if I can trust myself not to go all weepy on you. Do write. Tell Dad I'm okay.

Kisses.

B xx.

Dora wryly noticed that she gave a P.O. box in Chicago as an address, apparently not trusting a mother's weak resolve.

Lawrence's envelope was sealed. He was still in bed having drunk most of a bottle of wine the night before. She knocked. There was no reply. She let herself in. He had pushed the bedding half off him in his restless slumbers. He had not pulled the curtains properly so a broad shaft of morning light fell across the mattress. She had not seen him naked since she had stumbled in on him in the bathroom when he was fifteen. She was amazed at how lean and gnarled his body looked and how many cuts and scratches it had received, presumably in the course of his work. She gently pulled the quilt up over his shoulders again then left the envelope on his bedside table. He woke as she was leaving the room.

'She's written to you,' she told him and gestured awkwardly towards the letter. She made to go.

'No,' he said. 'Hang on.'

So she sat on the edge of the bed while he tore open the envelope and read. Bonnie had written barely one side of paper. He read it again, frowning, then passed her the letter.

'Are you sure?'

'Read it.'

The words were not laid out like a letter but ran together in a small block of prose. There were no crossings out. Dora pictured the cluster of discarded rough drafts, scrumpled up and tossed in some tastefully architectural receptacle.

Lawrence, she read, *I'm in America now with Craig. I don't know how long for. Lucy is well. She misses you but I didn't see what else I could do. I had to bring her. Maybe we can come to some arrangement in a few months but for now you have to understand that I can't see you so that means she can't see you. I was going to say I was sorry for getting*

*you involved with the police and the press like that but
now that I'm here and I can see more clearly, I can't. I'm
too angry. You fucked up, Lawrence, and I won't be made
to feel bad for your mistakes. I've done with feeling bad.
Now it's your turn. Look after Dora. She's more than you
deserve. Steer clear of Dad. He might kill you. Bonnie.*

Dora was astonished that the tone of this indignant para-
graph and that of the tender, nostalgic letter she had received
should be so crudely polarized. She began to read it again
then realized that, at long last, Lawrence had broken down
into wracked, tearless weeping, his sobs like bitter mirth.

'I drove her to him,' he said. 'I made it happen.'

She held him to her, hands flat against his hot back,
thinking how she too had played her part and imagining the
anguish of having *her* child taken from her as a punishment
for wrongdoing.

He seemed quite calm when he came down. He ate
breakfast and pleased her by taking a saw out to the
little orchard and tidying her fruit trees. He spurned all
offers of mid-morning coffee but came inside for lunch,
then announced that he was returning to his house.

'Would you drive me over?' he asked.

'Of course,' she said, bewildered. 'But you don't think it's
a bit soon? I mean, the press – '

'Fuck the press.'

'You're welcome to stay on here.'

'I want to go. I've got to get working again, even without
John. There'll be bills to pay.' He scowled. 'I'll go in a taxi
if you'd rather.'

'Don't be silly. Just let me finish my coffee.'

She had always faintly envied them their farmhouse. An
old place, mainly eighteenth century, it was set at the end of a
winding track at one corner of what had been the local great
estate before hard times and death duties forced Bonnie's
former beau, the young Lord Barrow, to sell up two-thirds

of his birthright and see his ancestral home converted into a management training centre. From the upper windows of the farmhouse one could watch business people tackling a distant assault course where two centuries of pedigree cattle had grazed. Bonnie had planted an attractive garden on two sides, which one could enter by French windows from the sitting room. There were a yard and stable block to the rear where Lucy had been promised she could house a pony once she was old enough and provided horsehair did not make her wheeze the way that cat fur did. It was a house where one could imagine a young family growing older. There was room for two more children. Dora, normally so independent, had never left it after a visit without an unguarded pang of covetousness, less of the building than of the snug, ordinary domesticity it encompassed.

Returning there now she fancied the house had lost its heart and become a melancholy shell, its brightly painted windows mere sockets onto a void. She helped Lawrence in with the two cardboard boxes of bagged up 'evidence' the police had returned. While he sorted through a great fistful of letters and free newspapers, she discreetly replaced the chainsaw in the back of the pick-up then unloaded a bag of groceries she had brought from her own kitchen – bread, milk, cheese, eggs, bacon and a bag of crisp New Zealand apples. The house felt freezing and unlived-in already. She glanced at the sink, remembering the tabloids' stories of blood, violence and uprooted hair.

'Call me if you need anything, darling,' she said and hugged him as he perused a bank statement.

'Don't worry,' he said. 'I'll be fine. Thanks.'

Perhaps he would be. Divorces were commonplace now. Lucy would travel between them for double the holidays. He might remarry. He might have more children. It was always possible, she told herself. Anything was possible. She could not, however, suppress the thought that her son was marked now, branded unweddable and unapproachable as a village outcast. He would have no second chances. He would not be fine.

She had just made herself an eggy supper to eat with a glass of sherry in front of a television programme on antiques, when the telephone rang making her start and slop sherry on her skirt. Cursing, mopping herself with a napkin, she was in no hurry to answer it.

'Mrs Frost?' A woman's voice.

'Yes?'

'It's Hecate Murray here. Your son's neighbour.'

'Oh yes. Hello.'

'I thought I'd better ring you. Oh dear.' The woman sounded distracted. 'Only there's been a bit of an accident. Don't worry. He's fine. But his van needs fixing and, well, I think you'd better – '

'Thank you. You're very kind. I'll be right over.'

Lawrence had made himself falling-down drunk then somehow made it into his van and driven down the drive and onto the Barrowcester Road. Driving on the wrong side, he had swerved to avoid an oncoming car and ended up in a ditch. The other vehicle was Hecate Murray's Morris 1000 Traveller. Its headlamps were lighting the scene as Dora pulled up. Lawrence was slumped in the back of the Morris, wrapped in a yellow tartan rug. A small woman in a duffel coat hurried over to greet her. One knew from her apologetic manner and unmade-up face precisely what sort of ten-year-old she must have been four decades or so before.

'Mrs Frost? Hecate Murray. So sorry to call you out.'

'Not at all. God!'

'Don't worry. The van's not too bad; just a light gone and a tyre and, well, the front end doesn't look too good does it? Still. We can get it towed out tomorrow. My other neighbour can do it with her tractor if we ask her nicely. He was very lucky.'

'So were you. He might have killed you.'

'Oh. I don't think so.' She seemed entirely certain. 'He's just woken up. He hit his head. I thought we should drive him to the hospital in case he's concussed.'

'Really?'

'I think so. Don't worry about the police or anything. We can just say he got drunk at home and fell over. That's it. If you get in that side – '

'Oh but I can drive him.'

'Actually it was quite a job getting him where he is,' Mrs Murray said firmly. 'I think we should leave him be. Really it's no bother.'

Dora winced as she opened the door, smelling the alcohol. And something else. An old-fashioned, inefficient sort of odour. Paraffin. Lawrence half opened his eyes and mumbled as she reached out to touch his jacket.

'That's the other thing,' Mrs Murray said, starting the car. 'He's soaked in the stuff so don't go smoking. Heaven knows what he was doing. Funny how smells take one back. We always had to get dressed by a paraffin stove in the bathroom. Warm undies on winter mornings. Very cosy. Sorry. Here.' She tugged another rug from behind her seat and settled it across Dora's lap. 'You're probably a bit shocked. Have this.'

'Thank you.'

Hecate Murray gave off a powerful aura of capability which enveloped Dora as warmly as the rug.

'You've been going through a very dark valley,' she said. 'I've been praying for you.'

'I should never have let him go home. He could have killed himself. He could have killed someone else!' Dora imagined the police, the papers, fresh scandal.

'Prayer is amazingly efficacious,' Hecate Murray continued. 'Even for non-believers. You'd be surprised.'

'Oh it's never really been my thing. Lawrence? Lawrence, can you hear me? Darling, everything's going to be fine. You're safe now.'

'Let's pray now. It will still your thoughts so you can be strong for him. Say after me. Eternal Father.'

'Eternal father,' Dora repeated thoughtlessly.

'Whose cleansing flames smote Babel and the Cities of the Plain.' Mrs Murray was a small woman but her voice was sternly compelling as an archangel's. 'Whose fire burned before Moses in the bush and came to Gideon's aid against the infidel, whose burning coals purified Isaiah's lips . . .'

The two of them prayed aloud all the way into the hospital car park. Inexorable as a dentist's probe, Hecate Murray named the unnameable: alcohol, scars, violence, broken families, maternal insufficiency, lost grandchildren, secrets. Her complete lack of diplomacy burned off all Dora's inhibitions so that Dora cried, wailed even, as she stumblingly repeated the near-stranger's solemn sentences. Still profoundly drunk but picking up the religious tone like a radio signal, Lawrence began to half-mumble, half-sing *Eternal Father Strong to Save* as he lolled from side to side on the back seat. Dora wanted to laugh, felt drunk herself. Any passing policeman would surely have flagged them down. She felt considerably stronger when she stepped out again into the chill night air. Hecate Murray gently took the rug, which Dora had forgotten was still wrapped about her. Dora assumed she would leave them there but Mrs Murray, who was plainly quite mad, tugged Lawrence out of the car and threw one of his arms over Dora's shoulder while she took the other across her own.

'Be brave,' she said. 'The Lord is with us. Take the strain.'

She steered them forwards, Lawrence still singing and with legs like untrustworthy rubber, Dora staggering under his weight, and she moved as stoutly as if the revolving doors before them were the mouth of Hell itself and they were come to liberate the souls of the lost.

Lawrence had indeed been concussed where he had struck his head on the windscreen. There might also be a touch of whiplash injury. The doctor in the casualty department wanted him kept in overnight while he sobered up and x-rays were taken.

When Hecate Murray drove Dora back to her car, she suggested they check all was well at the farmhouse. Inured by now to the curious woman's intrusiveness, Dora agreed. They found the back door swinging open and the bantams, still perilously at large, making themselves messily at home. Lawrence had made a mound of possessions in the middle of the kitchen floor. Clothes, papers, shoes, photographs, bottles of scent, greying, second-best bras, trays of cuttings from the kitchen windowsill, vitamins, old calendars, even a bottle of Tia Maria.

'What the – ?'

Dora regarded the chaos with horrified confusion for a few moments before she realized it was made up of things that were Bonnie's. The exhaustive catalogue of the fragments that accumulated around a life, thrown together became mere stuff. Like Lawrence's clothes, the pile was soaked in paraffin.

Shocked, Dora began to clear up, picking a few things off the floor, rinsing the liqueur bottle under the tap, vaguely sorting the wrecked from the salvageable. Then she gave up and slumped in a chair, beyond tears. Hecate Murray spoke with quiet authority behind her. She had forgotten the woman was still with her.

'I think it's time you involved your brother. Don't you?'

CHAPTER EIGHT

Darius and Dora were twins but it was as though they had spent their lives compensating for the early compromise of sharing a womb by each unconsciously colonizing the territory the other had passed over. Yin and Yang, they were so entirely different as to be therefore a perfect fit. Open where she was secretive, he betrayed nothing where she laid bare. He thought nothing of driving two hours to lunch on a particular partridge and could grow misty-eyed at the mere memory of a wine while she could live quite happily off Cyprus sherry and cream crackers and owed her excellent figure to a habit of forgetting mealtimes if there was anything more interesting to occupy her. She thought herself all dithering feeling while he believed himself incapable of abandoning intellectual control. (In fact, she was the one whose spirit verged on spartan while his brittle exterior concealed a spirit of violet cream.) He was lamentably stout but dressed so well that few people noticed. Dark where his sister was all English rose wispy blondeness, he liked to joke that he was Goneril to her Cordelia. Picking up on this, Dora tended to speak to Lawrence of his 'wicked uncle' while Darius referred to Dora as 'your poor mother'.

True to his ambitions, he had become rich but not from sitting in glamorous boardrooms or fighting to the top of some vast corporation. A born opportunist, he had played at business the way he had always played at Monopoly, acquiring cheap property and small businesses so that his capital was thinly invested across a broad base with minimal risk. He now owned dry-cleaning outlets, a few minicab firms, a chain of off-licences in Kent, and small hotels in Brighton, Deal and Eastbourne. He had indirectly acquired a cider factory near Taunton whose product had become unexpectedly fashionable and been handsomely bought out by a national drinks consortium. He was now taking tentative steps into the sheltered housing market. He delighted in answering enquiries with a vague,

'Oh. I'm just a businessman.'

On the side he was a keen bridge player and wrote a column on the subject for a monthly magazine, whose circulation figures were reassuringly low.

Darius was appalled at his parents' callous treatment of his twin and, liberated by his mother's death and father's foolish remarriage, had followed her to England with the intention of supporting her as they had not. He loved his nephew with an uncomplicated selflessness, loved him, low marks, unruliness and all, and was saddened when it became clear that Lawrence had neither the drive nor the inclination to go into business alongside him.

As a child, Lawrence found his uncle bewildering, full of swift speeches he did not understand and jokes whose humour he failed to grasp. At the same time, since his life with his mother was quiet and countrified, his uncle brought with him a tantalizing waft of city life. He also brought chocolates, ingenious toys, and Marvel comics. Ever alert to market trends, he told the boy to collect the comics carefully as they would be worth something one day. A complete ten-year library of the things was now tied in bundles in the farmhouse loft. Extremely male – he smoked cigars and wore enormous, heavy brogues – he also seemed at times more feminine than his independent sister – curling up in an armchair rather than sitting on the thing foursquarely, sucking crystallized violets from a small silver tin to sweeten his breath when not smoking. As a father figure, he was consistent only in his ambivalence, at once alluring and alarming, pressingly attentive one week, then coolly absent for weeks at a stretch.

Occasionally he would whisk Lawrence up to London with him for a week at his anonymous house in Pimlico, taking him on day trips in the car to check up on his various business interests, buying him new clothes, feeding him in antiquated restaurants and dazzling him with theatre or incomprehensible trips to the opera. Since these rather tense little holidays were designed to enable Dora's discreet love affairs, Lawrence always returned from them to find his mother in wistful good spirits and so came to appreciate his uncle's value elliptically, from the effect his interventions took on her.

Darius foresaw the problems in Lawrence's marriage as Dora did not. He had perceived in Lawrence a kindred, unweddable spirit. Where Lawrence became wordless and remote when cornered or overruled, Darius told the unadorned truth, which had just as devastating consequences within a relationship. He was not charmed by Bonnie; quite the contrary in fact, finding her spoiled, young for her age and, as he put it to a horrified Dora, 'falsely winsome'. He hid his distaste well, but Lawrence could not fail to notice a withdrawal on his part and a faint air of disappointment. Bonnie misread Darius' character entirely and made the fatal error of treating him with jovial disrespect, as an eccentric figure of fun, and reminding him on every occasion when he and Lucy coincided that he was now a great-uncle. He repaid her by misspelling her name or even calling her Georgie or Roberta. He did his duty by the young family, setting up a trust fund for Lucy and remembering her birthdays, did some business with Charlie Knights and even hired Bonnie to design some low-maintenance gardens for his proposed sheltered housing developments, while privately nicknaming her Capability Mauve.

If Dora had scant knowledge of Darius' private life, it was because there was so little to be known. In truth, he was far more romantic, far less independent than she. While she could often not wait to have the house to herself again, he would frequently abandon the matrimonial divan in his bedroom to sleep on the narrow Biedermeier day bed in his study because it wounded him to feel so much of a former lover's territory coldly unoccupied beside him. He hid his loneliness expertly, always buying theatre and concert tickets in pairs and entertaining couples and a string of ambiguous young men who tended to flirt, take his hospitality and opera tickets then turn up to long prepared seduction dinners with a previously undisclosed girlfriend in tow. Good, unattached bridge players were always in demand of an evening to make up fourths. Bridge was one significant level cooler than ordinary socializing and the hunger for play and the built-in formalities of the game overrode the usual etiquette whereby friendship evolved through fixed gradations of drinks for many, then dinners for eight, and on to intimate suppers for four. He often found himself cordially summoned to the houses of players he had encountered only once.

It was at one such occasion that he met the latest of the young men, a pianist called Rufus Barbour, who toyed with him blatantly all evening and made up for his poor play by a flattering thirst to learn. He had since attended two of Darius's dinners, three trips to the opera and two seduction dinners. There were two of the latter and would probably have to be a third because Rufus somehow slipped out of the first two unscathed, having soothed Darius' *amour propre* with steamily flirtatious telephone calls which managed to suggest that he was at once persuadable and heart-warmingly scared. Before risking a third, Darius opted for one of the grander gestures in his arsenal – the free holiday. As a bridge correspondent, he had been invited on a Caribbean cruise and could bring a companion. Rufus was suitably impressed and accepted with alacrity. The thought of this sustained Darius on a tour of German fake fur factories with some rivals who wanted him to participate in an import deal. He trusted that good food and unseasonal sunshine and balmy Caribbean nights would succeed where a scandalous Meyerbeer revival and his most *outré* recipe for pigeon breasts had failed.

There were only two messages on his answering machine when he returned. One was from Rufus, dryly announcing that he was unable to come cruising after all because his 'sort-of fiancée' had been summoned to a psychiatry conference in Oslo and wanted him to come with. The other was one of Dora's. Dora tended to talk to the machine at length, much as though Darius were listening but somehow unable to respond. Her tone was confidential. She was worried about being overheard.

'I'm going quietly out of my tiny mind,' she announced. 'First he crashed the van. Blind drunk. Almost killed Hecate Murray. Then he was so hopeless I brought him back here and now he's become a sort of cuckoo and refuses to go home or start work again. I talk to him. I try to make him talk. But we don't seem to connect.' She sighed and Darius heard her gulp from a drink. There was a sound of machinery in the background as though someone were ploughing up her garden with a tractor. 'It's as though I'm having one conversation and he's having another. In another room. A day later. Oh God. Darius, I think he's having a sort of breakdown.' She broke off again and, after another clink of ice in her glass, she added, in a brighter tone, 'Come down when you can. It would be lovely.'

He found Lawrence in the garden, digging a new border in the middle of Dora's lawn.

'Darius!' The boy greeted him cheerfully enough. 'Can't shake, sorry.' He indicated the mud that caked his fingers and forearms.

'I stopped by your place to look at the van,' Darius told him. 'Christ what a mess! What have your insurers said?'

It was as though his question had bounced off glass.

'I thought with a new border here we could have some peonies. She's always hankered after peonies. Then I can move that rose, which should *never* have been put over there, it's far too big, and divide up some of the delphiniums to re-establish some here at the back. What do you think?'

'Great,' said Darius uncertainly. He saw that the garden was one great scene of transformation. There were heaps of earth everywhere on old fertilizer bags. Every tool in Dora's small armoury seemed to be in use and Lawrence had even hired a bright orange diesel-powered rotovator. A bonfire crackled threateningly in one corner and the hedges and fruit trees had been cut back so heavily that they were stumpy shadows of their former selves. 'Shouldn't you be watching that fire?' Darius asked. Lawrence glanced over his shoulder at the smoking blaze.

'Oh no,' he said carelessly. 'It's fine as it is,' and he turned back to cut away more of Dora's precious turf. Backing off, Darius was startled by some bantams which appeared to be running wild. He nearly tripped over one and thought he heard Lawrence laugh.

Dora tapped on the window and threw him a wan smile. Darius hurried inside. She was in her study, a small nest of tapestried cushions, ticking clocks and glittering bibelots. A formal photograph of their parents stood on the desk. It was taken in carefree youth yet even then the couple emanated a scornful indignation, ripe for outrage. Dora saw it catch his eye and turned to look at it too for a moment before she walked into his embrace and held on.

'Thank God you've come.'

'He doesn't seem so bad.'

'Darius, I'll have no garden *left* if he stays much longer. Sorry. Sit down. You must be tired after the drive. Tea? Gin?'

'Stop it,' he checked her and made her sit too. 'What about the van?'

'They're dragging their feet. I'm sure it's a write-off – the engine seems to be stoved in – but they're havering. He'll lose his no-claims bonus and, from what I can make out, he barely has enough in his account to pay his excess on the repair bill much less put down the deposit on a new pick-up.'

'But when that's sorted out, can't he go back to work?'

'That bastard John Docherty stitched him up. He got Lawrence to sign some document which effectively surrendered the clients with the partnership. Anyway, he needs to get away from Barrowcester. People are still gossiping. So horrible. If he went somewhere new he could start afresh maybe.'

'What about therapy?'

'Hecate found us someone and he went two or three times but he retreated into stony silence and it was all a waste of money. The therapist spoke to me in the end and said she felt he had "unfinished business" with Bonnie and couldn't begin to progress until he'd spoken with her. Strange woman. Oh Darius he's so *hopeless*! Why did he have to be so hopeless? And I miss Bonnie. And Lucy. And I can't even mention them in front of him and – Oh God.'

She had been walking fretfully about the room as she talked, fingering paperweights, minutely adjusting lampshades.

'Never mind him. You need a break. This has all been too much for you.'

'Oh don't pay any attention to me. I'm just rabbiting because I haven't seen you for weeks. Anyway, Hecate's been a huge help.'

'Who's this woman?'

'Hecate Murray. She lives near him. She's quite peculiar, very religious. You'd probably hate her.'

'I probably should. Listen. There's a cruise I've been asked to go on. You know. As a bridge coach. It's the SS *Paulina*. They'd pay for me plus a companion. Three weeks. Southampton to Miami then down to the Bahamas and the Virgin Islands and back to Miami to fly home. Quite fun. Probably hideous people, Americans mainly, but – '

'But that would be *perfect*.'

'You think so? I'm so glad.'

'It would take him right out of himself. No one on board would know about, well, his being arrested and everything.'

'But I meant it for you. You and me. You never go on holiday.'

'Oh. But I couldn't possibly leave him alone, even if Hecate offered to help. No, darling, take Lawrence. You haven't spent time with him for such ages. You'd be helping him and giving me a rest. If he grants me power of attorney, I can deal with the insurance claim and have things a little more organized by the time he gets back. Yes that's *such* a good idea. How kind of you. Now. Let me fix us both a nice drink and call Lawrence in to tell him.'

She kissed his cheek with a gratitude that bordered on triumph and crossed the hall to the kitchen. Darius looked through the window to where Lawrence, a roughly handsome version of his mother in the low autumn sunlight, broke off from heaving earth back into a fertilized trench to stretch his straining back. In his wistful mind's eye, Darius saw Rufus in neat white shorts and deck shoes and a suggestive smirk.

'Well you had better teach him the fundamentals at least. Lend him that book on basic bridge bidding I gave you . . .' He tried to picture Lawrence with a fistful of cards, grimacing with the effort of assessing the hand dealt him. 'Are you sure you couldn't get away?' he asked, plaintively.

'Only three weeks. It might be fun. I was looking forward to spending time with *you*.'

Dora came into the kitchen doorway, listening at the

mouth of a half-used bottle of tonic water to see if the stuff were undrinkably flat or merely a little tired.

'I get seasick,' she reminded him. 'Lawrence will be much better company.'

CHAPTER NINE

Seating plans for dinner on the *Paulina* were rigorously fixed so as to avoid anarchy and, presumably, the hideous embarrassment of unseemly scrambles to avoid dining with the unattractive or disadvantaged. Darius and Lawrence had a good table in the second sitting, as befitted the resident bridge expert and companion, but not too good a one, because they were travelling gratis and already had corner cabins with balconies and bathrooms that actually contained baths. (Rejecting the first, poky cabins they were shown to, Darius had snorted that a second glance at the shipping line's brochure would probably reveal an admission in tiny print that the photographs of accommodation were printed 'actual size'.)

Lawrence's nerves had been rattled since an ugly scene at Southampton. As they passed through passport control, an immigration officer recognized his name, took one look at his baseball cap and dark glasses and hauled him out of the queue, taking him for a fugitive from justice. Darius protested, had a police officer summoned and a telephone call made and Lawrence was released, with apologies, but not before several of the passengers had been led to recognize him. He had already glanced at the dining room as Darius dragged him on a quick tour of the *Paulina*'s public areas, so he knew the room was reached by descending a theatrical glass and chrome staircase in full view of the assembled company and he was dreading further exposure.

'I'll be fine,' he assured Darius. 'I'll just eat something up here. Some sandwiches. A glass of wine. I'll be fine.'

'Nonsense,' his uncle protested. 'You can't hide up here indefinitely. You've got to face them all some time. We have to dine in public tonight as we're guests of the shipping line. Anyway, those ghastly people in customs are probably travelling down on Mariner Deck or whatever it was called, and will have asked to eat at six-thirty. There are nearly five hundred people on board, probably more including all the staff and crew. It's like a floating city. You'll hardly ever see the same people twice unless you try to.'

When his mother and Darius had presented him with the cruise invitation, they had been so busy talking, trying to convince him, possibly trying to convince themselves, that they had not noticed his lack of response. He had not said no, but he had not agreed either. Truth to say, he found the very idea bewildering. He continued to feel a profound sense of blame. In the rapid dissolution of his home and his work, no one was at fault but he and he felt he merited some punishment. Even if the removal of his daughter were considered punishment enough, he still did not feel worthy of worldly treats. Yet here he was, royally treated.

He had seized on various large-scale projects in his mother's garden because planting and pruning seemed to be the only area in which he was not left paralysed by indecision and he could not bear inactivity, as it turned him in on himself. He could not pursue Bonnie for fear that might drive her away still further. She knew how much he loved the child, she knew how much this was hurting him. She held a gun to his heart. The next move had to be hers. If, from all his conflicting needs he had to select one, it would be to have Lucy back. Bonnie he could accept as lost, a hostage to his own ingratitude and crass stupidity, but Lucy had become such a vital component of his life that the loss of her was like a removal of sunlight or water and he could not function in her absence. Without her it was all one to him whether he was in his house or his mother's, in a prison cell or a liner stateroom. He entered into a bland passivity, mindful that if he could not please himself, he might, at least, avoid displeasing others. If his uncle wanted his unrewarding company suddenly, he should have it. If his mother suddenly required him to learn bridge, he would try his level best.

She lent him a book on the subject but he found he only stared at the text and diagrams without taking anything in. Perceiving the problem, she set up a card table in the sitting room and, for several successive afternoons, her odd new friend, Hecate Murray, was pressed in as a fourth while his mother played both first and third player.

'The game falls into three parts,' she explained. 'Hand assessment, bidding and play. Play is exactly like whist. You remember whist, don't you, darling?'

'No.'

'Oh. Well. Never mind. We cut for dealer. Aces high and the suits go spades, hearts, diamonds, clubs in descending order. So. You're dealer, see?'

'No.'

'It's quite easy. Hecate cuts to you as she's on your right. That's it. Now you deal the whole pack out into four piles of thirteen. That's it. Now we sort out hands into suits and assess their worth. Aces are four, kings three, queens two, knaves one. You count points for voids, singletons and doubletons but that's later.'

'You've lost me. Sorry.'

'Surely not. Am I going too fast, Hecate?'

'Just a little, dear. But I'm with you. I think.'

'Well the trick is not to question anything yet. Just accept and remember.'

'Like a new religion.'

'Yes, Hecate. If you like.'

The week before their departure, Darius had swooped down

on his sister's house and taken Lawrence to London to buy him a wardrobe.

'Something I've been meaning to do for years.'

Lawrence watched his reflection in a succession of mahogany looking-glasses as he was kitted out with a dinner jacket, a linen suit the colour of old newspaper, black shoes, suede brogues, deck shoes, swimming trunks, shorts, impenetrable tortoiseshell sunglasses and a bouquet of shirts of startling hues but impeccable quality.

'People will think I'm your boyfriend,' he said, who had worn nothing but jeans and rugger shirts for as long as he could remember. Darius stared at him a moment as they stood on a Jermyn Street pavement.

'What better alias could you hope for? You're fixed in the public mind as a suspected uxoricide, not a rich man's clothes horse.'

Before dinner, they had to attend the captain's drinks party. It was a strained affair. Darius was keen to meet the officers but found they were all Norwegian and spoke only strenuously polite English devoid of ironic nuance. Nobody had met anyone else before, so passengers stood about with their travelling companions, overtures were muted, introductions led only to doomed dribbles of conversation. The sole genuine revelry emerged when a group of Norwegian Englishwomen boarded. They had all married British soldiers after the last world war, left their homeland for love and now, apparently, formed a loyal social club which organized group holidays for them. The officers fell on them with Norse cries of delight and a bottle of highly toxic warmed aquavit began to circulate. It was served in small Viking helmets of translucent plastic. Darius and Lawrence downed two apiece before braving the dining room.

This was an oval, windowless space the size and style of an Odeon cinema, plunging down through three deck levels in the SS *Paulina*'s heart. It glittered with chrome railings, bevelled glass and polished wood and was plainly one of the few areas where the ship's original 1930s details had been left unaltered. On panels of beaten tin, Art Deco imagery was chosen to remind one of none but the tamest, sand-bordered water. Muscular boys carried a swimsuited girl aloft, hatchet-faced children tossed a ball, women raced on bicycles, men on foot. There was not an iceberg, breaker, lighthouse or shark in sight. As throughout the ship, there were no curtains nor any freely dangling soft furnishings whose sudden change in angle to the walls might emphasize the great boat's churning motion through the ocean.

Lawrence was sure heads turned and people stared as they made their entrance but Darius assured him they were glancing up at everyone who entered.

'It's first night curiosity, that's all. Besides, if they do recognize you, they won't show it. Those sort of people will have eaten earlier. Now. Something to take away the filthy taste of that dry-cleaning fluid, I think . . .'

They shared their table with two other non-matrimonial pairs. There was a mother travelling with her grown-up daughter. The daughter, who had Down's syndrome, was wreathed in smiles but struck dumb by shy confusion. Her mother had been abandoned by her husband when the girl was still a child, had taken to bridge to fill her lonely evenings and, she confessed, had become 'quite obsessed' with the game to the point of teaching it in her local adult education centre. The daughter, Jess, would occasionally lean her head on her mother's shoulder or reach out to squeeze her arm. The mother pretended to be embarrassed at such displays of powerful affection but Lawrence noticed how they warmed her and disarmed, even now the afflicted girl had lost the sweetness of childhood. Lawrence smiled at Jess as he offered her the bread basket. She shied away at first then, deciding he was friendly, smiled broadly at him whenever she fancied his face was turned in her direction.

The other pair were an attractive brother and sister in their thirties. Reuben Calder, whose manner was too calm for comfort, his eyes too bright, his teeth too sharp, had been hired to write about the cruise for a leading women's magazine and, like Darius, had brought a spare relative along for the free ride. He and Darius promptly fell to high-octane small talk, while Jess began to have difficulties with her food and annexed all her mother's attention. Thus the spare relatives were thrown together. Bee was convention-ally pretty, with a heart-shaped face, generous lips and dark brown hair which she tucked repeatedly behind her ears. He was not surprised to notice her wedding ring or learn that she taught the junior form at a cathedral choir school, but he was when she said the school was in his home town.

'But I'm from Barrowcester too,' he exclaimed. 'I was even at your school.'

'I know,' she said, adding in a rapid undertone. 'I'm sure you don't want to talk about it but I think the newspapers have treated you and your mother dreadfully. I'm so very sorry. I – er – Well. News travels fast in a place like that.'

Her kindness wrong-footed him. Something about him – the illusion held in common with half the country, perhaps, that she knew all the salient points of his intimate life – caused her to drop her guard as well. As they talked of their ambivalent feelings towards life in a provincial backwater, she told him how her husband, the cathedral organist, had died a few years ago of a brain haemorrhage and she had subsequently suffered a faintly disgraceful romantic disappointment with a rugger-playing colleague who had gone on to marry her best friend. He saw that she was so given to frowning in self-deprecation that her high forehead was permanently marked, scarred by care. She saw him glance at her wedding ring and instinctively covered it with her other hand, then twisted it about.

'I thought quite seriously about leaving it off for the cruise,' she said. 'Reuben said it would mislead people and cramp my style. Anyway, I'd never taken it off, never, and my finger must have grown fatter since poor Tony married me because it wouldn't budge and I had to use olive oil to slide it off. But it left this awful ring of pale, yellowy skin, like a kind of brand – the merry widow's mark – which never seemed to fade, so I put the ring back on. I mean, better to be passed over and taken for a married woman than mistaken for a would-be adulteress. Sorry. That sounds rather old-fashioned. I teach too much divinity. Adulteress. Fornication. Whore. There are no kind words. No neutral ones.'

Lawrence discarded his inedibly tough lamb cutlet and helped himself to more potatoes and gravy.

'Do you think marriage is so respectable?' he asked.

'Sorry. I'm putting my foot in it.'

'No you're not. Do you?' he repeated.

She teased her ring again.

'I always used to.' She smiled to herself, frowning. 'Funny. I couldn't wait to be Mrs Some Man's Name. I thought it sounded so grown-up. I still do, when I'm addressing Christmas cards. All those invisible, stately female presences. Mrs Clive Hart. Mrs St John Delaney-Siedentrop. And I still find Miss sounds brave and rather sad and Ms is inaudible really, because no one knows how to pronounce it so that it sounds different, and if they do, they pull a silly face when they do it, as if to apologize for being modern. Of course marriage is respectable,' she went on firmly. 'It's hypocritical, it's outdated, but what else is there? Supported by law and church, it's rock solid.' She eased off her ring with another small frown. 'There,' she said, and dropped it on her side plate with a clatter that made the others turn to look at her. 'I've just become a merry widow for the duration,' she told them and laughed in a way that made Lawrence want to shield her from the room.

'Tell me about trees,' Jess's mother asked Lawrence firmly as if to say that she thought things needed bringing back to less slippery territory. 'Do we have any native varieties left or has the whole country been invaded by imports?' And as Lawrence began to answer her, he watched Bee fall to a nervously rapid consumption of her cutlet.

It was marketed as a bridge cruise. The *Paulina* also hosted cruises for ballroom dancing, country and western music, detoxification, chess and weight loss. In fact all its cruises followed roughly the same routes and daily timetables with fruit carving demonstrations, fancy dress parties, gambling, bingo and nightly entertainment while the particular theme of each cruise was merely slotted into a few spare hours a day. On the bridge cruises, the library and the largest bar were permanently set up with card tables and stocked with fresh decks of cards, pencils, duplicate wallets and score sheets, though nothing so fearsome as bidding boxes. As the on-board expert, Darius had to be available every morning and evening to act as tournament director, tutor or match pathologist as required. Avoid blundering novices as he might, strictly speaking he was to refuse no one a game.

Jess's mother had clearly been living in hope but Jess became seasick and they were forced to abandon the dining room before the arrival of some glutinous yellow puddings fringed with pineapple. Reuben, who was clearly better than proficient, had already agreed to play and Lawrence, who had hoped to escape, was alarmed to find brother and sister pressing him to join them.

'You've read the book, haven't you?' Darius asked him.

'Yes,' Lawrence lied, 'but – '

'And Dora laid on a few rubbers for you?'

'Yes, only – '

'Well then.'

'It's only glorified whist,' Reuben added. 'You'll love it. We'll only play rubber bridge. Nothing scary like duplicate.'

'You're on this boat for three weeks,' Darius reminded him. 'You can't escape indefinitely and I'm relying on you to save me in case Mrs Night-School comes back.'

'Tell you what,' Bee suggested kindly. 'You can partner

me. Reuben has to win, whatever he says, and would only get cross with you. I never get cross.'

'Oh all right. But I'm going to be useless.'

'So?' She smiled. 'How do you know I'm not?'

'This is Hell. This is Hell. I'm so bad you've no idea,' he muttered as they all headed upstairs to the library and coffee. He was surprised to feel her take his arm.

'Don't *worry*!' she chuckled. 'We'll play no conventions but a strong no trump – that's sixteen to eighteen points and a flat hand . . .' And she reassured him by repeating the old wives' sayings of the game which his mother had already striven to impress on him during his period of intensive tuition. *Lead into Dummy's strength and round to his weakness. Cover an honour with an honour. Three noes and a fool goes. If in doubt, lead trumps out. Second plays low, third plays high.*

He followed these sayings obediently. He led his singletons, he high-lowed his doubletons, he led the highest of his partner's suit and duly returned her opening leads but Reuben and Darius tripped him up with their low cunning. They misleadingly discarded picture cards then devastated his humble tactics and won tricks with mere twos and threes. They somehow calculated precisely what he held in his hand so that his hard-saved aces and kings, which he had trusted would flummox them, were rendered powerless by coolly dropped junior trumps or by an aching lack of appropriate leads. Reuben showed a nasty tendency to crow that was made no better by Darius's impatient sighs.

Bee's patience was saintly however.

'Never mind,' she would say, as he laid down a woefully underbid dummy or gave their opponents extra tricks by discarding apparently insignificant fives and sevens that would otherwise have mysteriously brought them in one trick short of a contract. Having won his assurance that he did not mind her doing so, she quietly and concisely explained where he had gone wrong after each game.

'Never mind,' she said sweetly as he apologized as yet another rubber fell to the enemy. 'You'll soon learn. We were all beginners once anyway. Their contract was impregnable. Your lead was fine. You weren't to know Rube had a void. It was just bad luck and after that we didn't stand a chance.' Where anyone else might reasonably have shown anger or at least a mild vexation, she gave merely a wry, private smile. He thought of her husband's death and tried to imagine her wild with grief.

When Bee pleaded exhaustion after five rubbers, Lawrence seized the opportunity to leave the library with her, thus freeing Reuben and Darius to find another pair to trounce.

'I wasn't really tired,' she confessed. 'I just felt them itching to move on to greater things and Reuben can be such hell when he's winning too much.'

The third deck from the top, the deck above the library, was dedicated to fitness. There was a large, glass-walled gym at one end, a swimming pool for those who scorned the lazy pleasures of the bubbling lounge pools on the sun deck, and a squash court. The rest of the deck was open to the elements. A basketball court was marked out at the stern and the outer perimeter formed a jogging track, punctuated by benches for the breathless and the idle. Lawrence walked with Bee about the track, enjoying the buffeting of the wind and the sickening roll of the ship as it ploughed the black wastes of the Atlantic. They passed a few intrepid moonlit joggers and a grey-faced family evidently trying the fresh air method for battling their sea sickness. She reminisced about childhood crossings to the Isle of Wight and suddenly he was pouring out his heart about how much he missed Lucy and how he would probably not see her now for years. Bonnie had taken her to America. The child would be raised an American, with a rich American father. Lawrence would be denied access and when, at last, he met Lucy again, they would be strangers.

'Sorry,' he said. 'I'm being pathetic and melodramatic. And pissed. Don't encourage me. I moan with no encouragement. And I've no right.'

'You've every right,' she said and suddenly they were kissing.

She was the only woman apart from Bonnie who had kissed him in years and the effect was as electrifying as any teenage grope. Had he considered her earlier in a sexual light, it would never have happened. He would have considered her, rejected the possibility and passed on safely unperturbed. He usually did. Any new woman to enter his orbit was immediately assessed, albeit from a purely theoretical angle. He assumed this was something all men did, like sniffing shirts to see if they could wear them twice or shaking a few times after they finished having a piss in case of drips. Bee, however, had somehow eluded the usual process and been simply the person she was, a sympathetic ear, a kind smile, a pensive gaze.

He pressed her against one of the steel girders that held the lifeboats aloft, newly aware that she had unexpectedly generous breasts, and felt his heart pound as if he had drunk too much coffee.

'Sorry,' she stammered. 'You wanted to talk, didn't you?'

'Did I?'

He kissed her again with a hunger that was, he felt sure, as impersonal for her as it was for him. Judging from her narrative, she had slept with no one since her romantic disappointment with the rugger master. She smelled of soap and tasted of lamb cutlet and red wine. Strictly speaking, this was adultery, yet he felt no guilt, only an overmastering, automatic desire. But suddenly she was fighting him off.

'No. Lawrence? Er. No. I'm ... I'm so sorry,' she stammered.

'What's up?'

'I'm ... It's nothing to do with you. Nothing wrong, I mean. It's just that I'm not ready for ...'

'I rushed you.'

'No. I rushed. I shouldn't have. Too much wine on top of seasick pills. Or something. Sorry.'

Flustered, she smiled, and kissed his cheek, which he took as his dismissal. He backed away, grateful at least that he did not have to fumble after lost socks or tangled underwear.

'Night, then,' he muttered and watched her slip away and disappear through a door.

A party of laughing Italians emerged in her wake. Lawrence fled up the stairs all the way to the sun deck. There he stood on the Astroturf and leaned against a railing to look up at the vapour cloud that billowed from a towering smokestack, until he grew dizzy at the way the great silhouette pitched up and down against the pattern of stars beyond. Turning to stare back at where the boat's myriad portholes cast a ghostly glow across its churning wake, he thought nothing of his uncle, of the woman he had just lunged at, of how he was to get through the three purgatorial weeks ahead. He felt only a profound, calming sense of detachment and thought, if it were possible with the wind flapping his clothes and the sea boiling all about him, of nothing at all.

CHAPTER TEN

Only with the following morning did the folly of what he had done dawn on Lawrence. This was no casual encounter in a pub or ordinary holiday fling. He had crudely pounced on a perfectly nice, actually rather sweet woman, possibly the only remotely sweet woman on the entire boat, and now she would avoid him, mortified, and they were trapped in this floating purgatory for another three weeks under five hundred pairs of watchful eyes.

Darius had already formed some kind of alliance with her brother – doubtless based on smug supremacy at the card table. The two men were heartily breakfasting together when he shuffled out onto the aft restaurant deck in search of toast and coffee. Reuben was got up in a jaunty, faintly nautical outfit. Darius had relaxed sufficiently to wear one of his more overtly woolly weekend suits. Lawrence decided to play innocent in the hope of their ignorance.

'Ah. Three down, one to go,' Darius said as he joined them. 'Sleep well? It got pretty rough in the small hours.'

'Yes thanks,' said Lawrence, although he had spent half the night clinging to his mattress for fear of rolling off his bed and the other half suffering cramps as a result. 'Your sister's not up yet, then?' he asked Reuben.

'Amazingly not. She's normally up for hours before anyone else, reading and writing letters and taking walks and generally putting everyone else to shame. A lie-in's a very good sign. She needed a holiday so badly.'

'Unless she's sick, of course,' put in Darius.

'Oh she's definitely not sick,' Reuben went on. 'I heard

her singing to herself in the bath as I was leaving my cabin.'

'Sea air must agree with her.'

'She so deserves a good break. I expect she told you, Lawrence, she's had a run of bad luck. Shitty men. She's always had hopeless taste in men. I mean it was hideous to have him drop dead like that but Tony was a pimple of a husband really. Then there was the bloody rugger bugger – '

'Well good morning!' Darius stood with a pointed smile, to indicate that Bee was approaching beyond Reuben's sight line. Lawrence, like Reuben, remained firmly in his chair. She waved, passed on to the buffet table and returned with a bowl of lurid fruit salad and a pot of natural yoghurt. Even with dark glasses on, she had a certain glow.

'Morning,' Lawrence said, his voice emerging strangled. He fell to buttering his toast, which had dried out and so shattered disloyally under pressure. He caught her eye, smiled and saw just a terribly sweet woman who did nothing for him. Whatever had possessed him? Judging from her satisfied feline smile, she was not remotely put out by the memory of the night before; she was prepared, indeed, for some vengeful teasing.

'You both missed the midnight buffet last night,' said Darius.

'What's that?' she asked. 'Leftovers from dinner?'

'No,' Reuben enthused, 'a whole new meal. These people live to eat, I tell you. Their ticket price includes food so nothing is to pass them by. There's a different theme every night. Mexican. Italian. Tutti Frutti.'

'What was last night's?'

'Scapa Flow, I think. There was a lot of soused herring.'

'I'll see you all later.' Lawrence could bear it no longer, so jumped up, taking his coffee with him.

'Vegetable Sculpture at eleven,' Reuben called after him. 'Be there or be square.'

'Bridge Basics at twelve,' Darius added.

Lawrence drank his coffee on a wrought-iron bench outside an ersatz French patisserie where all cakes were free. It lay at one end of what had once been a promenade open to the elements. He tried to imagine rows of passengers tucked up beneath liveried blankets on steamer chairs; sour older women with wide-eyed daughters, honeymooners too exhausted by passion to do more than clutch hands and gaze out at the passing desert of grey-blue wave, long-married couples united by a tacit agreement to read away a morning in silence. The passengers who strolled here now, however, in their acid-toned tracksuits and unwise shorts, were a far cry from the elegant ghosts they trampled. The bracing spaces in the former promenade had been filled with windows that did not open and the resultant long corridor was left largely chairless, the better to encourage passengers to shop in a string of pointless boutiques. Lawrence frowned at his 'orientation map' and saw that he was sitting on the Champs Elysées and could cross to a corresponding deckside 'street' no less confidently dubbed Fifth Avenue, which he did in a spirit of depressed curiosity. These were the shops advertised whenever he had turned on his cabin television. They sold cultured pearls and ugly overpriced 'fashion wear' with stitched-on motifs, glittery beads and sequins. There was a chemist, a barbershop called Herr Kutz, a beauty parlour called Cheeky Miss, a thinly stocked bookshop-cum-newsagent and rack upon dispiriting rack of souvenirs which bore no discernible relation to any of their Caribbean destinations.

He caught sight of Bee at the other end of Fifth Avenue. She smiled and seemed to want to speak so he held her at bay with a quick wave and ducked into a stairwell. He began to pace, furiously retracing the tour he had taken with Darius the afternoon before. The sun deck was unpleasantly windy, since they were still mid-Atlantic, and short on sun. Undeterred, a gang of children was already larking around in the outdoor pools, shrieking at the way the dipping and rolling of the ship caused the pool water to slap up over the sides and knock them about. A *Paulina* childminder, evidently forced to accompany them, was trying to interest them in an inflated plastic beach ball. Her arms were grey and goose-bumped with cold. In the bingo lounge he stumbled on the crowd already assembling for the chef's vegetable carving demonstration and hurried out again. He passed the ballroom, where another crowd was solemnly learning to chachacha and, realizing he was hungry, ordered more coffee and a chocolate muffin in an area perkily defined as Polly Pretzel's Milk Bar. He gained no thrill from being served without money changing hands.

A tall, thin, white-haired man in a check shirt pulled out the other stool at his table.

'Mind if I join you?'

Lawrence tried not to frown. His mouth was full so he merely shrugged. The man, who was American, sat parallel to Lawrence, also watching the passing groups of passengers. He stirred some Sweet 'n' Low into his coffee, sipped it and sighed.

'So what are you doing in this hell hole?'

'My uncle had a free ticket.'

'You too, huh? Martha won ours in some magazine competition she filled in at the dentist's. They flew us to London for a week first. I already feel as if we've been away for months. Crazy. You don't look like a bridge player.'

'I'm not. My mother is. He wanted to bring her but she sent me instead. I'm starting to see why.'

'We could always jump ship in Miami.'

'Do we get to go ashore there?'

'We get a whole day. They need to restock the kitchens and take on more gimcrackety crap to sell in these stores, I guess. They'll be bussing us all out to some remote shopping mall they've done some deal with. It's not exactly *An Affair to Remember*.'

'Sorry?'

'What? Oh. It's just a film. A very old film.'

The American drained his coffee and made a face at it.

'Poodle's piss,' he muttered. 'The name's George.'

'Lawrence.'

They shook hands and Lawrence noticed he was as tanned and weather-beaten as a cowboy.

'So what do you do, Lawrence?'

'I'm a kind of tree surgeon.'

'Well either you are or you ain't.'

'I am. I'm a tree surgeon.' Lawrence felt himself smile. George nodded slowly, watching him.

'That's good,' he said. 'It's good to work outside. Too much indoors drives a man mad. So why's that?'

'I dunno.' Lawrence shrugged. 'I like trees. I like the feel of them. I spent a lot of time climbing them as a boy. I could have been a carpenter, I suppose. I liked the smell of cut timber.'

'And trees don't yabber all the time, right?'

'Something like that.' Lawrence smiled again. 'How about you?'

'I used to farm. Now I'm retired and we've moved to the coast. Martha's a potter. She's got her kiln and a workshop. Takes it quite seriously now. People have started buying her stuff. Say, if you like trees you should get your hands round one of our sequoias. Now *that's* a tree.'

'There you are!'

A middle-aged woman was approaching them. She might have been George's twin but for the fact that she was nearly two feet shorter; same tan, same checked shirt, same short white hair. George reached out to take her hand briefly as she pulled up another stool.

'Found another refugee,' he murmured. 'Missing his trees.'

'Oh. I hope he hasn't been depressing you too much, young man.'

'This is Lawrence.'

'I'm Martha. George and Martha. We've heard all the jokes and we *hate* Virginia Woolf.'

'I'm sorry?'

Seeing Lawrence's confusion, she patted his arm.

'Oh, nothing. Just an old play. So you miss trees? I just want some grass, tired old cow that I am. Do you play bridge, then, Lawrence?'

'We've been through all that. He's a refugee like us.'

'Oh but I want to learn. There's a Bridge Basics class at twelve with Darius Blake who's a real expert so I thought we should – '

'That's my uncle.'

'No!'

'He brought me along on this.'

'Well then we *must* go. George? Just the once? We might love it and we'd get to meet folks.'

'Just what I was afraid of.'

'Oh baloney.' Martha laughed, showing wonderfully white teeth and smacked her husband playfully on the chest with the back of her hand. 'I told him when we won this that we didn't have to come, it wasn't costing us any, but he was keen as mustard. Deep down,' she confided to Lawrence, lowering her voice, 'very deep down, I think he's sort of enjoying himself. We lead such a quiet life since we sold the farm. Is your wife with you, Lawrence?' she asked suddenly, having glanced at his battered wedding ring.

'My – er. We're not together any more.'

'Oh. I'm sorry to hear that,' she sighed. 'Any kids?'

'Just the one. A little girl.'

'What's she called?'

'Lucy.'

'Well that's the strangest thing. That's our girl's name too. She's long grown up and left us of course. Lives in Seattle now in a converted meat fridge – the darnedest weird place. But her lady friend's from round there. Rosanna. I'm sorry. Does that shock you?'

'What? Oh. Not really.'

'Quit yabbering, woman.'

'Am I yabbering? I'm sorry. I've had women showing me photos of their grandchildren all morning and I reckon it's got to my brain somehow.'

She smiled mischievously and Lawrence could not help smiling back, so that she patted the back of his hand.

'Larry here's a tree surgeon,' George said gruffly.

'Well isn't that great. I could tell you worked with your hands on account of the state of them, poor things. You should see the trees up by our place. Hundreds of years old and wider than my Chevy.'

'I was just telling him that when you came along.'

Lawrence felt almost happy. There was something soothing about the way this couple talked, their bickering speech rhythms mirroring each other like the question and answer calls of two foraging birds. He was disarmed too by their natural admiration of what he did for a living. He had been too long exposed to Bonnie's friends who plainly viewed the fact that he was not a doctor or a solicitor as a social stile to be scaled with the maximum show of gracious condescension.

'Hello.' Suddenly Bee was amongst them, wanly smiling, in jeans and a crisp white shirt. She had caught him. She kissed him slyly on the cheek and pulled over a stool so that she was between him and Martha. 'You vanished so suddenly at breakfast. I missed you,' she said.

'Oh. Well. I've been walking around. Er. This is Martha. This is George. This is Bee.'

'Hello.'

'Hello, dear.'

He could see Martha brightly assessing the new arrival. Woman who broke up marriage? Not the type. So she must be Girl he turned to when Wicked Wife left him, poor boy.

'Bee's a teacher,' he said. 'Martha's a potter.'

'So are you two engaged?' Martha asked, eyes twinkling as George studiously ignored them all to read an ice cream menu. Bee gasped.

'Well, no,' she said. 'Hardly. We've barely met.'

Lawrence pushed back his chair.

'Time for Bridge Basics,' he mumbled. 'Darius will kill me if I don't show willing.'

'Oh but we're coming with you,' Martha said.

'Me too,' added Bee, rising with him. 'My bidding's got so rusty.'

'Well I'll see you down there. I just need to get something. Erm. Bye, George.'

Face hot with confusion and anger, he hurried away before they could gather themselves to follow. He headed towards his cabin, then realized they could find him there; he had no intention of being dragged off to Bridge Basics for further humiliation after last night's display.

How could she? She had seemed so sweet. He had been feeling bad for making a vulgar pass at someone so vulnerable and open. He need not have bothered. He remembered the way she had coyly insinuated herself between him and the old woman, shyly pecking him on the cheek, coming on like a lovebird. He had never been able to take teasing as a child, as a man he found it intolerable. She was going to be merciless, secure in the knowledge that she was unanswerable.

He angrily punched the button to summon a lift. As he waited, however, he heard Darius's distinctively fruity tones approaching up the stairwell so he turned aside, hurried back onto the Champs Elysées and dived in at the first open door.

It was a chapel. Panting, Lawrence barely had time to take in the abstract stained glass, electrically lit from behind, the soft organ music piped from below a gaudy flower arrangement, the stripped pine pews, the flickering sanctuary lamp, before a man dressed like a Mormon with a buzz cut like a marine's, had sprung out of the shadows to trap him in a sunny smile and outstretched, seemingly elastic arms. He could have been any age between a sun-wrinkled forty and a sinisterly apple-cheeked sixty-five.

'Welcome welcome. I'm Father Xavier or just Xavier if you prefer, or indeed Father.' He laughed. It was as though Lawrence had tripped an invisible switch that flung him into motion like some sophisticated puppet. There was a cluster of emblematic badges on his lapel – a crucifix, a star of David, a red ribbon, a pink triangle, a shamrock leaf, a CND symbol and an Islamic moon. 'Have I left anything out?' he asked, following Lawrence's gaze. 'I am the boat's all-purpose faith resource and holy person and I tell you the strain can be bewildering sometimes. Come in, come in. What can I do for you?'

'Well actually I was just hiding from somebody.'

'Quite understandable. And so many of them to hide from now.' He guffawed. His accent was either Welsh, Irish or American and had perhaps started as one, travelled towards the other and become mired between all three in mid-Atlantic. 'Sit down do. The seats are hard you'll find but the reception's soft and non-judgmental. Ha ha. Only my little joke. Come. Sit.'

Warily, coerced by goodwill, Lawrence sat in the best lit pew. Father Xavier twitched a remote control gadget from his breast pocket and fired it at the flower arrangement. The organ music retreated slightly but the lights, Lawrence was happy to see, dimmed no further.

'Do you have many people seeking you out?' he asked defensively.

'Not too many. I find if I keep the lights dim and sit with my back to the door, they don't realise I'm here. Only joking. It's weddings mainly. You'd be amazed how many people meet on board and want to get married. Of course, I can only bless their union when we're out at sea but there's always quite a rush for the full works when we put into a port.' He sighed. 'There's the occasional death, of course. Usually too much alcohol and midnight buffet on top of the wrong medication. Either that or they've just blown their life savings and an overwhelming sense of anticlimax carries them off. But you're not dead and I can see you're married already, lucky man, so you must be a lost soul.'

'No. I'm just hiding. She's probably gone by now.'

Lawrence made as if to go but the priest's silky prattle held him there.

'Of course. Did she want you to play bridge?'

Lawrence nodded.

'You're wise not to learn. It can be a tyranny.'

'You play, then?'

'Used to. It took over my life. I began only to see people who played. I neglected my friends, my work, my appearance. It took me into a life without love. I don't know why it has such a respectable image; it can be just as destructive as poker and even more expensive. Tell me, er – '

'Lawrence.'

'Lawrence. Lawrence of the gridiron. Tell me, are you a believer?'

'No.'

'Not even in the broadest sense?'

'No. Why?'

'Professional curiosity. I just wondered why you chose to hide in a place of worship rather than a broom cupboard or a washroom.'

'The door was open. It was near. I didn't know it was a – Look. I can't stand church actually and I think God's all crap.'

'So you do believe.'

'No!'

'But you think he's all crap? If he didn't exist, you wouldn't have an opinion of him.'

'I mean the whole God business. I . . . I believe in nature.

Seasons. Seeds. They make faith pay. Religion's just there to control people, to make them afraid or guilty.'

'It can comfort. It can offer hope.'

'False hope. If it was all true, you'd never need to convert anyone. We'd all be religious. We'd believe because we'd know, like we feel the heat of the sun or know that rain is wet.'

'Ah but with faith you can – '

'Faith? The whole thing's a con. Who takes invisible things on trust? Men used to worship trees and that made sense. Trees shelter and hold land together and let you plant crops. Yew trees cure cancer. God doesn't – '

'The power of prayer is – '

'Gobshite! I – I can't believe I'm even having this conversation.'

'You're very angry. I could feel the anger about you the moment you came in. It was crackling like an electric storm.'

'Well I'm angry because I got talked into coming on this fucking cruise and now I'm trapped on a boat with a bunch of brain-free morons and there are no trees anywhere and it makes me want to – '

A glance from the priest made him see that he was clutching the bench so hard that his knuckles were white. He loosened his grip, embarrassed. Father Xavier watched and waited a moment then said quietly,

'They're not *all* that bad.'

'I don't like people at the best of times.'

'And this isn't . . . ?'

'You don't want to know.'

'It's my job.'

'Well piss off.'

Apparently accepting defeat, the priest held up the palms of his hands. Lawrence began to leave but Xavier was following him.

'Actually there *are* some trees in the theatre lobby, but

they're not well and the sight of them so neglected makes my heart bleed. Do you know anything about them?'

Lawrence stopped, a hand on the door. He had to smile, however grimly, at the man's cunning persistence.

'It's my job,' he said.

'That makes sense.'

'Why?'

'Bad-tempered man, doesn't like people, worships nature.'

'I'm not bad-tempered.'

'Short-tempered, then. It's no bad thing. St Peter was quick to anger. It just needs a useful channel. You should try the gym. For your anger, that is; I'm sure your body needs no work at all. Here. I'll show you those trees.'

They took the lift up two floors and walked along an internal corridor. The entrance to the casino lay at one end, that to the theatre at the other. In the foyer, four miserable weeping figs were arranged, each one beneath a grimy skylight. Even as the priest led him over to them, Lawrence saw leaves drifting down to join the scattering of them on the carpet. The problem was easy to spot.

'They've got enough light, just about,' he said, 'although those skylights could do with a scrub. But they hate being so close to the heating grilles. They need humidity either way. If the pots are set on gravel . . .'

'Ordinary gravel?'

'Yes. Or the kind you put in fish tanks. You need about an inch. Then that needs to be kept wet at all times. The compost's fine, it's obviously getting enough water, but the air around the pots is dry from the heating and water in the gravel would evaporate slowly and help them. But you can't just stand them in water or the roots'll rot.'

'Excellent. The works department should have some. Or maybe the florist. Thank you. It was so depressing watching them die.'

'Not at all.'

'You've saved four lives.'

He accompanied Lawrence back to the lift, apparently reluctant to let him go.

'You must come back here tonight. Lala's doing her first show.'

'Lala?'

'The singer. Surely you've heard of her?' His tone implied an accusatory 'even you'. Lawrence shook his head. 'Actually her records always sold better in Catholic countries. She's big in Ireland. But you *must* hear her.'

'Must I?'

'You'll be glad you did. She's a phenomenon.'

The lift arrived. Cruelly, Lawrence allowed the priest to step in first then ducked out to escape him.

'I'm going this way,' he said.

Unabashed, used perhaps to being avoided or abandoned by his reluctant, floating flock, Xavier slapped a broad finger on the Open Doors button.

'You should try the gym. Really you should,' he said.

'Why the fuck?'

'Instead of the chapel,' he went on calmly. 'Nobody goes there either and the instructor's, well, he's your kind of guy.' He took his hand off the button and the doors began to close. 'Peace of the Lord,' he said, winking as he raised it in blessing.

CHAPTER ELEVEN

Of the five hundred passengers on board, forty or so had discovered the indoor pool. They swam stately, mind-my-hair breast stroke, hauled anxious children across in the shallows or merely floated, clutching the edge bar for security, and staring, slack featured, at the watery scene, as though surprised or even indignant at finding themselves so publicly naked and so wet. By contrast, only one older couple had braved the gym. In matching yellow tracksuits and redundant flannel headbands, they were off to one side, riding exercise bicycles so gently as to produce little more than a faint, constipated flush on their cheeks. Reading stands were clipped to the handlebars and each rider was flicking through a magazine. Judging from the photographs, the woman appeared to be reading recipes for comforting winter puddings.

A man with the build of an oak, in tee shirt, socks, shorts and plimsolls of uniform whiteness, was polishing the chrome on one of a daunting array of weightlifting machines. He looked up eagerly as Lawrence came in and revealed the lined and humourless face of a sergeant major. Lawrence could not imagine that he and the chaplain had much in common.

'What can I do you for?' he asked and his endearing lack of charm lent Lawrence confidence to be candid.

'I'm on this boat for three weeks,' he said. 'I don't play bridge, I've no money to gamble and I'm not big on fruit carving. Someone suggested you could help me make good use of my time.'

'Right.' He all but rubbed his hands. 'My name's Spencer. Your name is?'

'Lawrence.'

'Lawrence. Right.' He seized Lawrence's hand in a powerful shake. 'Got any sports gear, Lawrence?'

'Er. No.'

'That's fine. Pick out what you want from the display in the corner there and we'll bill your cabin number. Changing room's through there. I'm ready when you are and we'll see what you can do.'

Lawrence picked the plainest clothes in his size – not an easy feat since most were adorned with dayglo flashes and other meaningless decoration – and put himself at Spencer's mercy.

'Right,' said Spencer. 'What we'll do is begin with a thorough assessment – muscle tone, elasticity, weight, heart rate, aerobic levels and so on – then we'll draw you up a routine. You can come in every day, stick to the routine, do more if you feel like it but never less or I'll be disappointed in you. Three weeks and you'll feel like a whole new you. On those scales, then, then I'll take your stationary pulse and stick you on the treadmill till you lose your puff, alright?'

Lawrence had thought himself quite fit. Climbing trees, even with a safety harness, sawing off branches, and heaving away the debris kept his arm and leg muscles taut. He was not a smoker, but he drove more often than he walked and he rarely ran if walking would do. After ten minutes on the rotating rubber belt of an electric treadmill, he was gasping like an old man. After five on the Stairmaster, he was gasping like an old man with a cheroot habit. He fared better when Spencer tested his strength, asking him to raise clusters of shiny metal weights with forearms, legs and chest, but the humiliation continued when Spencer led him into his office and, getting him to roll up his tee shirt, used some callipers to measure the fat deposits at his waist and under his arms.

'No worries,' said Spencer, filling the shaming details in

on a form. 'You're in good shape for a bloke of fifty-two. Only kidding. Now. Did you plan to go to the tango class or do you want to go for your first work-out right away?'

Lawrence pedalled a bicycle for ten minutes while a computer screen illustrated the imaginary hills his legs told him he was climbing, then he had another five minutes climbing imaginary stairs before Spencer moved him onto weight machines and worked his back, biceps, triceps, lats, gluts, pecs and whatever until he was inwardly whimpering for rest. Spencer was as merciless as his fat-busting gadgets. He stood over each machine, clearly thrilled to have a willing victim at last, and gauged Lawrence's every gesture. When he ordered a set of twelve reps, he expected twelve, since, he explained, the last two, the two where Lawrence could barely clunk the weights off their resting place, were the crucial muscle-building movements that the other ten were only leading up to. After each set, it seemed, he declared,

'Nice set. Now. Deep breaths then give me twelve more. Water?'

After an agonizing series of sit-ups, by which time it felt as if every muscle in Lawrence's frame but his tongue had been stretched to powerlessness, Spencer marched to the sound system and switched from the thudding, road-middling rock to the kind of breathy slow number Bonnie dismissed as 'Celtic Whale music', and led Lawrence through a series of deliciously relaxing stretches. Many of these involved his grasping Lawrence's aching limbs –

'Relax,' he commanded. 'I said *relax*!'

– and easing them with surprising gentleness a few centimetres beyond the point where Lawrence's exhausted muscles would carry them. Finally he made him lie on a mat with his eyes closed and concentrate on breathing while he crouched beside him as though keeping guard.

Lawrence experienced the euphoria of pure exercise, when concentration on muscle, on movement, on pain and the longing for it to stop, drove out all other thoughts and allowed him to exist as simple body. Showered and changed, his sweaty clothes furled in a towel, he felt light-headed and almost in shock on re-entering the world of the *Paulina*. Although the Atlantic breeze was still bracing, the sun had come out, luring passengers onto the decks and making the ship feel twice the size. He was ravenous. Noisy queues were already forming for lunch and he planned to join them after he had left his gym kit to dry on his balcony. He could not resist the sight of his bed, however, sat for a few seconds then lay back and fell into a deep doze within seconds of reaching the horizontal.

'Lawrence? Lawrence, it's me.' He stirred at the sound of knocking. 'Lawrence?' The voice was Bee's. He froze then saw that, with the curtains drawn, she could see in through the porthole beside the door. He was too shattered to hide in the bathroom, incapable even of leaving the bed to lock the door. 'Lawrence?'

'Come in,' he called out.

She still looked fresh, her hair slightly tousled by the wind on deck. She shut the door behind her and leaned on it.

'Sorry,' he said. 'I can't move.'

'Are you sick? We missed you at the bridge class.'

'No I – I chickened out. I went to the gym. Christ.' He laboured into a sitting position and rubbed his eyes. 'I'm wiped out.'

'The others are all eating lunch. I wondered if you wanted to join us.'

'Er. Well. I'm not so hungry.'

'You must be starving if you've been to the gym.'

'Not really,' he said, raising his voice to cover the rumbling of his stomach. 'Maybe I'll get something later.'

'You don't have to hide from me, Lawrence.'

'I'm not.'

'You are.' She grinned. 'It's okay. I haven't told a soul about last night and, judging from the way you've been avoiding my gaze and running away from me all morning, you're relieved I didn't encourage you as far as the ooh-ah-I-think-I-really-love-you bit.'

'Shit,' he muttered, still unable to meet her eye. 'I feel so stupid.'

She came to sit on the edge of the bed and rubbed his feet through his socks. Somehow she managed to do this without tickling.

'Why? We had a nice talk and I lent a sympathetic ear and you kissed me because you were grateful and that's the way you relate to women you like and maybe you'll grow out of it and maybe you won't.'

'But. Well, I – '

'Yes yes. You *really* like me and I *really* like you and you're a good kisser and so am I but we're neither of us so desperate or so bored that we have to lunge into some ghastly, misjudged affair. So if you think you can manage to be friends without plunging your extraordinarily big tongue down my throat whenever a conversation's getting interesting, and yes, if I promise not to refer to this again, I suggest we go and find some lunch before the gannets scoff the lot.' She laughed. 'Don't look so shocked. Honestly, I've been walking about all morning and there are so few half-way bearable people on this boat it would have been madness to risk sleeping together in case it was a disaster and we had to spend the next three weeks hiding from each other. And the others have no idea. About the lunge, that is. Just in case you were wondering.'

'They certainly haven't. Reuben thinks of you as a sort of sad virgin.'

'I wouldn't have it any other way. He's such a gossip. If he knew half of what I do, I'd have lost my job and had to leave Barrowcester by now. Lunch?'

'I'm *starving.*'

'Good. And then I'm going to teach you some more bridge.'

'But – '

'You can't escape. There's no point trying.' She smiled and leaned over to push the hair off his face so that he felt like a small boy suddenly. It was not entirely unpleasant and he wondered if perhaps a second kiss might not be out of the question eventually. 'So let's say you've got nine points and no five card suit and I open a no trump and nobody bids in between. How do you respond?'

CHAPTER TWELVE

Throughout dinner, Darius kept his end of the table enthralled and scandalized with Lala anecdotes. Lawrence was trapped between a retired riveter from Tyneside who shouted because he was deaf and the riveter's wife who, hardened by years of trying to make herself understood, shouted at everybody.

'We took to cards,' she bellowed at Lawrence, 'because he could play without talking! We started with cribbage and gin! But we switched to bridge because you meet a more varied class of person and I do like breadth in my society! Especially since Malcolm's disability payments came through!'

'How do you bid, though?' Lawrence asked her, beginning to bellow in sympathy. 'Surely he has to hear you for that?'

'She writes her bids down!' Malcolm roared back. 'The whole auction goes down on a piece of card that we pass around!'

'It comes in handy as an *aide-mémoire*!' she added, then swung round indignantly on the waitress who had just served her. 'Is this the chicken? It looks like chicken! I asked for the pork!'

He saw Bee laugh and watched as Reuben and the passengers nearest Darius leaned forward to catch some other highly spiced morsel he was throwing them. He wondered at his uncle's unshakeable poise, at his ability to hold forth and chatter with complete strangers. His mother had the gift too. She could chat in queues at the post office or butcher. Stranded in a waiting room, where Lawrence would shield himself with magazines, she entered the lives of the other patients, daring to ask what seemed to him outrageously searching questions. How long have you been trying for a baby? What form did your wife's cancer take? She happily bartered confidence for confidence and left each encounter seemingly unscathed by the self-exposure.

'They're only people,' she would protest. 'We were only talking. It's fun to pass the time of day with people you'll never see again.'

'It's all in the questions,' Bee had explained to him that afternoon as they sat in deck chairs, she failing to read, he failing to write Bonnie a letter. 'However grim they are, however dull, ask the right question and they'll do all the talking. Before you know it they'll be telling you really quite interesting things about themselves, you'll be able to get on with eating and, hey presto, you'll be passing for human.'

He watched for a few minutes as the retired riveter's wife sawed a strip of fat from her pork chop and he strove to remember the sort of questions Bee had suggested.

'So,' he asked her. 'Tell me about yourself.'

It worked like a charm. For a moment she downed her knife and fork and stared and he feared he might have offended her, then she began to talk. Dropping her voice to a level nearer ordinary, thus leaving her husband adrift in a pool of silence, she told him of her childhood in North Shields, of her memories of the war and handsome Italian POWs near her aunt's farm, of her young marriage, her large family, her vexation with her wayward daughters, the consolation of her sons and her recent hip operation. She asked no questions so, while she talked, Lawrence could listen, half interested, and eat his mediocre meal in peace.

Darius was adamant they should move to the theatre early to be sure of a good table.

'I'll probably head off for an early night,' Lawrence began but was shouted down by the others.

'You must see her once. She's probably past her best, but she's still a legend,' Reuben insisted.

'So why haven't I heard of her?'

'You just don't move in the right circles. Maybe you led a more sheltered childhood than most of us.'

He allowed Bee to persuade him.

'Come on,' she said quietly. 'It might be fun. And you need to sit for a while to digest that revolting pudding.'

Lawrence had never been musical. He sometimes thought he lacked the requisite gene. He saw no reason to sing something that could be spoken in a fraction of the time. His mother loved musicals and when he was a boy would encourage him to watch television matinées with her but he found something faintly embarrassing about the moments where the characters prepared to burst into song. The artful line or two of I-feel-a-song-coming-on dialogue and the sudden, intrusive swell of an invisible orchestra filled him with a kind of rage. Live performances of any kind were even worse. He took long detours to avoid walking near the tribes of Morris dancers, folk singers and buskers who invaded the pedestrianized part of Barrowcester High Street on a Saturday. He could not bear to catch their eye or watch them fail. He was horrified on their behalf.

When Darius found them a table, Lawrence resolutely chose the seat with its back to the low apron stage. As the waiters hurried to deliver the last orders and the overhead lights dimmed, leaving only the pink glow of the shaded table lamps and Darius's Havana, he tried to keep up a conversation with Bee but Reuben shushed him.

'Look,' he said. 'She's coming. It's Lala!'

He pointed. Lawrence twisted as if by reflex and then was unable to turn away. The little band struck up, a follow spot swung across the stage to some blue velvet curtains. A black-gloved forearm emerged, diamonds sparkling at its wrist, and began to tease the curtains apart. This was evidently one of the performer's signatures for several people in the audience let out cheers before everyone began to applaud. Then the hand flicked a curtain aside and a woman appeared.

> *'How glad the many millions*
> *Of Timothies and Williams would be,'* she sang,
> *'To capture me . . .'*

From where Lawrence sat, she seemed tall, at least six feet including her coiled and stacked up hair, and her voice was as deep as she was tall, an almost masculine purr with an edge of burnished copper. Her hair was so beetle-black as to seem almost blue and she had netted it with black beads which glittered as she walked sinuously forward and revealed, through a thigh-length split in her spangled, petrol-coloured dress, a huge but well-turned leg in lethal spike heels.

> *'But you had such persistence*
> *You wore down my resistance*
> *I fell and it was swell.*
> *You're my big and brave and handsome Romeo . . .'*

She sashayed along the catwalk, making a show of inspecting the men within reach. Then Lawrence saw to his alarm that she was advancing towards their table, towards him. He froze as she stopped, stepped off the low stage and singled him out.

> *'I've got a crush on you, Sweetie pie,'* she crooned.

There were a few titters, not least from Reuben, as Lala stroked Lawrence's cheek with a gloved finger then, in a gesture as potent as it was tawdry, tossed her silk wrap about his neck like a halter then slithered it away again. She moved back to the catwalk but she sang the rest of the song to him and he could only stare, paralysed with mixed fear and shame. He realized, with revulsion, that the wrap was sprayed so heavily with scent that the fabric had felt wet on his skin. He disliked scent as a rule, preferring that people should smell of people. But the one enveloping him from the scarf was incredibly rich stuff, something made of animals not flowers, something shockingly suggestive. As she moved away to accept applause with her odd, lopsided smile and begin another song, he felt assaulted by it, marked, claimed. He was furious but he had a hard-on. He knew the music was drab, old-timer stuff that was old even when Darius and Dora were young, but it had him entranced. Doused in her scent, sweating with embarrassment, he watched her slink through her set.

She favoured weary songs of desire and enslavement. *That Old Black Magic, Night and Day, Lilac Wine, So in Love.* She conjured up a world where nothing existed but idolatrous passion, self-destructive, addictive, immolating desire. Lawrence was no linguist but when she sang in Italian, in German, even in Arabic, he could tell the theme was being continued. It was ridiculous, outdated and she was old enough to be his mother. Why then did he find her so . . . so . . . ? He would have laughed out loud at her for a worn old tart, only his hard-on was verging on painful and he had to cross his legs.

Bonnie used to say that men were little more than animals in the simplicity of their response to sex. The woman's face and age and nature were immaterial, she claimed, provided she wore the right clothes and pressed all the usual buttons. For all his occasional fantasies, Lawrence had never used a prostitute. He could not bear to see Bonnie proved right, that desire could be demystified, revealed as a matter of casual professional manipulation.

Lala sang just nine songs. She bowed a little stiffly. She accepted flowers with downcast eyes and a murmured thank you. She paused with one arm raised on the curtain to throw them a smile from her huge mouth. Then she slid out of view. The applause continued but she gave no encores. She would be performing several more times in the course of the cruise and clearly sensed that hunger in a captive audience was preferable to satiety. Lawrence quite forgot to clap. As he turned back to face the others he found them staring at him with expectant grins.

'So what did you think?' Reuben asked.

'I . . . I dunno.'

'She seemed very keen on *you*,' Bee mocked.

'She'd have gone for whoever was sitting here,' he protested. 'It was obviously all planned. But . . . But she was rather amazing. Her voice is very deep.'

'Deeper than mine, in fact,' said Darius airily, topping up everyone's wine.

'Yes. Only she's so . . . feminine.'

'So did you think she was sexy?' Bee asked.

'Oh piss off.'

'No but did you? Go on. I'm interested.'

'Well.' Lawrence hesitated. The others leaned forward a fraction to catch his answer. The band struck up again and a few couples stood to dance. 'I dunno. What did you think?'

'She's bliss,' Reuben sighed.

'Oh there's no point asking them,' Bee said. 'They'll just think she was camp and there's no point asking me because I'm a girl. What did *you* think?'

'Well . . .' Lawrence felt hot, aware again of the singer's pungent scent on his collar and fingertips. He gulped for air. 'Yes. I suppose I did. Think she was. You know. Sexy.'

'Interesting,' said Bee. 'You see to my eyes she's still too obviously masculine. That big jaw. Those muscular legs.'

'Like Sophia Loren crossed with Tony Curtis,' said Darius admiringly, frowning as he relit his cigar.

'What's all this about her being masculine?' Lawrence protested. 'She's not some bloke in drag.'

'Not exactly,' Reuben began and Lawrence wanted to punch his self-satisfied little face. 'She's only notoriously transsexual.'

'Rumoured to be. Only rumoured to be,' Darius qualified. 'Of course, you missed out on the conversation at dinner, trapped as you were with Darby and Joan.' Lawrence gulped his wine.

'So tell me now,' he said.

'Well Lala obviously isn't her real name. No one knows what that is. Though La is A in the sol-fa scale so her initials might be A.A. I suppose. The story goes that she or rather he was born in a slum in Naples, born a boy, and the mother sold him to an Egyptian pimp who trained him as a transvestite prostitute. Then some wealthy French client hears him singing one day in the brothel in Alexandria, falls madly in love, buys him, whisks him to Casablanca for the operation then on to Paris where he launches the new-born Lala in a nightclub. The Berkeley, I think it was. She's a huge star in some countries – Italy, Latin America, Egypt – but her style, well, you saw it. I mean, she's hardly hip.'

'Wasn't there a disco album?' Reuben asked.

Darius shuddered.

'Dreadful. Dreadful. No wonder the poor creature's reduced to working cruise lines. She's a dinosaur.'

'He . . . She's not *that* old,' Lawrence protested.

'Very good legs still,' Bee murmured. 'Neck like a swan's.'

'Nobody knows her age,' Darius conceded with a shrug. 'Her myth has been so cultivated and elaborated that the truth vanished long ago. One version has her working as a double agent in occupied Paris. You know the sort of thing. Sleeping with a Nazi general to obtain secrets for the Resistance. That would make her ancient. But another has the first rich patron as Sacha Distel or Charles Aznavour or someone, which would only make her, what, Brigitte Bardot's age?'

'Just fairly ancient,' Reuben said.

'Of course,' Bee pointed out, 'she might just be a forty-year-old woman with a very cunning PR stunt and a respectable, loving background in Dinard or Auteuil.'

'Oh please,' said Reuben. 'Leave me my dreams.'

'I mean, when I said she was sexy,' Lawrence began to backtrack, 'I didn't mean I actually *fancied* her.'

'Really, Lawrence. There's nothing to be ashamed of,' Darius assured him. 'I'm just thrilled to find your tastes less conventional than I'd always feared.'

'In fact,' Lawrence battled on, 'it was pretty ridiculous, really, with that gravelly voice and those big hands. And she must be at least six foot, even without the hair.'

It was too late, however. They had laid the trap and he had sauntered straight into it. They teased him more and more, Darius making matters worse by saying things like, 'Careful. We must stop or he'll lose his temper . . .'

At last he made a clumsy exit, pleading exhaustion, despite their relenting pleas for him to sit down again. Rather than return to his cabin however, he was lured by the winking lights of the casino, where he drank a succession of free margaritas and ran into George and Martha. They taught him how to play blackjack and, drunkenly convinced that he had seen a sure-fire way of winning, he lost sixty pounds before Martha tapped him on the elbow and suggested that maybe it was time he called it a night.

CHAPTER THIRTEEN

Fight it as he might, Lala entered Lawrence's system like a virus and took tenacious possession. Prompted by the trace of her scent on his fingers as he slept, he had erotic nightmares. She tied him to a dinner table and dressed his genitals with salt, pepper and hollandaise before setting about them with a knife, fork and lip-licking relish. She made him undress her, garment by garment, until her breasts were revealed to be no more than melting ice cream. Most disturbing of all, he dreamed of catching her giggling and naked in the same bath as Bonnie and Lucy and sensed that the shame this represented was known to every passenger on the ship.

Waking, he strove to drive her from his thoughts. Despite muscles still aching from the exertions of the previous day, he let Spencer drive him through a session of circuit training, goading himself on with the thought of how disgusted Spencer would be at the thought of desire for some ageing she-man. He sat with George and Martha through his uncle's second Bridge Basics class, even taking laborious notes, which afterwards read like gibberish to him because he had been concentrating so little when he wrote them. He hired an hour's clay pigeon shooting off the stern and tried to teach Reuben how to use a rifle. But all the time, all he could think of was the notice he had seen announcing that, due to popular demand, Lala's second appearance would be after dinner that very evening. Drinking a cocktail amid the chlorinated steam of an outdoor lounge pool, he overheard two Canadian women discussing her, what suite she was said to be living in, what diet she was said to be on, whether her hair was her own and, if so, how she achieved such wiggish perfection in it. He took the lift with them and tailed them all the way to their cabin door to glean every last gobbet of dubious information. In his desperation, he nearly paid a second visit to Father Xavier's omnidenominational god closet, only checking himself with the memory that Father Xavier counted himself Lala's number one fan so would scarcely provide the impartial voice of reason.

Late in the afternoon he found himself back on the windy sun deck, huddled in a deck chair beside Bee, still failing to write the letter to Bonnie.

Dear Bonnie, he had written so far. *Guess what? Darius has taken me on a cruise with him. A bridge cruise. I wish you were here too. Lucy would love it. There are lots of kids on board. Some parents must be made of money. I got your letter. You were right about the police and the press. I deserved to be locked up. I know I did. I'm so sorry though I know those are just words. I don't know how to get this to you but when we get to Miami I'll try to find out –* (here he had tried and failed to write McBugger's Christian name) *– your address in the States. Did you hear about the van? I . . .*

He could write no further. He tore it off and made a neat copy in the hope that, like a run-up, this would lend him the necessary impetus to proceed but, as he tore the new sheet off the pad to write on the other side, the wind whisked it out of his grasp.

'Don't you want to save that?' Bee asked when he made no move after it.

'No,' he said and they watched the paper dance through the railings and out over the ocean.

'Was it to your wife?'

'Yes. I've got the rough copy still. I don't even have her address. I don't know why I'm bothering.'

'After Tony died I used to write him long, careful letters then burn them on the fire.' She sighed, adjusting her dark glasses. 'It was like writing to Father Christmas only I wasn't asking for presents. I was just saying how angry he'd made me.'

'Did it help?'

'Not really.'

'Do you really think that singer last night is a . . . used to be a man?'

She smiled, possibly at the abrupt change in topic.

'She's singing again tonight. Let's go and take a really close look this time,' she suggested.

'No but *do* you?'

She shrugged.

'It's impossible to tell. Look around us. So many women could be, once someone puts the idea in your head. Men tend to have better legs but then a lot of women are cursed with big hands or moustaches or size nines. What does it matter?'

'I'm just curious. Do you think she *feels* like a woman, if she used to be a man, that is?'

'God. I dunno. She probably *feels* like a transsexual. However that feels. *Transsexualus Transatlanticus Regina*. You'll have to bribe a cabin boy to take a peek at her passport. Has she *got* to you?'

'No.' Lawrence pretended to reread his rough copy.

'She has, hasn't she? She's *got* to you!'

'Fuck off.'

'Sorry.' She smiled to herself then added confidentially, 'For what it's worth, I lied last night because Reuben was there and I like him to think I'm, well, you know, quiet. In fact I think she's sex on wheels. And I hadn't a Sapphic bone in my body till now. But she's like a, well, you feel she's seen it all and is entirely blasé.'

'Like a whore.'

'Yes. A mature but still very expensive whore. By appointment only. I'd be curious.'

'To go to bed with her?'

She wriggled, adjusted her glasses again.

'Ssh,' she said.

'Could I watch?'

'Ssh! Write your letter. They're playing in the tournament tonight. We can duck out and go to hear her sing again. I'll talk to someone and try to bag us that good table again.'

He lost his nerve. As promised, Bee reserved them the same table. They left the others to play bridge and sat beside the catwalk drinking while she talked and he pretended to listen. But his nerve failed him. He could not cope. As the house lights began to dim, he jumped up.

'Sorry,' he said. 'I feel a bit dodgy. Must have been that mushroom starter I had.'

Then he stumbled out leaving Bee alone in pride of place. Outside he paced a while but was drawn back to the foyer by the sound of applause engulfing the band. He watched through a window in the door then pushed through to stand in the darkness at the back of the auditorium. Lala made her entrance. She sang her songs. Perhaps he only imagined it, but he could have sworn she paused at Bee's table, registering an absence there. She was trailing the perfumed scarf again and he waited to see who she would pick out this time. But she picked out nobody. She was a woman. He was certain of it. Older, vampish, but undeniably female.

When Reuben found him an hour and a half later, Lawrence was taking refuge in a figure-hugging thirties armchair in a corner of a leather-panelled bar where a few elderly passengers nursed drinks and talked softly, looking about them in a shell-shocked fashion. One pair was attempting to waltz to the barely audible slithery strings of Mantovani. After one brandy he had stopped thinking about Lala. After a second he had realized afresh how profoundly he missed his daughter. His mind had become locked on the lack of her as in a kind of groove, uselessly locked. Reuben arrived just in time.

'You look almost pleased to see me.'

'You came just in time. This place is . . .' Lawrence cast gloomy eyes about him. Reuben looked, drew in his breath in mock astonishment and whispered,

'The Ballroom of the Undead!' He flopped into a chair and helped himself to Lawrence's third brandy. 'Do you mind?' Lawrence waved it away.

'You'd be doing me a favour. How was the tournament?'

'The cards were against us.'

'You lost?'

'No. But there weren't any slams so it was a bit subdued.'

'I left your sister watching the show.'

'That's over. I left her tucking into the midnight buffet, which happens to be an all-chocolate one tonight, and Darius has gone to bed to escape all those card fiends with problems they want him to solve.'

Lawrence yawned.

'I should turn in too. Go to bed and dream of woods and fields and empty space.'

'But I was hoping you'd help me research my article.'

'How?'

'Well,' Reuben stood, staring in absentmindedly candid revulsion at a powder-blue tuxedo that was passing, 'it involves going somewhere much more lively than this I'm afraid.'

'Where?' Wariness stirred beneath the liquor fog in Lawrence's skull. When they were children, Reuben would have been the kind forever getting him into trouble from which only Reuben emerged blame-free.

'I've talked to passengers till I'm numb and they're all polite as hell. I think it's time for a trip below stairs, if only for our own sanity. Hang on a sec.'

He darted to the bar and chatted briefly with the grizzle-haired barman who smiled, nodded and called a waiter over to take his place.

'This way, gentlemen. I should warn you, it's not like up here. It's pretty rough.'

'Pretty rough sounds just fine,' Reuben purred, eagerly following.

The barman led them out onto the deck, along a corridor, through a series of low-slung doors and into another, parallel ship where pipes were not boxed away, floors were uncarpeted and the walls were painted a uniform white gloss, sweaty to the touch. It looked like a proper ship rather than a ship trying to pass for an hotel. They ducked past cramped, shared cabins where Lawrence could barely have stood much less fitted himself into a bunk bed. They passed a galley slovenly with crumbs, used tea bags and bacon grease.

'There you go, sirs,' said the barman and held open a door. 'Just ask anyone when you want to find your way out again.'

It was the staff bar, a kind of windowless pub. There was a darts board and a pool table and a bar strung round with winking fairy lights and a collection of Ken dolls and Action Men, none of them in the clothes their maker had intended. The sound system was blasting out Motown songs and seventies disco hits. Lawrence had feared they would be resented as trespassers on out-of-hours privacy, but the crowd of waiters, cooks, chambermaids and beauticians absorbed them without question. Perhaps they were used to refugees – paid companions and dutiful sons desperate to let their hair down. Father Xavier raised a glass in greeting from his corner of the snug and Lawrence was greeted by Spencer who was working a shift behind the bar.

Drunker than he had realized, Lawrence leaned on a pinball machine and listened as Reuben, entirely without fear, gatecrashed a gathering of boys and girls from the ship's health spa.

'I thought all the masseuses were European,' he said. 'Italian, French and so on.'

'So?' asked one. 'Dudley's European too. Anyway, most of the clients down there are American so Brum's as exotic as Dubrovnik to them. They can't understand half of what I say. You should slip down tomorrow. Afternoons are quietest, and we'll give you a working over for nothing. You can bring your friend, if you like.'

Perhaps inevitably the gossip swung round to the resident star and a hard-faced young coiffeur told how suddenly all the women on board wanted hair like Lala's.

'I haven't the heart to tell them it's a wig, not at that price.'

'It's never.'

'She's got terrible scars. You know. *Surgical.* Denise gave her aromatherapy so she should know.'

'And what about electrolysis? I'd heard she had a chest on her like Sean Connery.'

The competitive swapping and capping of stories grew ever more lurid, the laughter more cruel. Lawrence tried not to listen. He turned aside to watch the crowd, amazed that they were not too worn out by vocational sycophancy towards passengers to socialize with each other. He felt his eyelids grow heavy as he heard piano music cutting through the malicious chatter and the fevered bounce of disco. There was shouting and Reuben dug him in the ribs.

'It's *her!*' he hissed.

The music was abruptly unplugged as Lawrence turned sleepily to see an off-duty Lala being persuaded to the piano's side. Someone offered her champagne but she rejected it in favour of a deckhand's glass of Guinness.

'Alright alright,' she muttered. 'One. Just one. Jesus. I've been working my tits off upstairs and I came down here for a bit of relaxation. Oh alright already!'

Her speaking voice was pure gravel, her accent bizarrely multinational but principally American. Lawrence watched her mutter something in the ear of the childminder at the piano and wondered afresh at her gender. The childminder struck up an introduction. Lala frowned, her thick, black eyebrows and began to sing.

'*You made me love you.*
I didn't want to do it. I didn't want to do it.'

Without a microphone, her singing voice was as soft and smoky as her speech. She leaned on the piano, apparently enjoying the crowd's intimate enthusiasm. She dropped all the grand gestures, all the theatrics. She simply leaned and sipped her Guinness and growled. The song was over in seconds. The crowd cheered and called out for more. Men shouted requests:

'*Mad About the Boy!*'

'*Ich Bin von Kopf!*' but she waved them away.

'Shut up shut up. Leave me alone. You had that for nothing now let a woman drink in peace.' Then she walked a little way through the crowd, saw Lawrence and stopped. 'Hello,' she said softly. He opened his mouth, thinking of spiders and flies, but could think of nothing to say. 'Where were you tonight?' she asked.

'What?'

'You weren't there. Your girlfriend was there. I saw her. But you weren't. Didn't you want to hear it all again?' She stopped. Lawrence was on hot coals. The room seemed to have fallen entirely silent. He felt every eye in the place fall on him. Lala looked about her and flapped a hand dismissively. 'Talk amongst yourselves,' she said, laughter in her voice. 'Don't mind us.'

There was a guffaw and obediently people turned away. Spencer plugged the music back in and the atmosphere was levelled out with blare.

'She's not my girlfriend,' Lawrence stammered and cleared his throat because his voice had come out squeaky. 'She's just a friend. I met her on board.'

'Uh huh.'

Lala drank, watching him. She had removed her stage make-up and tied her hair back in a black scarf. It made her look younger.

'Well you know my name,' she said.

'I'm Lawrence.'

'Lala and Larry,' she chuckled. 'It's destiny. We sound like some hideous variety act. Buy me a drink?'

'Sure.'

Happy to escape the glare of her orbit, he pushed through to the bar where Spencer was already pulling her another Guinness.

'Hope you know what you're doing,' he muttered, concentrating on the drink.

'I'm . . . I'm not doing anything.'

Spencer passed him the brimming glass, eyebrows raised. He waved aside Lawrence's money, eyes still downcast. Lawrence wanted to remonstrate with him but sensed he was too drunk to do so without making a fool of himself.

Lala had been drawn into the adoring circle formed by Reuben and the beauticians. She thanked him for the drink with a flicker of a smile and carried on talking, so it was the easiest thing in the world to pass her the glass and slip away. He could not, however, resist the temptation to glance back as he reached the door. She was smiling politely at something the Dudley girl was saying but her eyes alighted briefly on his and he felt their touch like a hand on his cheek.

CHAPTER FOURTEEN

'But they're amazing!' Bee laughed, plunging her face into the armful of flowers to sniff their heavy fragrance. When she lifted her face there was yellow pollen on her nose. 'It feels like my birthday,' she said.

'Well,' he mumbled. 'They're not from me actually. I mean. Well they *are* but I didn't buy them. She did.'

'Who?'

'Lala.'

'You're kidding!' She laughed again and took the flowers into her cabin. As he followed her, she found a little envelope stapled to the bouquet's wrapping by the ship's florist.

'May I?' she asked. Lawrence shrugged. 'Mmm,' she said, 'it's scented.' She tore open the envelope and took out a card. *Thanks for the drink*, she read.

'It was only a Guinness. I didn't even pay for it.'

There was a wine cooler on her dressing table. She stepped into the bathroom to fill it with water then set about arranging the lavish bouquet.

'What's the matter?' she asked, not looking up from her work. 'You're pacing.'

'I hate this.'

'Being sent flowers? You're mad. Have you any idea what these must have cost?'

'Not that.'

'What then?'

He slumped into her cabin's only armchair then jumped up again, walking to the porthole to peer out as some women in bathrobes sauntered by.

'Being singled out. I feel – I feel she's making a fool of me.'

'She's making a fool of herself, if anything. So. What are you going to do about it? She'll be hurt if she finds out you gave these away.'

'I don't care.'

'Aren't you interested, after all?'

'No. Well. It's only that I . . . Christ, why should you understand? I don't know why I'm telling you this.'

'Probably because I'm one of the only two women on the boat who isn't afraid of you.'

He stalled at that, surprised, and turned to lean on the wall and watch her carry the flowers to the table where she made a few final adjustments with her fingertips. Then she took a seat and looked at him.

'What's so upsetting?' she asked. 'So she used to be he. If you hadn't been told you'd never have guessed. Or is it that she's an older woman and she's taking the initiative?'

It was both these things, of course. He was unwilling, however, to pursue the subject he had started and angry at the ease with which she read his thoughts so he unscrupulously reminded her that he was still bruised at the loss of his wife and preoccupied with her abduction of his daughter.

'I'm not ready for anything, anyone. Least of all that.'

Lala sent more flowers, however; an armful of shocking pink gerberas with a card that merely read:

Well?

He gave these to Martha, who was bemused but delighted. That night however, as he wolfed his dinner, ravenous after a punishing session with Spencer, Lala singled him out more publicly, sending a waiter to his table with a bottle of champagne which he could scarcely turn away when Darius and the others were so delighted with it.

He avoided the theatre, where she was to perform a third time before they reached Miami. Desperate, he took refuge in bridge. Darius found him a table with some patient Danish Americans and he actually bid two part score contracts and made them. Reuben was taking Bee off to the below-stairs bar and she was keen for Lawrence to join them but he dreaded another close encounter and sloped off to his room. An overpowering scent hit him as he unlocked the door. He flicked the light switch and swore under his breath.

There were gardenias, growing gardenias, in pots, wherever he looked; one either side of the bed, on the table, on the balcony, around the television, on either side of the bath. A bloom had even been cut off and slipped through the lapel of the jacket he had left on the back of a chair. Another of her infernal little scented envelopes was tucked into the small potted bush on the coffee table. He tore it open.

Just try giving this lot away.

He slid open the balcony door and hurled a plant as hard as he could out over the dangling lifeboats and into the black abyss. With no splash and no sound of shattering pottery however this was less than satisfying, so he contented himself with lining the others up on the side of the balcony where he could not see them from the bed. He fetched a beer from the fridge and sat outside on a plastic chair to drink and ponder.

The air was humid and it was warm enough now to sit out in shirtsleeves. They were nearing land. The boat would soon dock in Miami where they had a little under sixteen hours and were free to pass through customs and disembark. The plan was to avoid the crowds and take an excursion of their own. Darius had been given details of that rare Florida phenomenon, an old house with an older garden, open to the public, and was keen to visit.

Lawrence made up his mind. He would duck out of the excursion at the last minute, wait until the others had left, then abandon the cruise and go in search of Lucy. As a working architect of note, McBugger could not be so hard to trace, nor Chicago so vast a city as to hide him. Whatever the state of his bank account, Lawrence had enough credit on his plastic to buy a flight. Bonnie might at least agree to a meeting. If he reassured her, gave her his passport as security, she might at least let him see Lucy again. He had to do this. The cruise, Lala, these flowers, were a nightmarish irrelevance. His family was real. He had to wake up and get real.

He did not sleep. He sat on through the night, steadily drinking his way through the contents of the fridge and listening to the distant rumble of the engines and hushed splash of the spray. He watched as the sun rose behind them and revealed the waterside sprawl of Miami's docks, watched as they slid into the slack grey maw of the harbour. Then he turned back to the cabin and began methodically to pack his bags. In the sheaf of embarkation papers on the bedside table he found an immigration form. He filled it out slowly, pausing to look up his travel dates, ticket code and passport number.

There was a loud, excitable atmosphere over breakfast, as though the overnight arrival of land, immobile and reassuring after days at sea, had brought with it shaming relief. Long queues were already forming at the tables where the American immigration officials were setting up their temporary office. Heavy with beer however, Lawrence had fallen into a deep, uncomfortable sleep in the cramped space left on his bed by his suitcases, clutching his passport in slumber as a child might a security blanket.

CHAPTER FIFTEEN

By the time Lawrence had washed, shaved, changed and found the others, he had lost much of his resolve. Darius, Reuben and Bee had been joined by George and Martha who were also keen to visit somewhere more interesting than a shopping plaza. As Lawrence ate some soupily syruped grapefruit segments, Darius read from a guide book a description of the house and garden they were to visit and Lawrence felt himself a traitor in their midst. When Dora had first announced that his uncle would be bringing him on this cruise, he had envisaged them functioning as a simple pair, not as part of a merry band. Dreading the thought of explaining his decision to leave the cruise to all five perplexed and wounded faces, he repeatedly missed his moment and sat on in surly silence.

Then a white-jacketed waiter appeared at Bee's elbow. 'Mrs Martin?'

'Yes?' Bee lowered her sunglasses.

'A delivery for you.'

He handed Bee a large envelope and walked off. Mystified, Bee opened it and drew out a small map of Miami with a route marked out in yellow highlighter and a bunch of hire car keys and registration details.

'What on earth?' she laughed and, peering inside the envelope, drew out a familiar-looking card.

Dear Mrs Martin, she read, *Or may I call you Bee? I wonder if you and a friend would like to join me for a little lunch today. I feel we could all do with a break from shipboard life. I'll be at a girlfriend's house – details enclosed – and have taken the liberty of hiring you a car because taxi drivers here are notoriously indiscreet. Come as soon as you like. Bring swimming things as the pool there is divine. Yours.*

'Who's it from, Sugar?' Martha asked.

Bee grinned at Lawrence and sniffed the card.

'Guess,' she said. 'Want to be my friend for the day, Lawrence?'

'It would be a shame to miss this garden of Darius's though,' Lawrence said and was immediately shouted down.

'Are you *mad*?' they laughed.

'The *girlfriend* is probably some star,' George suggested. 'I was hearing how a bunch of them have places round here now.'

'Otherwise I'll just have to take Reuben.'

'Oh much though I'd love it,' her brother told her, 'I don't think I'm quite the friend she has in mind.'

'You'll be utterly safe,' Bee went on, 'with me there to protect you.'

Lawrence glowered, then it struck him that this could prove the perfect way to abandon the cruise. Going with Bee, he would leave the others, get as far as the car then he would plead sickness or claim to have forgotten something, grab his luggage and slip away into the dockside crowds. Bee would forgive him, and if she did not, they were unlikely to meet again so it was of little significance. Lucy was what mattered, he reminded himself, finding Lucy.

'Okay,' he sighed. 'But I'm not swimming.'

'Huh,' laughed Martha. 'The vanity of the boy!'

Bee changed quickly in honour of their hostess and reappeared in a cream linen dress, yellow beads and a straw hat. She looked fresh and worldly, like a wedding guest, definitely Mrs Anthony Martin rather than sweet, homely Bee. As they walked down the gangplank together, she in her outfit, he in the linen suit Darius had bought him, they looked, it struck him, like an ideal married couple. Bonnie and he had never looked so matched. Whereas some mismatched pairs grew ever more alike, as George and Martha had evidently done, they had come to resemble each other still less with the passing of time.

They reached the car. Bee took the wheel since it was booked in her name and he began his escape.

'Shit,' he said.

'What?'

'I forgot something. Er. Hang on. I won't be a sec.'

He began to open the door but she accelerated.

'No you don't,' she said.

'But I – '

'It's only lunch. It'll be fun.'

'Stop the car. I've got to – Bee, bloody stop the car!'

'No!' she laughed.

She swerved to avoid a bollard and he reached instinctively for his seat belt. Strapped in, powerless, he felt a spasm of black rage pass through him. In the last twenty-four hours he had been thinking of Lucy so much, it was as though his daughter were waiting for him, sunnily alone and accessible at the quayside and did not still have to be tracked the country's vast length. Teasing, oblivious Bee was driving him away from her, for something as transitory as a laugh. Then Bee turned briefly, saw his expression and, shocked, indicated right and pulled over near the entrance to the docks.

'I'm sorry,' she said. 'I'm being childish. You really don't want to go, do you? I'll drive us back.' She was quite unafraid of him, as she had said the day before. She was only stopping because she saw he was upset and she respected his feelings.

'No,' he said, looking at the empty benches on the quayside and telling himself it was all one whether he set off for Chicago and Lucy now or in a few hours' time. And he was, perhaps, just a little curious to see if Lala would be diminished when encountered beyond the unnatural confines of a liner. 'I was the one being childish. Drive on.'

'Sure?'

'Honest.' He looked at the map. 'It's only lunch. What can she do? Eat me?'

She drove on, and smiled to herself.

'So,' she said. 'Is it left or right when we hit the main road?'

It was, indeed, the house of a star, one of several waterside mansions with high fences, densely planted gardens and security cameras. It was older than the Art Deco concoctions they had passed along South Beach; a fanciful, almost Moorish structure with a bell tower and arched colonnades like an old Spanish mission. Lawrence climbed out and was evidently seen on a camera because the gates began to swing open by remote control before he even reached out a hand to the bellpull. As they rolled onto the drive and the gates swung shut behind them, Bee threw him a mischievous glance.

'Beauty arrives at Beast Castle,' she said. 'Nervous?'

'Shut up and drive.'

'God! The size of those palms!'

Lala greeted them on the steps, for all the world as if she lived there and had not left the ship a mere hour before them. Like Bee, she had dressed for a wedding, only in French navy and without the hat.

'What a pretty hat,' she said kissing Bee's cheek. 'So glad you could come. Oh and you brought young Larry. Good. Come on in. I'll show you around. It's the loveliest place. For a rock singer, she's a clever shopper.'

She did not ignore Lawrence exactly, but she treated him like the sweet but slightly dull spouse of a cherished friend. All her attention, all her seductive attention, was devoted to Bee. As she showed them around the ground floor of the mansion – which had, in fact, been a home to Spanish

missionary nuns and still retained a cloister planted with
citrus trees – she gently took Bee's arm in hers and patted
it from time to time with an unringed hand. She made no
allusion to the attentions she had paid Lawrence on the boat,
to the flowers, the champagne, the gardenias now wilting in
the fierce sun on his cabin balcony. Occasionally she drew
him in with a casual 'Don't you find that, Larry?' or 'What
do you think, Larry?' only to proceed with her wooing of
his companion before he could muster much of an answer.

There was a manicured garden at the rear of the house
which descended in graceful stages to a balcony overlooking a kind of lagoon and a landing stage. There was an
inviting swimming pool, lined with midnight-blue tiles and
the occasional flash of gold, which made it seem far deeper
than it probably was. Unseen hands – surely not Lala's – had
laid lunch out on a table beside it in the relative cool of a
vast cotton shade. White cloth, white plates, white napkins,
gaudy food.

'Fruit punch? You must both be thirsty after the drive and
it's my own recipe.'

She filled three tall glasses with an orangey pink liquid and
handed them round. It tasted of strawberry, mango, banana
and something indefinable but alcoholic.

'Nectar,' Bee exclaimed. 'I must be careful if I'm to
drive back.'

'Oh there's hardly a thing in it,' Lala assured her. 'Nearly
all fruit. Now I want you here on my right and perhaps
Larry could sit on the other side. You don't mind if I call
you Larry? Now Bee, tell me all about your work. Children,
isn't it?'

'Little boys, God help me.'

'Delightful.'

The three of them ate. Cold fried chicken. Char-grilled
peppers. Rice salad. Baby artichokes in tomato vinaigrette.
They ate and the women talked. Seas of talk, about children
and childhood, marriage, death, chance, twins, astrology.

Lawrence lost all track of the conversation, consumed as he was by the glimpses he was gaining of Lala's body. She had discarded her jacket to reveal a sleeveless dress. When she raised her glass to her lips, or reached out a hand for a dish, he could see a braless breast. When she stooped to retrieve Bee's tumbled napkin, she afforded him a generous view of her cleavage. It was ironic that the conversation should have begun with a discussion of little boys for he could not remember having his thoughts so jangled by the suggestiveness of a clothed female form since he fell in love with his French teacher at ten and began to receive even poorer marks than usual because he was too busy watching for flashes of her chaste, white bra strap to concentrate on what she was saying. When Lala stood to offer him coffee, she had to ask twice because he was too intently wondering if she were wearing any underwear at all.

'Isn't it heaven?' Bee asked happily, pouring herself yet another glass of punch. 'Aren't you glad you came after all? Better than trudging round some dreary house.' She moved to a reclining chair, sat in it rather heavily, sipped her drink, pushed her sunglasses higher on her nose and kicked off her shoes. 'Bliss,' she confirmed.

Lala returned from the house with a silver coffee pot and two white cups. As if in sympathy, she too had removed her shoes but Lawrence noticed that she continued to walk on tiptoe, as though on the ghosts of heels. She said nothing but threw him a strange, direct glance as she filled his cup. She held out a cup to Bee.

'Bee, darling?' Bee did not stir. She had fallen fast sleep. 'Looks like the sort that burns,' Lala murmured and softly trundled the shade into place over Bee's head and shoulders, leaving her thin legs to toast. Lawrence had risen, ostensibly to walk about the pool. The sun was now full overhead and catching on the small gold tiles so that they shot darts of cold fire about the unstirred water. 'Here.' Lala took his cup from him. 'Come and see.'

He followed her into the house, where the sudden shadow blinded him at first, and up a wide, wooden staircase. The blue dress, which had seemed so respectable at first glance, was actually far sexier than the blatant outfits she wore to perform. As she climbed the stairs in front of him, it revealed the alternate squeezing motions of her buttocks and laid bare the muscular length of her legs. He had thought she was wearing no scent but now that they were indoors and he was walking close in her wake, he breathed it again and felt a pit in his guts and a constriction in his chest. He itched to lay hands on her. When she led him to a huge, white, shaded room where thin drapes drifted in the breeze about a great boat of a bed and, with one neat movement, unzipped her dress and let it fall so that she stood naked before him, he had never been so grateful for a lack of wordy preliminaries.

She let him kiss her lips, her breasts, her belly, her bush, while she stood, still on tip toe, swaying under his grasps and mouthings, then she stepped aside to part the bed drapes.

'Medusa's raft,' she said.

He clambered up past her, pulled her beside him and continued to rifle through her like a hungry burglar. She helped him undress, produced a condom from somewhere and, with a small purr, somehow slid it onto him with her mouth.

'What about Bee?' he muttered.

'How many drinks did she get down her?'

'Three or four.'

'We've got hours, then.'

'Did you put something in them? We all drank from the same jug.'

'Oldest trick in the world; I spiked her ice. Just a little something I get on prescription for long flights. She'll be having *fabulous* dreams down there. Dear girl. Now. Go back to where you were at. I *liked* that.'

Making love with Bonnie, Lawrence had felt constrained, both by his fear lest she detect any slackening of his desire for her and by a sense that it was not enough to be merely himself. Even when they were making up after a quarrel, sex between them tended to occur within a vacuum. It always felt as though she were striving to lose herself in bed and play some role and there was a corresponding onus on him to do the same. While she became someone else, non-wife, non-mother, a kind of temporary, amateur whore, so he must become some ideal stud rather than mere husband. He closed himself in for her, became impregnable, invulnerable, tireless. The result was that those times when they should have felt most intimately open to one another were the times of least communication. It was easier to maintain a show of appetite if he made himself a stranger to her for the duration. For the seconds when he raged at her in jealousy, she became an it to him, a thing. For the long minutes when he strove to satisfy her, he objectified himself in turn. He was often tempted to rise early before she woke and tire himself out with work so that he nodded off in an armchair after dinner and had to be gently woken and sent to bed wrapped in an invalid's chastity. But once there he would worry about McBugger and the comparisons between them, and rouse himself to the challenge.

Perhaps it was merely a condition of it being their first encounter or perhaps it was an effect of making love in such broad daylight in a space which belonged to neither of them, but with Lala he felt doubly naked, unable to be other than himself. Her gaze was a magnifying glass, her touch an entomologist's pin. Just as the filtered sunlight exposed the slight crepiness of her upper arms and his incipient belly, so he felt she knew him for what he was and, in each case, the exposure was at once unnerving and a relief.

Her hair was clearly her own – she winced when he pulled it slightly and tugged his own in retaliation. So were her breasts, great soft globes which weighed heavily in his hands as he cupped them from behind. She was unscarred, unhairy. Everyone had lied about her. She was very tall, that was all, and long-limbed. And yet, as she twined strong legs about him, as she pushed his face hard against the bank of pillows, as she pinned his hands above his head and trailed a nipple across his straining lips like a questing fingertip, he could not rid his mind of the ambiguity the slander had sown there or deny the covert excitement it was causing him. She came like a man too, letting him work her to a single climax in which she flexed herself and ground spasmodically against him as though to wring out the last drop of strength he had to offer. He fell asleep afterwards. In that respect, the experience was not unusual.

When he came to, the light in the room had softened considerably and Lala was standing at the foot of the bed, dressed again, sipping a glass of water and watching him.

'You should be getting back to the boat,' she said.

'Who needs to go anywhere?' he murmured, his head full of sleep. After nearly a week of his monastic cabin, the bed was too comfortable to leave, the heavy sheets too cool.

'Mrs Anthony Martin does for one.'

'I forgot all about her.'

She muttered something in a foreign language. It sounded ironic and she released one of her distant, crooked smiles.

'What?' he asked.

'Nothing. She's still asleep. Concepcion's made some fresh coffee. I must go. The launch is waiting for me.'

And she was gone. He heard a boat revving away on the water. Not a kiss. Not a farewell. Not a word to acknowledge what had passed between them.

He slept again. He woke. He dozed. He forced himself to shake the drowsiness from him, took a moment to find his bearings then lurched off the bed in search of clothes. Now that she had left, he felt like an intruder in the house. Fastening his belt as he bounded down the stairs again, he wondered if this was indeed her friend's house or whether Lala had not merely forced an entry by way of setting him up for some elaborate punishment. Cooling coffee was indeed waiting at the poolside but there was not a sign of the maid she had mentioned.

'Bee? Bee, wake up. It's – shit! It's late. We've got to hurry. Here. Coffee. Drink!' Bee rubbed bleary eyes, groaned and reached for the tepid cup automatically, as a baby would a bottle. He imagined wailing sirens, flashing blue lights, a sudden swarm of heavily armed police over the wall and up from the landing stage. 'Bee, hurry. Come on. You've been asleep for hours.'

'When – God!'

She lurched to her feet then sank drunkenly back, clutching her head.

'Come on. I'll hold you. We're going to be late. Where are the keys?'

'Er . . . I dunno.' She found the keys and dropped them inches from the pool's brim. He lunged for them as she sank back into the chair.

Somehow he half-walked, half-dragged her to the car, leaped in on the driver's side and negotiated his way back through Miami, snatching perilous glances at the map fluttering on his knees. He caught sight of clocks as he drove by shops or offices. He still had time to get Bee back through customs and on to the ship and, if he ran, snatch up his luggage and leave. It was madness to contemplate the alternative.

Immigration was a nightmare, however, as Bee was barely capable of standing unassisted, still less of answering for herself. He apologized profusely, said she had drunk too much at lunch without realizing it would react badly with the medication she was on. Medication was a foolish word to use. Increasingly suspicious, the officials wanted to know what drugs she was taking and, when he could not say and when it emerged that he was neither her lover nor blood relative, were all for performing a blood test for narcotics on both of them. Luckily, Father Xavier appeared behind them, breathless from some lone foray on the mainland, and insisted he could vouch for the young people's probity. He even had them procure Bee a wheelchair.

'Touch of Florida sunstroke, I've no doubt,' he said as they parted company. 'She's naturally pale. Just like me. Celtic skin. We burn in a flash. Peace of the Lord.'

The next obstacle was settling Bee into her cabin. All the fuss had apparently caused her dopiness to wear off and replaced it with a mounting, drug-enhanced panic attack.

'Don't leave me!' she cried. 'Where are you going? What happened to me? Why am I in a wheelchair?'

Hating himself for his irresponsibility, he poured her a stiff brandy from her mini-fridge 'for medicinal purposes' and sat with her till she passed out afresh.

He ran so hard to his cabin that he thought his lungs would burst, flung open the door and let out a groan of frustration. A new chambermaid, freshly embarked, had seen his cases and, assuming them to belong to a passenger joining the cruise from Miami onwards, had kindly unpacked them and hung or folded everything back into the cupboards. She had even slipped some crumpled chinos into the trouser press. He threw everything back in the cases pell-mell, crushing fabric, snagging buttons, and broke a tooth glass in his rush to retrieve the wash things so conscientiously rearranged on the bathroom shelf. Matters were not made easier by the chambermaid returning, realizing her awful blunder, trying to make amends by refolding clothes and, when he shouted at her to get out of the bloody way, melting into loud Cuban lamentations.

'Lucy,' he thought, as he ran down seven flights of stairs rather than wait for a crowded lift. 'Hold the doors. Make them hold the doors, Lucy.' All his efforts were in vain, however. The doors were closing, the last gangplank about to be withdrawn. He tried to explain himself, got caught up in a confrontation with the purser, who misunderstood and thought he wanted to leave because the cruise was not up to standard in some way, and was then sneered at when it emerged that he was travelling in a luxury cabin free of charge and merely wanted to leave to pursue some mother and child to a Midwestern address for which he had neither telephone number nor zip code.

Defeated, Lawrence returned to his cabin and placated and tipped the chambermaid who was near prostration at the thought of how foolish and obstructive her helpfulness had proved. As the *Paulina* throbbed into motion once more, he unpacked his cases a third time then mournfully chose clothes for dinner. He had already learned that there was nothing so shaming as a child disappointed by assurances given then broken. As he set about watering the parched gardenias he suffered a shame so profound he felt it should be displayed livid on his face for all to see.

CHAPTER SIXTEEN

Leaving Miami as the sun was setting, the *Paulina* sailed out past Cuba and down into the Caribbean. There were to be three nights at sea before its arrival on the Dutch side of St Martin. The atmosphere on board underwent subtle changes, emphasized by the departure of some passengers and the intake of new ones. The temperature rose dramatically, some parts of the ship becoming as stickily humid as a palm house. Passengers wore less and began to colonize the broad outdoor spaces, where the waiting staff were kept busy as consumption of sickly faux-Caribbean cocktails soared. Where the Atlantic crossing had been marked by a near frantic struggle against boredom as passengers rushed from activity to class to social gathering, the leisured passage into calmer, warmer waters saw them neglecting bridge clinic and dance class to spend hour on sweltering hour basking on serried rows of plastic couches. The lifts and bars were sweet with sun tan lotion, the faces at dinner browner, more relaxed. More used to heat, perhaps, the American passengers maintained a more energetic front, bouncing around the jogging track and assembling noisy games of basketball. The British showed a tendency to bewail delightedly how lazy the warmth was making them.

While Darius saw his bridge groups decimated by inertia, Reuben and Bee produced fat nineteenth-century novels and sat in the least populous corner of the sun deck in companionable, frowning silence, paperbacks held aloft like insufficient shields. They broke off their reading only to order fresh Tom Collinses or to shift their loungers so as to remain in a shrinking patch of protective shade. Reuben and Darius appeared to have quarrelled during the Miami excursion. At least, neither spoke of it and each was pointedly incurious as to the details of the lunch *chez* Lala, as though the entire day were something to be shunned.

In the air-conditioned gym, Lawrence rowed substanceless leagues and pedalled uneventful miles, punishing himself for his weakness as a father, thrashing his body through its paces as though he could reverse the mechanical process that was dragging him further and further from Lucy. He worried at first about being approached by Lala as he dreaded further gossip. She was not due to perform again until their night in St Martin however, and meanwhile she kept closely to her quarters, even for her meals, so that rumours began to circulate that she might be ill. Receiving no further fruit or flowers, he wondered if he might somehow have caused her offence. Far from hiding away as he had first, absurdly, planned to do, he haunted those parts of the deck he knew would be visible from her lofty suite.

Self-conscious at the thought of her possible scrutiny, he sustained a long vigil, sharing his table now with strangers, now with those who knew him. Jess, the teenager with Down's syndrome joined him. Infected by the omnipresence of bridge, she had acquired a sticky pack of cards and grinningly taught him a futile game called Go Fish, seemingly endless, full of minor retributions and small triumphs. It ate time and required little concentration or speed. They played for over an hour, drawing patronizing smiles from passers-by, and he was saddened when her mother took her away, red-faced and indignant from a long search. Clumsy, dark, the antithesis of Lucy, Jess's gentle approach and quiet confidence in his interest had nonetheless set off sad echoes within him. She left the cards with him and before long he was joined by Martha, puffed from an over-fifties basketball game, who taught him a version of patience.

'It's great for small tabletops and trains,' she said, 'because it uses little space and it's satisfying too because it hardly ever works. You place the pack so, draw four cards off the top and look at them. If the first and the fourth are the same number, you discard all four. If they're the same suit, you discard the two in between and draw two more and if they've nothing in common, you draw another card and see how that matches what was the second card but is now the first to your new fourth. See?'

'Show me again,' he asked. 'Slowly.'

He saw eventually and he continued to play while the afternoon drew on and a succession of strangers came to sit beside him and talk with one another in lowered voices. It became a form of moneyless gambling.

'If I can make it work,' he told himself, 'if I can discard the whole pack, then I can go and tap on her door.'

So of course he had to play on. And on. He thought through the events in Miami, seeking what insult he might unwittingly have offered her and found nothing. If anything, she had insulted him. She had treated him as a thing. She had used and, apparently, discarded him. He narrowed the field of risk.

'If I can discard half the pack, I *have* to call on her,' he conceded, and later: 'If the last card I can discard is a red card less than eight.'

Afternoon drew in to evening and a light coming on in one of her ungiving windows only spurred him on. At last the cards gained him permission but it was too late to act on it as it was time for dinner and he had promised to play bridge with Bee afterwards. He could, of course, have skipped dinner and barged upstairs anyway but he was uncertain of her dining habits. She might be entertaining. He imagined formal clothes, smart, enquiring faces turned with a touch of mockery at his sudden interruption of a witty conversation. He imagined Lala's feigned ignorance, imagined her cruelty, and he shied away.

After several attempts and much encouragement, Lawrence

was at last coming to see the appeal of bridge. At heart it was the simplest of courteous card games, a kind of whist, but the codified bidding, indeed the codified play, made it also a test and celebration of partnership. At first he made repeated blunders because he was too intent on viewing the game as a solitary struggle in which each player stood or fell on their own strengths. Then Bee made him see that, with the right communication, two relatively weak-handed partners could tumble a lone Goliath.

'I don't need to know about your clubs,' she said. 'I've got good clubs. That's why I bid them twice. But your queen and jack in hearts are perfect, you see? And your long diamonds may look like nothing to you but paired with my singleton ace, they're dynamite.'

He began to see that, in theory, if everyone played by the rules and bid with textbook precision, there could be perfect, unambiguous communication. Pride, he saw, was his downfall. Playing football at school he used to find himself surging up the field in hot-headed command of the ball and, ignoring the shouts of his team-mates, make a bid to score on his own only to find himself ignominiously offside. So now he had to learn to listen and accept that if his partner rejected his powerful spades in favour of diamonds, he must offer up his four feeble diamonds as humble support and let his partner play rather than pursue his own suit into disaster.

That night, for the first time he played rubber after rubber rather than making his excuses and sloping off. He became the one determined to play on when all around him were pointedly yawning and murmuring about calling it a day. Only when Bee finally insisted on breaking up the party and congratulated him, as she pecked him goodnight, on how he was progressing did he remember his earlier resolution to call on Lala.

He pretended to head for his cabin then ducked into a stairwell and hurried upstairs. There was no light coming from under her door, however. He lingered a few minutes, heart racing, but, intimidated by the rude stares of an overdressed couple mounting to their suite and shaken by the pointed marches past of a cabin boy who seemed to be doubling as the mistress's night watchman, he lost his resolve.

CHAPTER SEVENTEEN

Until now, Lawrence had imagined Caribbean islands as low-lying arrangements of cocoa palms, sandy beaches and rush-thatched seaside cafés at which one arrived by a small, putt-putting launch. Emerging from his cabin to watch their arrival at St Martin he realized his imaginings were fed by rum advertisements and wishful thinking. He saw no palms, only a dense mass of scrubby woodland, and black rocks where he had expected beaches. Instead of picturesque huts, a bustling commercial centre had been thrown up, much of it in crude concrete. It was also disillusioning to find that, far from cruising the Caribbean in isolation along a route of its own, the *Paulina* had been accompanied all the way from Miami by three other cruise ships. All four were easing into St Martin's deep harbour in preparation for a simultaneous credit card invasion. Darius had been here before, however, and took command.

'The Dutch side's a nightmare,' he said with his customary snobbery. 'Even more so when this lot have landed and started shopping. We'll hire a Jeep and head over the mountain ridge to the French side. No one bothers to go there as they all want to be back on board to eat a lunch they think they can trust. We'll find a good restaurant on the water somewhere. Maybe a beach, if there's time.'

Bee and Reuben were to come too – apparently Reuben and Darius had settled their differences over a card table – but not George and Martha as Darius was finding them a little wearing and Jeeps only took four comfortably. Imperious as a dowager at a car boot sale, he swept them through the hordes who were already snatching up 'cut price' jewels and imported tee shirts from the waterfront traders, and led them up a confusing network of side streets to a hire car lot where he began to haggle impressively over the price of a white, open-topped Jeep.

It transpired that the Jeep only came with a guide-cum-driver thrown in and all the self-drive cars had been reserved for passengers from one of the other liners.

'Why would we need a guide?' Darius huffed. 'I've been here before. There are barely three main roads on the entire island and with five of us the Jeep would be so cramped.'

The clerk was adamant however.

'My brother is an expert on flora and fauna,' she said. 'But if you only want a silent chauffeur then he'll be happy to oblige.'

At that moment she glanced across to a Sidney Poitier lookalike in white jeans and flame-red shirt who was drinking a cup of water from a dispenser. The others all glanced the same way, the man smiled and Bee said,

'Oh, I think having a proper guide might be rather fun. That's if you don't mind, Darius?'

'Who me? Not in the least.'

Forms were duly signed, the deposit paid and the brother, Jerome, introduced. He shook hands firmly all round and seemed relieved when he heard that they wanted to get as far from the shops and traders as possible. As they walked out to the Jeep, Lawrence noticed that Bee was more animated than usual and had removed her dark glasses as though to make herself more accessible.

'I'm sorry none of us speaks any Dutch,' she said.

'That's okay,' Jerome told her with a grin. 'Amelie and I are from the other side.'

'You speak French.'

'*Mais oui.*'

Bee laughed and promptly slipped into rapid French. Jerome banteringly responded in kind. Thus excluded, Lawrence thought it best he sit on the rear bench beside Darius and Reuben while she sat in front. They headed off through the outskirts of St Martin, bouncing out of town past lush gardens, shouting children and sly, scavenging dogs. Bee turned to call over her shoulder,

'Jerome says he'll take us up over the hills in the interior to see the trees and the view, which is marvellous apparently. Then down onto the French side to a beach where we can swim and eat a simple lunch.'

'Yes, dear,' said Darius acidly, one hand raised to stop his hat from blowing off. 'We understood perfectly.'

'I didn't,' Lawrence said but no one seemed to hear him. He saw Darius slip his other arm across the seat back behind Reuben to steady himself. The gesture excluded him as effectively as Bee's effortless, gurgling French.

He wondered what Lala would be doing. Perhaps she had left the ship to visit another friend. People like her must have friends everywhere, friends with large, secure houses. Maybe it was some other passenger's turn today. Some big-footed lunk of a Canadian was even now breaking out in a sweat as she unbuttoned his shirt at some borrowed poolside where his star-struck wife sprawled happily comatose from spiked fruit punch. Good luck to him.

He looked about them. Now he *did* feel as if he was in a rum commercial; five people in light, summer clothes and dark glasses driving heaven knew where and not caring, dazzling sunshine, balmy heat. As the road climbed, the houses to either side grew increasingly ramshackle and gaudy, concrete gave way to wood, garden to chicken run, then they were out in open country. The road surface began to deteriorate and the trees to encroach until they were climbing steeply through a kind of tunnel, flashing in and out of sunshine at the occasional breaks in the foliage overhead. Many of the trees were some kind of eucalypt, with dusty-blue leaves and gum that left a sensuous tang on the hot air. He looked at his uncle to see how he was managing.

Darius had taken off his hat to look up at the sunlight slanting through the trees. Sensing his nephew's eye on him, he turned back and smiled for the first time, it seemed to Lawrence, smiled with sincerity, with kindness, even.

Jerome drove them off the road up a dirt track which led to a hill's dry brow. They stopped to walk a few hundred yards to admire the view of undulating woods and distant beaches and the entire island coastline spread out around them with the simplicity of a treasure map. The air was resonant with eucalyptus scent.

'Bee tells me you are a tree expert,' Jerome told Lawrence in English.

'A tree *surgeon*,' Lawrence said. 'Hardly an expert. What are those?'

Jerome looked where he was pointing. Tall trees with ragged bark hanging off in strips and rustling, grey-green foliage.

'*Eucalyptus coccifera*,' he said and translated the Latin with a smile. '*Well covered berry-bearing*. Mount Wellington Peppermint. Here,' he added. He broke off a leaf, crushed it and held it under Lawrence's nose. Lawrence sneezed, apologized and took it from him to breathe in the intense peppermint scent.

'Delicious,' he said quietly. '*Delicieux*.'

Bee laughed at him and took a photograph.

Jerome then drove them down deep into the French side through a pretty village of old Colonial houses in painted timber, to a restaurant raised on stilts at one end of an empty beach. Chickens and fish were sizzling on a barbecue, red and white tablecloths fluttered in the warm breeze through the glassless windows and Lawrence realized with a delighted shock that what he had taken for pillars were actually the trunks of living coco palms growing up through holes in the wooden floor and disappearing through cunningly constructed sliding hatches in the roof. Another rum commercial.

*   *   *

Lunch – crab, chicken and a mound of fried christophine – was slow and delicious and foolishly alcoholic. The swaying of the palm pillars and the gentle plashing of low waves on warm sand was a tranquillizing combination even without wine and *p'tit ponches*. Although he felt obscurely peeved, jealous even, to see Bee insist that Jerome eat with them then continue to be so openly flirtatious with him, the setting and food conspired to leave Lawrence helplessly tongue-tied and aglow with love for his fellow man. Bee was beautiful and Reuben and Jerome were beautiful. Even Darius, puffing on his cigar and telling a rambling anecdote about his last visit to the island, seemed supremely distinguished.

Fortified by strong coffee, laughing at Darius's warnings against cramp, he wandered down the beach, stripped to his trunks and waded out into the impossibly warm and limpid water. He swam a few minutes of indolent backstroke then walked about in the sandy shallows, amazed at the spangled fish that darted fearlessly about his legs but vanished when he pursued them with his hands.

Lingering at the restaurant table, Jerome and Bee were deep in conversation. As he emerged, Bee waved to him and smiled invitingly. He raised a hand back but something in the intent way she had been listening reminded him of Bonnie listening to McBugger and he felt compelled to walk further along the beach, past the heap of his clothes, following the route he had seen the others take. The tawny sand formed a smooth-sloping, duneless shelf but the view along its length was broken here and there where clumps of the desiccated scrub and long grass had made inroads towards the water. Rounding one of these, he came across Darius and Reuben. Defeated by the after-effects of lunch, they were sitting on the sand, leaning against a fallen tree. Barefoot on sand as he went, they were unaware of his approach. When Reuben raised his hand to push Darius's hat off and run his fingers through his hair, Lawrence was as startled as if he had chanced on the two of them locked in a naked embrace. His uncle's expression showed a tender vulnerability of which Lawrence would never have believed him capable. Lawrence hastily backed off and turned towards the restaurant again then realized he might be *de trop* there as well. He sat in the shade, half-way between either couple, tossing sticks and shells into the waves' retreating foam and feeling the bonhomie of lunchtime curdle into the self-pity of the loveless inebriate.

'Lawrence? What are you all doing?!'

Bee was running along the beach to find him. He jumped up, thinking of her brother and his uncle, thinking fast.

'Hi,' he said in a clumsy stab at casual good cheer.

'Isn't it heaven here? Jerome wants to show us his house. It's only two bays on from here. Where are the others?'

'Ssh.'

'Why?'

'They're both sound asleep in the shade. Too much rum and sunshine. I think we should let them be.' He walked a little way past her towards the restaurant and succeeded in drawing her back with him. Jerome was waiting by the Jeep, tossing the keys on his palm and looking more like Sidney Poitier than ever. 'You go,' Lawrence said. 'I'll keep watch.'

'Are you sure?'

'Course I am. I quite enjoy just sitting and looking at the waves. I might swim again.'

'You are sweet,' she said and darted forward to kiss his cheek then hurried off. 'We shouldn't be more than an hour,' she called as she ran.

Lawrence watched the Jeep turn and vanish up the track to the village. He swam again, finding that the water felt still warmer second time around. Then, taking care not to cast so much as a glance towards Darius and Reuben, he carried his clothes into the shade, made a pillow of them and lay down to doze on the warm sand.

In his dream he was spreadeagled on a big white lilo, floating further and further from the beach where his mother, Bonnie, Lucy and McBugger were merrily dining with the others. He was powerless to swim against the current and could not cry out to them for help because he was naked. So he drifted and they dwindled. He was woken by Reuben's hand on his bare shoulder.

'Time to go,' Reuben said. 'You've been asleep for ages.'

'Rum,' Lawrence croaked, his mouth dry as the sand beneath him.

Bee had returned alone, apparently trusted by Jerome to take the Jeep back unassisted.

'Great excitement because there's a storm coming,' she said. 'His brother's out on a fishing trip with some tourists and he had to radio him to check he was on his way back to safety and the radio set's at some friend's house up in the hills. Do you think the *Paulina* should be sailing on? It's rather nerve-racking.'

Darius looked about them and shaded his eyes to stare out to sea.

'But the sky's so blue,' he said, faintly outraged. 'There *can't* be a storm.'

As she drove them back to the ship by a different, coastal route, Bee was full of chat. Jerome's house, apparently, was simple but charming. He was some sort of building contractor as well as a driver for his sister's firm in high season. He was unmarried. He had never been to England but he had a Scottish grandmother who had come to the island to study birdlife and never left. He was also an excellent cook. Darius tapped Lawrence's knee and discreetly pointed to where a fluttering label betrayed the fact that her tee shirt was now inside out.

'And did you swim?' he asked insouciantly.

'Oh no,' she murmured. 'Although his place is right on a tiny beach. We were far too busy talking. I'm so glad we came.' She laughed. 'I'm so glad no other cars were free.'

'Stop driving so fast,' Reuben told her.

'Am I? Sorry.' She slowed a little then gradually speeded up again.

'It's no use,' she said. 'I'm too happy. I can't pretend. He's asked me to jump ship and come to stay and I'm going to.'

Darius's eyes widened.

'You can't!' Reuben insisted.

'I can and I shall,' she said. 'I've got enough on my credit card to get home and school doesn't go back for weeks. Who knows, I might like it so much I might hand in my notice.'

'Bee!'

'Oh Reuben, I'm sorry. It was sweet of you to bring me and I've enjoyed the cruise enormously but – Oh God. Are you very cross?'

'I'm worried. That's all. This is so sudden.'

'But very romantic,' Darius added and Lawrence noted his private smile.

'Very,' she enthused. 'Oh Darius, you understand, don't you?' She swerved to avoid a clutch of chickens.

'Opportunity visits one less and less,' Darius pronounced. 'And regret is a harsh and unyielding companion.'

'But what about bridge?' Reuben asked, crestfallen.

'Bridge is going to be the consolation of my old age,' she said. 'But it's not a life substitute.'

The original plan had been to explore St Martin's French side a little further and even go to some of the better French shops but, with the careless selfishness of the supremely happy, Bee drove them directly to the *Paulina* with two hours still to spare. While Darius went to make enquiries on the bridge concerning the approaching storm, Reuben and Lawrence lolled drunkenly on her bed watching her pack and followed her to the purser's office where she paid her onboard bill with the credit card that was to be her lifeline. She signed a document to confirm that she was leaving the cruise of her own volition and would not hold the company responsible for her return to England. Then she kissed and hugged them both and left hurried verbal messages for Darius, George and Martha before hurrying down to catch a boat back to shore where Jerome had arranged to meet her in a waterfront café.

Her euphoria was palpable as sunlight. It was unassailable and self-sufficient and reminded Lawrence, with a pang, of Bonnie on their wedding day. She had faced her friends and family with a kind of brave triumph and made it seem that this was a rite of passage in which the joy or displeasure of the groom was immaterial, provided he was there, on time, dressed correctly and prepared to take her away somewhere special once it was all over. Watching Bee stirred up in him inevitable feelings of regret, so that he was left wondering if perhaps he should have pursued her after all. If nothing else, she had been his companion, an unobtrusive source of social support, a kind of ideal sister. Who would he talk to now? Who would help him through the remaining ordeal? Returning from seeing her off, he and Reuben passed a landing where a florist was arranging a vase of calla lilies beside a poster announcing Lala's fourth and final onboard concert.

'We're going,' Reuben sighed. 'No buts. Darius has a hangover. You can be my date for the evening.'

CHAPTER EIGHTEEN

Craig McBride's single-storey house was beautiful and strange. It was entirely his. He had designed everything down to the chopping board and shoe rack. In a city of architectural treasures, it was hard to resist comparisons, although Bonnie kept them to herself. It was as though Frank Lloyd Wright had collaborated with a Japanese craftsman. Presenting a blank, almost fortified air to the outside – although the outside was nothing more threatening than leafily suburban Oak Park – symmetrical yew hedge, concrete wall and *shoji*-screened windows concealed a series of serene interlocking rooms arranged in a perfect square about a sunny courtyard garden that held more stone and wood than unruly living matter. There was a deep, square pond in the centre, where white lilies and zandestechia flowered and ghostly koi rose to feed from one's fingers. There was a magnificently phallic menhir balanced by a more feminine cluster of smooth rocks which glistened and revealed colours when it rained. Inside, the walls and floors were made of wood but Craig had varied the wall panels so that each room's colour was dictated by its tree of origin. There was oak, of course, white pine, cork and beech but smaller areas had drawn on more luxurious timbers like walnut and maple. He had ordered successively sliced sheets of wood so that each wall contained an evolving pattern like a perverse wallpaper. The master bedroom was lined with incense cedar so that it smelled like a cigar box. Even the bath was wooden, made to a Japanese design with the aid of a bemused firm of Midwestern coopers. Bonnie's beloved

John Minton was the only painting in the entire place. She had not dared to request a picture hook, so it still rested at one end of a bookcase.

Blatantly charm the daughter though he might, if Craig had wooed the mother, he had done so with such stealthy sensitivity she was quite unaware of it.

'Come for three weeks,' he said at first. 'Then see. Relax. Take stock. I can find you some work if you want it. We're surrounded by gardens in need of you.'

He had clients to talk to and sites to check on but he took time off to show her and Lucy the city. They rode the lifts up the Sears Tower, went to a concert by the symphony orchestra, visited the Art Institute and paid homage at the altars of Frank Lloyd Wright, Mies Van de Rohe and Louis Sullivan. They took picnics to the beach. He found Lucy a cheerful dumpling of a baby-sitter some friends used and took Bonnie with him to a few parties. At first he merely walked her round easy, work-related receptions where there was no pressure on her. Then, as if it were the most natural thing in the world, he took her to a few dinner parties where she met his oldest friends and his sister, who Bonnie liked immediately. They then called on his widowed mother, who baked raisin bran cookies for Lucy and gently scrutinized her son's new, gardening friend under cover of asking her to identify some label-less plants she had picked up at a charity fair.

Little by little she was introduced, purely as a friend, but she was introduced. Little by little she picked up scraps and traces of Craig's ex-wife, Vi, who had left him suddenly for a man she met at the opera and who now lived in Boston. Little acrimony was held against Vi. Craig certainly dismissed it as a precipitous marriage of two people barely old enough to cook a meal, much less pay for it. Everyone spoke of her with a hint of laughter in their voices. She was plainly held to be a fool but they were all relieved at her folly for she was a fool who would surely have matured into a monster.

'Craig's a catch,' their tone conveyed to Bonnie. 'Don't make the same mistake Vi made . . .'

She felt some of them assume he was her lover but could hardly correct them when nothing was overtly declared. Adrift as she was in an emotional limbo, numbly recuperating, she found herself unable to speak firmly of the future or of her return to England in a way that would immediately clear up any misinterpretations of her state.

The end of the second week came and then of the third.

'Do you mind if I stay a bit?' she asked.

'I'll mind if you go,' he answered her.

He found her a near neighbour who wanted an English rose garden planning. He suggested she take the job on 'just for fun'. Just for fun, Lucy was introduced on a temporary basis at the lively neighbourhood nursery school, which she loved. The child was learning to swear allegiance to the flag of her new country and developed a taste for peanut butter and 'jelly' sandwiches and now she was having an all-American birthday when she would normally have had a few friends over for cake and party games and been spoiled by Dora.

Bonnie and Lucy were sitting at the kitchen breakfast bar. At the sound of a car engine and the garage doors purring into action, Bonnie looked up from the bulb catalogue she had been poring over. Lucy looked up simultaneously from the drawing pad that had been one of her birthday presents. The birthday girl had been sulking slightly since being thwarted in her desire to visit a neighbourhood ice cream parlour. In these last days, Bonnie had noticed, she tended to sulk only for her mother's benefit, setting her jaw, narrowing her mouth and becoming a small, watchful piece of Lawrence. Usually this look and the sullen behaviour that went with it vanished in Craig's presence, for the child was already a mistress of the manipulation of males. Just occasionally, when he was driving them somewhere, Bonnie would glance over her shoulder or peer in the rear-view mirror and see Lucy hunched on her booster cushion on the back seat, staring scornfully at Craig with her father's dark eyes. Bonnie could not fathom whether Lucy hated him and was hypocritically sweet to his face or loved him and merely mimed hating him behind his back to punish her mother.

'Is that Craig?' the child asked now.

Bonnie nodded and grinned.

'That's right. Which means it's time for someone's birth-day treat.'

'What are we doing?'

'You'll have to ask him.'

'No but what? The zoo? Ice skating? What?'

'I've no idea,' Bonnie laughed. 'He organized it all. It's his treat for you.'

Lucy hesitated a moment then, hearing the door that linked house to garage open, she flung down her felt tip and raced to meet him.

Hearing his laughter and her shouts, Bonnie could almost imagine her calling him Daddy. Lucy still missed her father, although the intervals when she forgot to mention him were already growing heartlessly longer. Once she asked, in a particularly irritating whine, whether he was ill or maybe lost.

'We can't see him for a while. Mummy and Daddy need to be apart for a bit. We – We make each other cross, remember?'

'But I want to see him. I want to see him *today*,' the child retorted.

Bonnie saw Lawrence in her petulant face and lost her temper.

'Don't you remember? You were there! You found me on the bloody kitchen floor!'

All child again, Lucy turned pale and wept so copiously that Bonnie worried she might have traumatized her. When Lucy mentioned him again, a few hours later, it was with almost comic caution as 'him'.

'Who?' Bonnie asked.

'Him. You know. *Lawrence.*'

Daddy had apparently become too conflict-ridden a concept to grasp. As mere *Lawrence*, he was demoted to the safer level of Black Bun or the characters in *Sesame Street* – to be invoked with the sheepish awareness that he was not entirely real. Today, however, Craig had anticipated she might begin to pine afresh when Lawrence failed to appear on her birthday so he had laid on a spectacular birthday treat: a trip to a theme park, then to a new Walt Disney film and then to a pizzeria.

She wondered anew if he were perhaps seducing her through her daughter, manoeuvring Lucy into playing Cupid like some Old Hollywood moppet matchmaker:

'Oh please say you love him, Mummy. Pretty please? He's said he'll buy me a pony and a kitten and a new pink party dress with seed pearls. Oh *please* Mummy!'

Tidying away the new felt tip set and sketch pad, Bonnie snorted at the very idea. She glanced at the pictures with a twinge of guilty anxiety, looking for codified images of sadness and loss amid the giant bumblebees, foursquare houses, triangle-skirted stick women and smiling flowers. Craig strode into view, bouncing Lucy on broad shoulders.

'Hi, honey. I'm home,' he said with a grin and she sniffed for truth beneath the satire.

She had always marvelled at how handsome he was – film star handsome, chiselled. His eyes were so true a blue she had heard him accused of wearing coloured contact lenses. His prematurely silver hair was thick and fell naturally into loose waves like the hair on a statue. With eyes only for Lawrence, she had been disconcerted when she first met Craig to discuss the university landscaping. His looks seemed so remarkable as to demand some acknowledgement. Then she had easily dismissed them. He was decorative, certainly, she told herself, but not specifically *sexy* like Lawrence. He was slightly *too* good-looking. He was no temptation. Thereafter she had unconsciously used humour as a Craig-vaccine, commenting satirically on his good looks in front of him to show that yes, she admired them but no, they stirred no dark unspoken longings.

In the pizzeria this evening, however, he looked at her and she changed her mind. Worn out by pleasure and so much stimulus, Lucy fell heavily asleep against him on the banquette across from Bonnie. He tucked an arm about the child to stop her sliding off, like a dad to the manner born, and reached for his coffee with his free, left hand. Raising the cup to his lips, his eyes met Bonnie's with such warm directness that she froze for a moment then had to look away. She felt that her chest, not her cheeks, was blushing. She thought of Mia Farrow as a star-struck waitress whose idol suddenly turns out of his celluloid setting to make public advances to her. This was an unscripted moment. She realized that, precisely because of his looks, she had not treated him as a flesh-and-blood male and had made no allowances for any emotional life, any vulnerable desire that might be uncoiling beneath that Hollywood exterior.

'So,' he said after a moment. 'You wrote to him.'

'Yes,' she said, snapping pieces of Lucy's half-munched bread stick. 'I wrote to Dora and I wrote to him.'

'No reply?'

'I didn't tell them where we are. But I doubt he'd write anyway. He's not a letter writer. Words unsettle him.'

Craig sighed.

'How did you two ever come together?'

'Girlhood crush. He was the hired help. I seduced him.'

'You're kidding me.' She nodded ruefully.

'Then, a bit later, he came to my rescue when a scumbag gave me a hard time.'

'Just like me.' He gave her that look again.

'He's not a scumbag,' she said quickly and waved to a waiter for the bill.

'If you say so.'

'Let's just . . .' She thought a moment. 'Let's just not discuss him, okay? There's nothing to agree on. It doesn't solve a thing.'

He drove them home solicitously, like a good cab driver, with them on the backseat, Lucy fast asleep with her head in Bonnie's lap. Neither spoke. She stared out at the still unfamiliar streets, the great, louring Loop, rich window displays, glittering, black-faced towers. While they were waiting at some lights, Lucy broke the silence by snoring softly and the adults laughed, catching each other's glance in the rear-view mirror, then Craig slid some quiet jazz cassette into the player. Thelonius Monk. It was one of the only two tapes in the car so, if only by virtue of enforced repetition, was fast becoming the theme tune of the trip, holiday, escape, whatever this was. *Their* tune.

Unlike Lawrence, whose silent presence was impossible to ignore, Craig had a way of melting away for hours at a stretch, suddenly absorbed like a thoughtful boy, at his drawing board or over a magazine. He vanished that night when they returned home. Bonnie swept a grouchily waking daughter off to bath and bed as soon as they were out of the garage. Sliding Lucy's door softly closed, she anticipated a mellow, companionate hour of sitting around with a bourbon and some music and was disappointed to find the living area and library in darkness. She took a delicious soak in the wooden tub instead, leaning back against its steep, warm side.

When she climbed into bed, she glanced across the courtyard as had become her habit. Lucy's window was dark, naturally, but she could see Craig in bed, tortoiseshell glasses sliding down his nose as he read the long novel he claimed to have been battling with for the last year and a half. She watched him for perhaps five minutes before he looked up and noticed her. He smiled and adjusted his glasses. She held his gaze until his smile melted then she pointedly flicked back the bedding on the other half of her bed and looked up at him again. Grinning now, he did the same.

Leaving her light on, she walked to the window, slid it back a couple of feet, then stole, naked and shivering, across the courtyard, treading the path of light from her bed to his. The brief, significant passage from one room to the other felt risky, yes, and transgressive, but, perhaps because of the light at her back, not irrevocable. There was a remote control panel at his bedside however and once he had taken her in his arms and kissed her, steering her through the giant cigar box to his bed, he used it to dim his own lights and plunge her distant room into darkness. As far as he was concerned, it seemed, her vote was cast.

CHAPTER NINETEEN

From the moment he knocked on her cabin door Lawrence was lost. In so far as there was a battle, he had ceded her the victory. She had already abased herself quite enough, apparently, and now it was his turn. At first she was all charmed, torturing surprise, as though he were some helpless fan in her dressing room and she had no idea, none whatsoever, why he should have come. She forced him to ask politely, worse, to beg, to spell out what he wanted.

'You,' he stammered. 'I want you. I can't stop thinking about you. No one need know. Please. Even if it's just once more. Please.'

He had never felt so humiliated. Even when he pleaded, she tortured him. She waited. She smiled. She crossed her legs and ate a grape.

'You took your time,' she said at last, still watching him.

'I'm sorry. I didn't know what you wanted. I thought perhaps . . .'

'What?'

'Nothing.'

'You tried to leave the ship.'

'No, I – '

'Don't lie. I find out everything. You tried to leave in Miami and you were too late. You could have left today, like Bee. Why didn't you?'

'I didn't – I don't know.'

'Well? What?'

'I didn't want to leave you.'

She ate another grape, leaving him to stand before her still.

'Doesn't it worry you, what people say about me?'

'What do you mean?'

'You tell me, Lawrence.'

'I – You mean about . . . about *you*?'

She nodded and looked at him expectantly, piercing a third grape with her nails.

'They . . . Some of them say that you used . . . I mean . . .' Her scent was everywhere in the cabin. He had surprised her as she changed from her performance dress and she had on a long silk wrap. The heat in the room seemed to emanate from her, from her neck and chest. He could hardly breathe. He realized they had left port again. The ship was swaying below his feet. 'They're just stupid stories.'

'What are?'

He gulped.

'They say . . . They say you used to be a man.'

There was a pause then she said,

'I know. Does that bother you?'

'I don't believe it.'

'But if it were true?' He shrugged. He wanted to look away but could not. He felt rooted to the carpet. 'If I used to be a man, what would that make you?'

'You're a woman.'

'*Now* I'm a woman.'

'So it is true.'

Now it was her turn to shrug.

'If you leave now,' she said, 'you're never coming back.'

'I don't want to leave.'

'Then take off your clothes. No. Stay where you are and take off your clothes.'

She sat eating grapes and watching him strip. He was ashamed at how excited this made him. He took deep breaths to no avail. She looked at his face, down to his groin then up at his face again.

'Now lie down,' she said. 'No. Not on the bed. I don't want the sheets all rucked up. Put this on that,' she added, tossing him a condom, 'and lie on that rug there.'

He did as she said and lay down, feeling the ship roll gently beneath him. If he shut his eyes, he could imagine them in an aeroplane, breasting clouds instead of waves. She did not join him immediately but walked to the bathroom where he heard her brushing her teeth, blowing her nose and using the loo. Then she turned out all the lights except for the dim one out on her balcony, sat astride him and rode him like a horse, brushing his hands aside whenever he tried to touch her. She did not kiss him and did not speak. He cried out when he came but she rode on in silence, only registering her pleasure, if that could describe something so focused and mirthless, by spasmodic pincer motions of her thighs against his waist and ribcage. She dismounted as tidily as if he had been a chair and pulled her wrap back on.

'Now you can go.'

'Can't I stay?'

'I need to sleep.'

'Can I . . . Can I see you – ' he began and she cut in.

'I'll let you know.'

He dressed clumsily in the shadows and hurried out. Being used like a male whore should have killed his interest in her, but the experience was novel and intoxicating. For the next few days, he experienced the sort of addictive degradation on which women's magazines grew fat. He had no shame. Under Darius and Reuben's satiric gaze, he became indeed a kind of prostitute. He worked out to make his body hard for her, he washed two or three times a day, he kept his clothes neat and fresh and otherwise spent his waking hours waiting for the cabin telephone to ring or for a smirking waiter to bring a summons from her.

She was not always cold. Sometimes she was nearly loving. Often she let him kiss her for hours but go no further, until his lips were tender and swollen as his insulted privates.

When he told her he loved her, and he did this often, she laughed, not always unkindly, but gave him no reason to hope.

'Don't be a fool,' she said. 'You hardly know me. Besides, we're hopelessly incompatible. Do you think that chair could take us both?'

Once she made him squeeze into one of her dresses and dolled him up with make-up and a wig as if he were less lover than toy. Once she spent hours teasing him.

'Now that you've had me you should try it with a real man. I know you'd enjoy it. You could surrender completely. Let him fuck you. It would be so good for you. One of the engineers, perhaps. That one with the red beard. So liberating. And Bee's brother's attractive. Why don't you let him have you?' When she refused to stop he pressed a hand over her mouth and she lashed out like a stevedore and knocked him down. She walked out and left the door open so that he had no option but to leave too. Her punch gave him a black eye.

'I'd had a bit too much to drink and I managed to hit my face on the bedside table,' he said, when Darius knowingly asked if he had walked into a door.

She never let him stay the night. She never encouraged him to talk about himself. Just once he tried to talk about Lucy, about how badly he missed her, and she turned on him, harshly rebuking him for his self-pity.

'You loused up,' she said.

It was one of the moments when she seemed at once most womanly and least female.

CHAPTER TWENTY

Jerome's information was correct. Ever since leaving St Martin, the captain had been warning them of the possibility that their cruise might be affected by the progress of a hurricane – hurricane Esmé. Sure enough, when they reached the Virgin Islands they were forced to spend an unscheduled night sheltering in the lee of St John and St Thomas as the terrible wind sped through. There were scenes of panic on board, spread by some passengers from Florida who knew what a hurricane could do, but the shelter had been chosen well; the wind barely winged them since the eye of the storm was several miles away. They rolled and pitched sickeningly as rain lashed the windows. Several passengers suffered falls on the staircases, many were nauseous from fear and motion and a few glasses and bottles were broken, but nothing more dramatic befell the *Paulina*. However it was thought best to remain where they were until a new, safer course could be decided on for their return.

As always, Lala had inside information. She came to Lawrence's cabin early in the morning, while it was barely light, and told him to get dressed quickly.

'We're stuck here another day,' she said, 'and I'm going stir crazy, so I've bribed an officer to put us ashore for a few hours. He's radioed for a boat. We can walk about. Maybe go for a drive. Come on. Don't bother shaving.'

'Is it safe?'

'A bit of wind. A bit of rain. No worse than what you get at home.'

They slipped down to the embarkation gate seen only

by maids and waiters and were helped down to a small water taxi.

There was a light drizzle and the air was hair-dryer warm. Lala had dressed in a black trouser suit with just an orange scarf tucked under the jacket to make her decent. With the heat, she grew careless of the scarf. The waiter in the shabby little café where they ordered breakfast was so transfixed by her cleavage that he poured juice on the table and had to move them in a flurry of apologetic mopping up. They sat where a hatch was swung up onto stilts to form a makeshift veranda decorated with scarlet hibiscus planted in old petrol cans. Out in the bay, the *Paulina* appeared almost delicate and spotlessly white against the storm-darkened waters. Framed by flowers and sun-bleached pink and blue paintwork, the view would have done a cruise brochure proud.

Lala drained her coffee cup and clicked it decisively back in her saucer.

'It's been fun,' she said.

'It still is.'

'Lawrence,' she said and laid a hand on his with unexpected solicitude. 'We're screwing on a luxury liner in a Caribbean hurricane zone. This is not life. This is holiday.'

'I've got no house, no business. I'm free,' he assured her. 'I could be your chauffeur.'

'I don't have a car.'

'Your secretary.'

'I never write letters.'

'Your gardener then.'

'I don't lay the help.'

'Please.'

'You're so cute when you beg.'

'Fuck off.'

'Sorry. I don't mean to tease. I just – I don't want you building châteaux in Spain, is all. We have a few more days. Let's keep it light.'

'But – '

'You've got a marriage to dismantle and a kid to find. When this is over you have to rebuild your life. I'm not the one to build it with. Just look on me as some kind of extreme therapy.'

'I love you.'

'Ssh. Stop it.' She glanced over at the waiter who was needlessly polishing a nearby ashtray.

'But I do. I've never felt like this.'

'Oh listen, you!' She smacked the tabletop impatiently. 'You've just never had a tranny before. For what it's worth, I'll never forget this either.'

'Really?'

'Really. You've left your mark.'

'Am I supposed to be flattered?'

'Believe me. When a girl this age opens both eyes wide, that's flattering.'

He ground up a dark brown sugar lump with his spoon, mashing it into his coffee dregs.

'You're not half so old as you like to make out. You just act older so no one will notice your age.'

'And sometimes for a woodcutter your perceptions are quite eerily camp. The drizzle's stopped. Pay for these and we can take a walk.'

The air was thick with the scents of moist earth and wind-damaged vegetation and so humid it felt like warm drizzle on the skin. They walked slowly up a lane out of the tiny port past waking households and dozing cats, radios playing *soca* and mothers calling impatiently to children. The hurricane's calling cards were everywhere. Palm leaves and tree branches dangled at unhealthy angles, windows were still spattered over with mud, bushes bore incongruous pieces of litter like scrappy, ill-matched flowers.

They walked close but not touching. The atmosphere was saddened but still sweet. With the deranged optimism of love, he decided, as they walked, that she was having second thoughts. She had been testing him in the café. She had opened a door to give him a chance to flee and if he could just prove his resolution to remain, she would relent and keep him with her.

They reached the preserved ruin of an eighteenth-century sugar plantation where a tower still commanded a view across to the British territories.

'I came on a holiday here,' she said. 'Years ago. Before the cruise ships started spoiling it all. I stayed round there. See those houses on the beach? Nutmeg Bay. I'd forgotten how lovely it was.'

He took her hand and kissed her, backing her against the cold stone wall of the look-out point. That was when he heard the growl.

It was almost inaudibly deep, like a far off engine. Looking over his shoulder, Lala tensed, her hands freezing in the act of caressing his back.

'Jesus,' she breathed. 'Don't move.'

Of course he had to then. He turned and froze also. It was orange, tawny white and black, beautiful and outlandish on the lawn where tour guides stood to assemble their groups. Its ears rode back, its tail thrashed in an awful parody of a domestic cat and it growled again, this time baring its fangs. It was thirty feet away, possibly less. Its paws seemed big as cushions. Its belly swung as it walked.

'Don't turn your back,' Lala hissed. 'Not unless it runs,' and she began to edge along the wall back towards the lane. Heart pounding he did the same. The tiger followed them. Then its slow padding quickened to a brisk walk.

'Run,' Lawrence said.

'No,' she muttered.

'Come on,' he shouted and tugging her hand, took to his heels.

She kept alongside him for a few seconds then cried out and fell. Stumbling, he looked back and saw the great cat had knocked her to the ground on her face and was nosing at her hair and neck.

'Get away!' he yelled at it. 'Gaarn!' Amazed at his own courage, he made a dash back at it, arms wide, eyes agog, letting out a kind of roar. It looked up from Lala's body and sprang after him instead. Now he ran, sprinted, yelling as he went. 'Help!' he shouted, 'For God's sake, help! Police! Anyone! Help me please!' As he sprinted, he sensed it closing on him, tensed his shoulders for the impact of steel claws and musky tonnage of fur. Some children ran shrieking behind a gate. A driver honked his horn. At last a group of men with sticks and shovels, road workers probably, stopped him, releasing his breathless, incoherent babble, and he saw that the beast was no longer in pursuit.

He explained what had happened and one of them ran to call the police while another darted into his house and returned with a rifle. Heart racing, lungs in a heaving agony, for all his sessions on Spencer's purgatorial Stairmaster, Lawrence led them back up the lane and along the track to the ruin. They glanced wildly about them, sensing teeth and claws in every bush, but there was no trace of the tiger beyond its footprints, clear in the mud, where it had pursued Lawrence down the hill.

There was no trace of Lala either. There was blood on the grass where she had fallen and Lawrence quickly spotted the orange chiffon scarf which had been torn off her neck and left snagged on a tree's trailing branches. He sagged onto his knees in the mud grasping it so tightly that the police had to prise it from his shaking fingers. It was torn and soaked at one end in blood that was still warm to the touch.

Within the hour the tiny island was in uproar, within two, the first television crews had arrived. The tiger, a mature male, had escaped from a small private zoo kept by a wealthy American eccentric, high in the island's interior. A tree had blown down in the hurricane and smashed a section of fence sufficiently to allow the beast to escape. The police tracked it down in the woods and shot it. Lala's body and other clothes were not found. A bloodhound was used but it was confused by the strong scent left by the tiger's spoor and merely led the police back to the eccentric's hideaway. The tiger's body was destroyed before anyone thought to suggest that an autopsy report on the contents of its stomach might have provided conclusive proof one way or the other. The worst was assumed.

The remainder of the cruise passed him by in a blur. He surprised himself and Darius by not going to pieces, even during Father Xavier's unctuous shipboard memorial service. He did not take to drink or medication, did not begin to abuse his fellow guests. He pursued an unwavering routine of swimming, working out in the gym and dutifully embarking on any excursion Darius suggested. His mind became entirely focused on remaining in America when the ship returned to Miami and finding Lucy. He talked it through quite calmly with Martha. (He had grown bolder at expressing himself – Bee and Lala's unsparing tutorials had seen to that.) He would find work in Chicago, if that was indeed where his wife and child had settled. Having been born in America, a permit should be easy enough to come by. He would encourage Bonnie to file for a divorce so that his position would be quite unambiguous and he could negotiate joint custody. In this at least he could prove himself. Raising the child and providing for her should be his one success.

'I'll do whatever Bonnie wants,' he told Martha. 'I'll see a therapist. Remarry. Anything. But she can't stop me being a father.'

After raising a difficult daughter and weathering a marriage forged in painful compromise, Martha was wise enough to know better than to question his resolve. Instead she made her mild attentiveness a kind of conversational mirror, enabling him to argue with himself, and in the process came to love him as the passionate, slightly dim son she had always wanted.

Lawrence and his family were saved a second scandal because Lala meant so little to British journalists. Only one newspaper ran a story, under the headline *Murder Suspect and Transsexual in Man-eating Tiger Horror*. However, because it was a paper notorious for grotesque distortions along the *Prayer Doubled My D Cup* and *Slugs Ate My Baby* line, nobody took the matter further. Elsewhere an international league of fans went into mourning and the café where the diva had downed her last coffee was renamed in her honour. Thereafter a small glass cabinet in Café Lala displayed, like a holy relic, an unwashed Pyrex coffee cup with a parting imprint of *rouge extrême* lipstick on its rim.

CHAPTER TWENTY-ONE

Dora had never expected to return to America. It was a country of which even her happier memories had been soured. This trip was no holiday and was scarcely going to leave them any sweeter. She had gained no experience of cruise ships since her arrival in England with a baby and two suitcases but had, for some reason, expected them to have been modernized at the same rate as aeroplanes. As she and Charlie shared a taxi to the dock in Miami she had anticipated a building with all the comforts of an airport arrivals lounge; sofas, shops, carpet, a bar. She found instead an expanse of drab waterside concrete with a high corrugated iron roof, a kind of salty barn.

The situation could not have been worse. The *Paulina* had docked and a trickle of passengers was already disembarking and heading for the taxi rank and the waiting airport and hotel shuttle buses. There was nowhere quiet she could lead him, nowhere with soft edges and soft lights where she could break the news. Added to which, she had Charlie in attendance, mournful, shell-shocked Charlie, whose scarecrow face alone announced a tragedy. In the extremity of his grief, he appeared to have forgotten the bad blood between him and his son-in-law and was all loving, button-lipped sorrow. She realized too late that she could undoubtedly have contacted an official of the shipping line and had Darius and Lawrence paged on arrival, whisked through a priority channel and summoned to a place of privacy.

The emerging crowd was beginning to engulf her so that she had to strain her neck to keep an eye on the gangplank.

She was just wondering whether she could divert Charlie for the few crucial minutes by sending him on some errand, when she saw them and they, in seconds, spotted her.

There was no need for any careful preambles, of course. Her worried rehearsals had been in vain. The mere shock of her being there, Charlie too, alerted them that something was badly wrong and involved either Bonnie or Lucy or both. All she had to do was tell them which and she heard herself do it with brutal swiftness, her words a lancing knife. Lawrence did not weep or cry out but all the blood drained from his face and he sank onto his suitcase while Darius asked all the questions for him. When? How? Did she suffer? What was the medical opinion? What about the funeral?

They had missed the funeral, naturally. That would be the hardest thing for Lawrence. Arriving too late, he was deprived of a body to hold, of the grim reassurance in planting a farewell kiss on ice-cold flesh, deprived too of a ritual to enact. All Dora could do was tell him – or rather tell him through Darius – who had been there, what music, what readings had been heard and where in Chicago the grave could be found. She hated the milling crowd, the suitcases that kept bumping her shins, the uncomprehending, gawping witnesses whose prurience inhibited her so she could not hug him, could not touch him, for fear of the torrent of grief the natural contact would unstop within her.

'I'm so sorry,' Charlie murmured. 'Christ, Lawrence, I'm so sorry.' His voice cracked and he turned aside. Dora glared at an old woman who was staring, then almost jumped as Lawrence spoke at last.

'Where does he live? I could be there by lunch time.'

'I . . .' She stammered. 'Lawrence, I can't. I promised. It's better not. We can see the grave, go there together, then we'll take you home.'

He looked away as he spoke, controlling his anger.

'Just give me the address.'

'The cemetery? It's easy, you – '

'The house. Where does he live?'

'I . . . Darling, I can't.'

'I have to see where it happened.'

'No. Come away. It's for the best. Honestly. Let it go. Come home with us.'

'I don't fucking want to come home.'

The venom in his voice roused Charlie who turned back and tried to intervene in the worst possible way.

'Don't talk to your mother like that! Don't you see, you idiot? She's promised Craig. We both have. You're to stay away.'

'For God's sake,' Lawrence hissed and shook Charlie off.

'Come on,' Darius said in a furious undertone. 'All of you. Let's get away from here. Somewhere quiet where we can talk this through.'

'Darius is right,' Dora said. 'Please, darling. No one's forcing you but please come home. We can take things one step at a time.'

At this moment Dora noticed two things: that there was a young man with Darius, actually holding one of Darius's cases, and that the rude woman who had been staring had slipped forward through the crowd and was talking softly. She was short, deeply tanned, with white hair and a face like an old apple. She was American. Holding Lawrence's hand and kissing it as Dora had longed to do, she actually invited him to stay with her for a while to decide what he wanted to do. The woman spoke as rudely as she had stared, ignoring Dora and Darius, ignoring everyone except Lawrence. Then to Dora's amazement and intense unhappiness, Lawrence nodded, stood, picked up his case and walked into the crowd with her without a backward glance. No one tried to stop him. They were too surprised. Darius later explained who the woman was, but for Dora the hurt remained. He had preferred someone else's mother to his own, and done it publicly.

They were late checking in for the flight home and even

when Darius pleaded compassionate grounds it proved impossible to find four seats together. She assumed Darius would travel with her but, to her surprise, he sat with the young man, whose name was Reuben Calder, and left her with Charlie. This worked out better than she had expected. It was as though the confrontation with Lawrence had flicked some switch in Charlie's brain or perhaps he was merely reassured that Lawrence was not returning to England with them. Whatever the reason, he was no longer frozen in mourning. He did not become a chattering charmer either but he was warmer, solicitous. He shielded Dora from the stewardesses, from the other passengers. He ordered her two drinks, sensing one was insufficient, fetched her a blanket and pillow, even asked a noisy neighbour, quite politely, to move rather than continue to chat across the aisle beside them.

'I'm sorry about Lawrence,' he said after they had each handed in their half-eaten dinners and ordered more whisky. 'I shouldn't have interfered.'

'It's not your fault,' she sighed. 'Nothing you said could have made the slightest difference. He hates me. I see that now.'

'No he doesn't.'

'I'm not what he needs and I've got to get used to it.'

As the other passengers began to watch a film and she downed a sleeping pill and nestled into her pillow, she felt him take her hand and hold it between his on his lap. This felt good. He was still holding her hand when he gently woke her, his voice husky from lack of sleep, as they began the slow descent to Birmingham. He retrieved her luggage for her, drove her home and slept off his jet lag beside her.

At long last, with no discussion, no seduction, no teasing glances or passionate embrace, they embarked on their long overdue affair. To start with, they often wept together as they made love and all her memories of his earliest, searching kisses, were tear-pickled. Tender from grief, she forgot all her old love of a solitary bed and habit of sleeping lightly. They spent night after night in his bed or hers and she slept for dreamless hours without waking. They laid no plans, recovering as they both were from a crisis, but when he gave her a necklace of garnets and said he loved her, she did not panic and did not try to escape, but accepted jewellery and adoration with a guarded, careful pleasure and realized she was falling in love in return. For the moment, however, Dora said nothing to anyone. Not to Hecate, whom she continued to see in the afternoons, and not to Darius. Used to secrecy, accepting as yet that they had little in common when they were up and dressed, Charlie obliged her with a similar discretion.

As for Darius's young man, she had assumed he offered no more to her brother than one of those short-lived friendships forged during the temporary adversity of a poorly planned holiday and she was embarrassed when Darius announced that he was bringing him to stay for a weekend, lest her indifference had given offence. Far from being on the defensive, however, Reuben Calder had come armed to charm. She had thought him a lightweight, a wastrel even, but once he had done with praising her house and garden, insisting she leave her hair just as it was and encouraging her to talk at length about Lawrence and Bonnie and poor little Lucy, and to show him photographs, she found him a witty and sensitive listener.

His sister had formed an unsuitable attachment, apparently on impulse, and had forsaken brother, house, teaching post, her life, in fact, to prolong it. Reuben was unnerved by this, and feigned an angry dismay, but Dora sensed that it was the withdrawal of his sister that had enabled him to form the blithe attachment she witnessed developing over a succession of months. He feared her sudden return, perhaps, and how it might affect his new happiness.

As for Darius, he was a man transformed. Compensating

for Lawrence's lack of a father, he had long affected a dignity beyond his years. Now his ageing had not merely halted on the kinder side of fifty but was perceptibly shifting into reverse gear. Weekend after weekend she watched his walk, his voice, his dress, his hair, his taste in music, even his vocabulary take a turn for the younger.

Ordinarily a twin in her position might have felt forlorn and obscurely slighted but, while it was true that she sometimes found the spectacle of his happiness a trifle too bright to bear at close quarters, she was experiencing fresh pleasures of her own. Just as Reuben seemed set free by the departure of his sister, so she had to admit that the continuing absence of her son and, indeed, her daughter-in-law, had loosened certain constraints upon her. She and, she supposed, Darius felt at once less responsible than they had done, and less *watched*.

Unlikely as it might have seemed two years ago, Hecate Murray was her new, best friend. Stern but true, a widow shunned by her more sophisticated children, she had set about saving Dora's soul with a mixture of slyness and zeal. She lent her novels with uplifting endings and coaxed her repeatedly into the cathedral or to various country churches, albeit on the pretext of admiring architecture or memorial tablets. She spoke of Jesus as of an intimate friend with such frequency that Dora caught herself thinking of him as someone they might run into any day. Realizing, to her surprise, that she was growing fond of this insistent and penetrating woman, Dora demanded that all evangelizing cease.

'I could no more become a Christian than I could a Hindu,' she declared firmly. 'You may pray for me as much as you like, but please do it out of my hearing. I believe that when we die we stop and there's an end. I am entirely for this world, Hecate, not the next. Your trying to convert me any further would be both insensitive and unfriendly.'

On the understanding that this world, unlike the next, could do with some immediate attention, she encouraged

Hecate to join her as a prison visitor at Barrowcester's jail and found her friend excelled at the work, not least because many of the hardened lifers, unlike Dora, were keen to embrace Jesus as an intimate friend, especially if his ambassadress could slip them packets of cigarettes and chocolate along with her uplifting texts.

'Jesus enjoyed a drink, clearly,' Hecate defended herself against Dora's sarcasm. 'So I know he'd have smoked too, if tobacco had been available to him.'

After cruel months of silence, Lawrence sent her a characteristically brief postcard of a giant redwood with a car driving through a hole in its trunk. It asked her to sell off his equipment and put his workshop and his house up for sale. She guessed, with a heavy heart, that he had found or was seeking work in California and would not be coming home. There was a firm of auctioneers on the edge of the city which held sales every Saturday of miscellanea including tools and furniture. They would gladly sell his filing cabinet, desk, chairs, even his pick-up truck, however their agent suggested that she find details of any service contracts or guarantees.

She had rarely set foot in his workshop. She never had any business there. She tried several keys before she found one that would let her in. There was a small, sad heap of mail on the other side of the door. The tools, kept spotless and well-oiled, hung on nails along one wall. There was an Easter cactus, thriving on neglect, an out-of-date calendar on which a topless model caressed a chain saw and a cheque from Charlie for ten thousand pounds, torn in two and framed. A thin layer of dust, the very image of redundancy, was already coating every surface. Dora spread her coat inside out across a chair to protect her clothes then began to work her way through the contents of the filing cabinet, picking out relevant papers and tossing everything else into a bin liner at her side.

Either Lawrence or John Docherty had been neat and

methodical. Each client had their own file containing correspondence and details of contracts and purchases. There was a file of invoices, a file of tax receipts and a file of all papers relating to the truck. There was also a file of guarantee slips. It was simple enough to check them off against the tools on the wall and the ones still in the back of the truck. He bought most of his equipment through the same trade supplier whose sales invoices, marked up with the buyer's name and address, were clearly printed with *Please Retain Proof of Purchase as Warranty – see over, note 4, for terms and conditions.* Many of the purchases had passed their guarantee period but the chain saw in the rear of the truck was apparently still covered. Then she noticed that the serial number on the chain saw failed to match the one written on the sales docket. She searched high and low and even rang John to check, but there was no second chain saw and no paperwork relating to the one she had found.

Heart racing, she locked up speedily and drove to the police station with saw and docket on the seat beside her. She was seen by the duty officer who promptly offered her a cup of tea, seeing the state she was in, and sent for Detective Inspector Faithe. Dora had not forgotten Faithe, a stocky woman with greying hair, a scarred cheek and a stare Dora felt could penetrate to the labels on one's underwear.

'It's only a thought,' Dora stammered, when she had explained how she had come by the things, 'but I remembered how the saw or one like this, was linked to . . . to what you found in Wumpett Woods. If they write names and addresses on their sales dockets, then presumably they keep copies and presumably if this saw isn't my son's it might belong to . . . I mean, with the serial number they could give you a name . . .'

There was indeed a name and an address and an arrest and a confession and a rapid, shamefaced trial. Charlie Knights had not needed to confess. He had been a client, after all, and there was no proof that Lawrence had not stolen the saw from him. He had no idea, either, that there was no longer conclusive forensic evidence linking this specific tool rather than an identical model, to the sawing up of the body. Guilt had proved an intolerable companion, however, and it was with deep sighs of relief that he told Faithe how he had killed his mistress, Carla Rushton, in a blind rage when she had announced that she was sleeping with someone else and thinking of marrying him because Charlie would not wed her. He had driven her body to Wumpett, dismembered it, broken its teeth with a rock, thrown it into a trench and set it alight. Once it was burned beyond recognition he buried it. He had not planned any of this and was not thinking clearly. He had rubbed the chain saw over with handfuls of beech leaves wet with dew but, uncertain in the pre-dawn light how clean it was, he had thoughts of driving back via the Bross and hurling it into the deepest part of the river. He was calm enough to sense, however, that to have a chain saw disappear was more suspicious than to have it still hanging innocently in one's workshop. If he drove home swiftly he might yet avoid being seen, then could clean it thoroughly at his leisure with bleach or disinfectant and further mask any traces with fresh oil.

It was pure chance that Charlie should have found Lawrence sleeping in the truck. Ducking out of sight, his initial panic was soothed by the memory that Lawrence had helped him buy just that saw when they were planning the arboretum because he had recently bought an identical one himself which was serving him well. It had not been his intention to frame his son-in-law, despise him as he might. The slumbering man, the unlocked truck door, were merely a perfect insurance policy thrown temptingly in his path. When he registered Bonnie as a missing person, he was not to know they had already found Carla Rushton's anonymized body and were looking for identifying clues.

The judge sentenced him to life imprisonment. His free

confession, she said, and his guilty plea might have mitigated in his favour had he not been so cold-bloodedly content to see another man pilloried for what he had done.

Bonnie remained in America. She was under doctor's orders to avoid stress. With her father's consent, she instructed Dora to put his house and contents up for sale and to make large donations from the proceeds to cover the cost of a burial plot and headstone for Carla Rushton, whose family, if she had any, had not claimed her, and towards starting a women's refuge in Barrowcester. Dora attended the trial on her behalf, leaning on Hecate Murray's moral support and observing bitterly that the press seemed far less interested in the truth than they had been in disseminating a calumny. Hecate urged Dora to call a press conference to draw attention to the affair and right the balance in Lawrence's favour, but she and Darius recoiled at the idea. Because of the guilty plea, it was soon over. She could not bring herself to look at the accused but Hecate assured her afterwards that he had faced his punishment with proper dignity and had stolen 'speaking glances' at Dora throughout.

Her love for Charlie was a fresh thing, as vigorous as any new growth. Even unavowed and shrouded in silence, it refused to wither all at once. When he was arrested and she was called to make fresh statements to Detective Inspector Faithe, she felt nauseous at the conflict within her, at the dreadful knowledge that her own zealously meddling hand had set the machinery of retribution in motion. Were it possible, she wondered, would she now *not* contact the police? She could not unknow new knowledge, but she was shocked at how little disgust she felt at what Charlie had done. She knew him. She had made love to him. She continued to remember the smell of his chest when she had lain in his arms and continued to wear the necklace he had fastened about her. He was a murderer now, there was proof and she had to believe it, but he was also a man who loved her, so she could not think him a monster. Carla Rushton was nothing to her, merely a name and a reputation, a sad postscript of a person. Only sitting in Barrowcester High Court, clutching at Hecate's dry little hand as the forensic details were read out, did it come home to her that the man in whose bed she had blithely slept had *cut a person up*.

Lawrence's card had given her no address so she wrote to him care of the elderly couple who had taken him under their wing in California, in the hope that they could forward her letter to wherever he had gone. She sent him the few clippings the trial gave rise to. Justice had a harsh, metallic taste and nothing could compensate him for the public exposure his wretched marriage had received or the savage loss but she hoped that it might at least help him in whatever new beginning he was attempting. She still missed Bonnie. Hecate was wayward and amusing and absorbed a great deal of time and emotion but she was more sister than daughter to her.

When his house and belongings were sold, Dora adopted Charlie's two Dobermans rather than have them put down or given to an animal shelter. In her mind, soulful Megan and foolish Rex were the better part of him. She had never owned dogs before and it amused her to have two such loyal creatures guard and follow her. She let them sleep on her bedroom sofa at night. Ignorant of any sentimental motive, Hecate approved wholeheartedly of what she saw only as a noble gesture.

'Dogs are higher beings than us,' she maintained. 'They know no malice. They teach us how to live.'

CHAPTER TWENTY-TWO

'I suppose I was spoilt,' Bonnie sighed. She was talking on automatic pilot, her attention taken up by the view. Dr Marcus lived near the top of a high-rise block on the Outer Drive facing Lake Michigan and back across Chicago. The extreme altitude rendered the lake and cityscape a crawling map. On grey days, Dr Marcus's apartment was often inside a bank of cloud. On windy days, Bonnie fancied she could feel the whole place sway like a ship. The sense of removal from the earth made it easier to talk, as though one had absentmindedly died, nothing mattered any more and Dr Marcus's apartment, with its elegant blond parquet and contemporary Italian furniture was a sparse but fashionably decorated staging post on the way to whatever came next.

'Yes?' Dr Marcus prompted. She rarely spoke. When she did, her voice was warm but studiedly neutral, interested but never prurient.

'My mother dying so young – I mean when I was so young – meant that I was his daughter and sort of wife too. I mean he didn't molest me or anything. But I had him all to myself. Every young girl's dream.' Bonnie broke off again, turning her head slightly as she lay back on the deep purple sofa to watch a seagull from the lake wheel and hover, riding the uprush of wind caused by the building. When Craig first brought them here, Lucy had insisted on calling the lake the sea, because it had beaches, boats and appropriate birdlife.

'You never mention your mother. Why do you think that is?' Dr Marcus asked.

'I never knew her. She meant nothing to me.'

'Are you sad about that?'

'Why should I be? I had no mother. Like I say, every young girl's dream.'

Silence floated down between them like a piece of gauze. Dr Marcus liked to use the silence, Bonnie realized. Silence was her thumbscrew. She looked at her watch. There were five minutes to go. It was always in these last minutes that she began to feel the need to talk properly, deeply, and time ran out on her and the next session always began back at a superficial first square. Bonnie watched the second hand on the watch. The silence oppressed her.

'I never realized this would involve me doing so much talking. You send me home hoarse,' she said. Dr Marcus said nothing. 'And no, I'm not twitchy because I'm used to being controlled and led. I'm not the bloodless English wimp you think I am,' she laughed bitterly. 'Just because I sit here and cry for a whole hour sometimes. I have a life. I stand on my own two feet. I'm not some victim, you know. I *left* him, remember. I got out. I'm rebuilding my life. I know Craig thinks I blame myself for what happened but he's wrong. I don't, any more than I think I blame myself for letting things get to the stage they did. It only happened once. I'm not a battered wife. I've read the books. I know there are meant to be these weird women who sort of attract violent men and connive in it all and manipulate themselves into a position where they *need* to be beaten. But I think that's a stupid, dangerous lie and anyway, as I say, I'm not one of them. The violence between us was a one-off, an accident. It happened to him as much as to me. Now I'm outside it, and it set me free. I can see that. And I can see he loved me. In a way. I think . . .' She tailed off. The minute hand had reached the vertical.

'And Craig?' Dr Marcus prompted.

'It's time to go.'

'That's alright. There's no one after you. What about Craig?'

'Craig.' Bonnie sat up. She let her feet slide to the floor and slip into her shoes, then she relaxed. She felt his arms about her, his sleeping breath on the back of her neck. 'Craig really loves me. It took me so by surprise. I think it surprised him too. First he was just helping me, holding open a door so I could run away and then I found he was the one I was running to. It's just that . . .'

'Yes?'

'Sometimes I think my sorrow, my confusion over Dad, whatever, I think it offends him.'

Dr Marcus raised her plucked eyebrows minutely, requesting more.

'Maybe if Craig had had children himself before Vi left him, he'd understand better. But he's an architect,' Bonnie explained. 'He requires perfection. He's not a monster, not some psycho who lines up all the towels just so, he doesn't want me to be perfect but. But I think that, well, Lucy and everything, since then, it's become a sort of blemish he wants taken away. You know he pays for these sessions?'

'I know.'

'He insisted. I don't mind. No reflection on you, but I don't think they're helping much. But it reassures him to feel he's doing something. He has faith in specialists. If some stone cracks, he gets a mason. If a plaster pigment comes out in blotches, he calls in a colourist. When his bereaved girlfriend's father turns out to be a murderer and she sits opposite him in expensive restaurants and cries on the foie gras, he calls in a soul doctor.'

Bonnie smiled wryly and stood up. 'Living up here,' she began. 'Don't you ever want a garden? Trees and things?'

Dr Marcus merely shrugged. She walked Bonnie to the door. She was all in grey as usual, right down to little grey suede ankle boots, which were a mistake. Bonnie imagined her wardrobes, shelves of thunder-cloud cashmere, silver silk, elephant moiré, pigeon-wing cotton, a whole rack of elegant non-commitment.

'I'll see you on Wednesday, Bonnie,' she said.

Bonnie took the glass lift rather than the internal one. Re-entering the world from this height was like suicide in slow motion.

On the way home through Oak Park, she stopped off to check on the rose garden she had completed for a client two months previously. She had several pieces of work on her drawing board now. Only one of them was for Craig, which was as it should be. The rose garden was the simplest project to date but, of its nature, the hardest to maintain. Because she liked to be able to send potential clients to view her previous work whenever possible, she needed to be sure the Balmains' gardener was doing his work correctly. The Balmains were away at their Cape Cod hideaway which was a relief because she found their attention oppressive. A childless couple, they were all too keen to treat her like a daughter, which she found faintly sinister.

She let herself in at the high gate in their unusual copper beech hedge and slipped around the side of the house to the lawn. The rose garden was settling in well. It was of a suitably unadventurous design; a perfect square divided into four equilateral triangles. Herringbone paths of slate and red brick ran from corner to corner, crossing through a central gazebo with a circular seat. Lavender bushes marked the entrances to each path and clipped box hedges delineated the four beds. The gazebo was to be grown over with jasmine for shade and scent.

Bonnie walked along one of the paths, noting that, as she had requested, the roses were not being too tightly trained yet. She frowned, seeing that one of the jasmine plants had died and tugged it up, making a mental note to complain to the nursery that the stock they sold her had not been sufficiently hardened off for bedding out.

'Bonnie, darling!'

'Hell.' Bonnie straightened up and turned to see Cindy

Balmain, broad, tanned and predatory, crossing the lawn to greet her.

'Welcome back,' she said aloud. 'We weren't expecting you for a week yet. Sorry. This jasmine's withered. I'll get you another from the nursery.'

'Really? Oh. Never mind that. How *are* you?'

'I'm fine.'

Cindy circled her shoulders in a beefy arm and steered her towards the house.

'Really? We've been so worried about you. It's the most horrible thing. I know it's months ago now but I just can't get over it. Dick kept saying the way I carry on people would think it was one of my own. But I can't help it.' She sniffed. 'But enough about me. You must come in and have a drink and tell me everything. How're you doing and dear, sweet Craig and that nice Doreen?'

'Dora. Her name's Dora.' Bonnie thought of Dora with a pang. Cindy Balmain's emotional blowziness always made her pine for Dora's elegant, citric restraint. 'Cindy, I'd love to but I'm late as it is and I promised Craig . . .'

'Now don't you let him control you like he did Vi.'

'I wouldn't dream of it. But thanks and I'll sort the jasmine out tomorrow.'

Bonnie ran for the car.

Returning to Craig's house, she walked round the building's entire square, opening all the doors, enjoying the sense that its quiet symmetry restored her equilibrium. Craig's cleaner amused herself by sliding the doors shut as she worked her way around the place, which left the house feeling clean but airless as an Egyptian tomb. Walking from door to door, Bonnie could not help recalling how Lucy, fractious after the long journey from Barrowcester – effectively from Paris – had immediately cheered up on arrival and run from room to room, laughing as though the building were one delightful puzzle, which in a dry, architectural sense, it was. Because most of the rooms were infinitely adaptable and the futons easy to move and reassemble, Craig let Lucy have a choice of five. Bonnie had expected her to choose the one nearest her and took it as a good sign that she selected one on the opposite side of the square, lined in creamy ash. The child had already realized that, though the housebound route was long, she could reach her mother quickly enough by sliding open the window onto the courtyard. At night, too, they were able to wave to one another from their beds, which Lucy thought funny. Craig's room, the cedar-lined one, was on yet another side of the square, so Bonnie could see him too.

She slid back another door, stepped forward then faltered and came to a staring standstill. She had arrived in the ash room before she could check herself. She had managed to avoid it for months until now, taking circuitous routes or crossing the courtyard and re-entering via their shared workroom. But now here she was. The cleaner had long since stripped and washed the bedding, but Craig had not thought to move the futon again and the drawers beneath it were still full of Lucy's clothes. A favourite bedtime book of hers, *Noisy Noises*, still lay on the bedside table along with a clutch of the plastic 'jewellery' she treasured, her toy rabbit, Black Bun and her inhaler and drugs. In a house where clutter was usually anathematized, neglect and queasy indecision had created a shrine. Surprised, unable to pass on now, Bonnie sank to the bed, kicked off her shoes and drew up her feet. She hugged the book. She reached for the rabbit. It began to rain. Streaks of sympathetic water turned the rocks from uniform grey to shades of pink and blue while the koi rose to kiss the lily pads in search of food.

Looking across the courtyard to one side, she gazed at the cedar room, now their bedroom. After her first night in there, she had slipped back to her own bed before dawn.

'I don't want Lucy waking and wondering where I am,'

she explained. 'Or still worse, seeing. Not yet. Not till she's ready.'

By the fourth day, Craig was growing impatient. 'I love the kid,' he said. 'I think she's starting to like me.'

'She adores you.'

'So tell her. Make her glad.'

'Okay. I'll tell her tomorrow.'

On the fifth day, a Saturday, Bonnie had woken to the sound of the coffee grinder. She lay in the big bed for a while, planning a shopping trip. Lucy was intensely materialistic, to the point of actually enjoying watching adults spend money on themselves as well as her. The promise of a shopping trip and a department store lunch would make her instantly receptive and amenable. Bonnie had pulled on one of Craig's thick kimonos and gone to Lucy's room all ready to sit calmly on the futon beside her, Black Bun between them for security, to tell her that Mummy was in love with Craig now and Craig was in love with Mummy and they both wanted to make Lucy happy and give her a new home here in Chicago for ever and ever.

She found Lucy still in bed but not asleep. Her bedding was on the floor and she lolled forward in a sitting position, as though she had sat up and fallen asleep there. She was a strange, pale colour. Her mouth was open in a frozen gasp.

'Darling? Lucy? Lucy!'

Bonnie fell forward onto the heap of quilt and blanket, clutching her daughter, patting her cheek, violently seizing her wrists, her chest. Lucy was cooler than the wood around her. She must have suffered an asthma attack hours ago, around midnight or earlier. They had all been in bed by eleven. Bonnie's first reaction was to snatch at the nebuliser and check it was working. It was fine and there was a supply of drugs.

It was only when Craig came running, white-faced, across the courtyard that Bonnie realized she was screaming.

* * *

When she had rung Dora to break the news, Bonnie heard that Lawrence was incongruously on a cruise and was not due back to Miami for a week. At Dora's advising, Bonnie held out against Craig's suggestion that they have a cable sent to him on the boat in case he wanted to get back in time for the funeral. Bonnie should meet the boat, Dora said. She should take him on one side as he came through customs and tell him face to face, lead him to a private room perhaps, if this was permitted.

Dora flew out with Bonnie's father on the first available flight. The funeral was held three days later. Her father was now Bonnie's sole blood relative, Dora, the nearest thing to a mother she possessed, and yet, under her belljar of grief, she would gladly have spurned them both to find Lawrence beside her. Only he could understand what she was feeling because only he was suffering as she was. Rather, he would be, once she scalded his ears with the news. His absence, his grotesque, holiday inaccessibility, wounded and enraged her more than his words had ever done. In the first, hot-eyed hours of shock, her need for him was as impatient as any frustrated lover's. Craig dealt with the doctor, who passed neatly from signing the death certificate to filling out a prescription for sedatives, and handled an odiously tremulous woman from the funeral parlour. Dora made and fielded countless phone calls. When the moment came to get the coffin from hearse to grave side, Bonnie's father broke from her side to intercept the undertakers and carry the wooden casket in his arms. When any of them came near her, Bonnie clung to them like an unsupported vine. She took her pills, tried to eat, did her dazed best to behave in a way that would not attract attention. Left alone, however, she watched them in a kind of mute, listless anger, resenting their ability to function as much as she resented their usurpation of Lawrence's role.

The time came, the ticket to Miami was bought, but her nerve failed her. Suddenly she turned anew to Craig, needing his strength, unable to face the battery of Lawrence's emotions.

'I'll go,' Dora said quietly. 'Perhaps it's for the best that way. I'll ring to warn you if he's coming to Chicago. He may – He may want to see the grave.'

But Lawrence had not come or, if he had, he had visited Lucy's grave in secret, without contacting his wife. This, she had come to perceive from the Olympian heights of Dr Marcus's consulting room, was entirely his right. His absence and silence also spared her some pain in the fresh ordeal that followed.

When her father was arrested, he rang her, reversing the charges from Barrowcester police station, and she judged him as he feared. She could not face him, would not return for the trial, happily acquiesced in the sale of his property and wanted no part of the tainted proceeds. His guilt, like Lucy's death and Lawrence's continued silence severed yet another rope that had tethered her to her old life.

A whole year had passed. It would be thirteen months to the day tomorrow. She had grown used to laying flowers before a tiny headstone, to telling other young women,

'I had a daughter but she died. An asthma attack. Yes. Terrible,' and to hearing them apologize as though their innocent enquiry made them somehow culpable. She could not, however, tell people what her father, her *dad*, had done. Strangely, unlike death, violent crime in the family was not something that slipped naturally into conversations. And she was deeply, however irrationally, ashamed. She had tried several churches. She had tried a support group. She had called helplines. She had even called a live radio phone-in. Now, because Craig worried that her grieving process, entwined with her shame about her father, was becoming irrationally morbid, she was in thrice-weekly consultation with Dr Ida Marcus of the American Psychiatric Association. Still, however, she froze over when Craig made even tentative reference to divorce and remarriage. She knew from Dora's monthly letters that Lawrence had gone to earth somewhere, had declined to return to England with her and Darius. She fantasized in secret about him coming to Chicago. Her old confused desire for him had been cauterized by Craig's touch and evident love. A powerful sense of guilt was prolonging her grief, however, holding it about her like an unnatural tide, and she felt, but dared not confess, that only the father of her child could cause it to ebb. She wondered whether Lucy would still be alive if she had not left England, and felt this to be her fault one moment, Lawrence's the next. A second, darker cause for guilt, however, was less easily dispelled by common sense. There was unfinished business between them, business that no psychiatrist could exorcise or divorce lawyer could begin to broke on her behalf.

She heard the electric garage door mechanism hum and thump into motion, heard his big car drive in. She continued to sit quite still on the futon, clutching book and rabbit, her face awash with tears. She would wait to let him find her. Sometimes he was distracted or had work to finish. He might head straight to his workroom and not find her for an hour or more. He saw her at once, however. There he was striding across the courtyard. He dropped his case on a chair and hurried over, falling onto the futon beside her and drawing her into his arms, knees, rabbit, book and all. He said nothing, kissed her hair, her ear, her neck, squeezed her tight as though the pain could be wrung from her like sour water from a flannel. He pulled out one of the coloured bandanas he used as handkerchiefs, gently wiped her face and eyes and encouraged her to blow her nose.

'Sorry,' she said at last. 'The sessions are helping. They really are. It's just that I came in here when I got back and it sort of took me by surprise.' She blew her nose again, taking the soaked cotton from him and clenching it in her fist till her nails gouged her palm painfully. 'We should clear all this out,' she muttered. 'We really should. Make it a spare room again. Have some friends to stay.'

'Time enough for that,' he said kissing her. 'Listen. I had a call from some new clients who want me to go see them. There's a place near them I helped build three years back and it's time I paid it a visit. See if everything's okay. It's a special place. Real peaceful. We can just lie in a tub and look at the trees or curl up by a fire and watch the stars. It's turning cold again and I want to take you for some sunshine.' He squeezed her again. 'You mustn't apologize,' he said. 'I just want you to – '

'I know,' she mumbled.

'– find some peace,' he finished.

She stroked his thick hair, felt his stubble on her cheek. With Lawrence it had so often been she who gave the solace, as if he were a second child. Craig only had to hold her and she felt safe. She wondered if it was dangerous to place so much trust in a man. What if he were to have a crisis and need her? It would be like God asking a favour. She felt the bony contours of his spine beneath his shirt and breathed deeply, breathed in the workaday cars and coffee maleness of him. She wondered if she should let him make her pregnant and whether that promise of new life, stretching before her as well as growing within, might change everything to the good or send her running, defenceless and self-destructive, back to the battle zone.

CHAPTER TWENTY-THREE

Lawrence was on his last task of the day. Watering the saplings was best left until the sun was well down towards the sea's horizon. Earlier on, the heat evaporated the precious moisture before the new roots could draw it in. He enjoyed the slow rhythm of the work, the repeated walk to and from the water truck to fill the can. It was repetitive, tedious even, but this meant that it freed his mind. He liked the sense that the saplings were thirsty. Of course he knew that it was really the bone-dry soil which absorbed the water, but he liked to pretend that the saplings sucked the fluid in. Each sapling wore an identical tall collar of rigid plastic to protect it from the deer and ground squirrels and he used these to measure a plant's water share, filling each collar to the brim. Often the water gurgled as it sank down around the skinny stem, as though a mouth were actually at work below ground level.

A stick snapped in the mature woods a few yards behind him. He turned in time to see a motion of leaves and undergrowth where something had scurried out of sight. He frowned and turned back to watching the stream of water from the truck splashing into his can. He was often haunted here by the sensation that someone was watching him, that Lucy, in fact, was watching him. She was always standing on the wood's edge, never in the sun's full glare, her skin white against the black-green gloom, absentmindedly clutching something she had brought for his inspection – a stick, a beetle's wing case, a sweet paper. Finding him had made her shy, however, and initiated a new game, more stimulating than nature study and she would always dart out of sight the moment he did more than view her from the corners of his eye. It was deer of course, just as it was racoons and gophers and not Lala's ghost, who shadowed him through the trees by night. The woods were alive with their thin, seemingly vulnerable legs and great, shocked eyes. They were used to him by now and drew closer to him than to any of the camera-wielding guests, but it was policy never to feed them, so they remained wild and continued to flee at the sound of his saw or striding boots.

An unsympathetic 1950s bungalow had stood here. It had been demolished and the rubble cleared as infill for where the service drive was to be extended. The plot was to be reclaimed as forest, an impossibly optimistic and far-sighted undertaking, given that the local redwoods were well beyond a thousand years old. Lawrence had ploughed it back and forth with a mechanical digger, enriching the compacted clay with spadefuls of the compost heaps all the staff were trained to maintain. Then he brought redwood saplings – or sequoias as the locals called them – collared them and erected a temporary fence to protect them further both from animals and the blundering legs of guests.

His work over, he drove the water truck back to its shady place beside the waste water reservoir. Not a drop of water was discarded here. Sewage was filtered through a system of reed beds and the resulting run-off 'grey water' stored in a covered reservoir from which the gardeners and estate fire truck could draw. All but the most organic cleaning products were banned. Guests were easily seduced by the delicious scents of the estate-produced honey soaps and lavender, pine and mint extract shampoos with which their bathrooms were stocked. Lawrence had never noticed shampoo or soap before, merely using whatever came to hand. With surprising swiftness however he had become sensitized by this additive-free environment. Now, when he stood near someone who used hair lacquer or fabric conditioner, the inside of his nose buzzed with the unfamiliar harshness that lingered in the air about them.

By the time they disembarked in Miami, Martha and George had already said their farewells and were looking forward to a return to their quiet, uncrowded life. But Martha saw the drawn, elegant woman with Lawrence's face, guessed on the instant that she brought bad news, and tugged George's sleeve indicating that he should wait on the quayside with the luggage while she lingered a moment or two in the customs hall. She saw Lawrence sink to his suitcase as though his mother had cut his strings, saw the mother talk and talk without ever touching him, as though words could make do for flesh and blood contact, saw her bite her lip and throw her brother a glance of covert desperation across her son's bowed head. Martha saw an ugly little scene break out as another man, tough-looking yet somehow broken, was pushed by Lawrence. She knew at once what must have happened, since Lawrence had been so determined and eager to find his daughter – he had talked of nothing else since Lala's death. She drew closer until she could feel the distress and discomfort radiating like heat from the little group. She stood quietly and waited.

When Lawrence looked up at last, sensing her presence, he met her level gaze and made a minute gesture towards her with one hand. That was all Martha needed. Ignoring Darius and the mother, she stepped forward and took his hand in both of hers and kissed it. The mother, who talked a bit like the Queen of England, was saying something about coming home and taking things one step at a time. She broke off, surprised by Martha's approach.

'You can come and stay with us, if you like,' Martha told him. 'It's very peaceful. Just the sea and the hills and miles of forest.'

He had travelled to California with them and had yet to

leave. It had been a long journey – a six-hour flight to San Francisco then a two-hour drive down the coast to near Big Sur. Even in his state of shock, he was amazed at the ease with which the old couple accommodated his brooding presence. When he tried to apologize during the flight for saying so little, George told him,

'It's alright, son. You don't have to talk if you don't have a mind to.'

While George was absorbed in watching a film after lunch, Martha slipped Lawrence a pill with a wink.

'Make things a little easier,' she said and he passed the rest of the journey drifting in and out of a thoughtless doze. They arrived after dark so that Lawrence, who went directly to bed, woke in an entirely new place with little sense of where it was or how he had come there.

Their house was an unpretentious three-bedroom bungalow tucked away down a steep drive off the coastal road; a house for people who had spent most of their lives out of doors. It was surrounded by coastal pine, juniper and tamarisk – native varieties Lawrence had only seen as cultivated specimens at home – which gave way to a flat rocky outcrop where one could sit looking out to sea or take a narrow path down to a tiny beach where icy waves thumped on the sand.

For a long-married couple, George and Martha spent little time together. She passed her days in the second garage, where she had rigged up her potter's wheel and kiln and an ad hoc shop where, very occasionally, she sold her work to a driver lured down by her hand-painted sign at the roadside. George spent his daylight hours fishing off the rocks or poring over celestial charts and books in preparation for his nightly stargazing sessions from the loft window. They handed Lawrence a set of car keys, gave him occasional errands, and left him to his own devices. He swam, bruising his feet on the stones. He took drives up and down their dramatic stretch of coastline and he spent whole hungry days following paths across the woods and hills with a battered map in one pocket and his only photograph of Lucy in the other.

He could not weep at first. He could not, in fact, acknowledge her death. It was impossible to accept so overwhelming a thing merely on trust. It was as if someone had informed him that Britain had sunk without trace during his absence; he needed proof, news footage, eloquent details. Poor, strange Lala had left a bloodstained scarf for him to grasp and sniff at and stow in his luggage – that at least helped him grieve for her. All that he had of Lucy were small proofs of her existence, the photograph, his memories, a small, coloured scribble she had done which was meant to be him up a tree. The knowledge of her being had lodged like a warm nugget in his belly on the day of her birth. It grew cold as steel when she was in danger, it beat like a second heart each time she reclaimed him as hers. It would not now dissolve to order but continued to pulse, to chill over, to ache like a phantom limb.

He lost all desire to see Bonnie again. Not only had the reason for seeking her been taken from him, but he sensed that, against all rational argument, tarring her possibly with the brush that had so spectacularly blackened her father, he was beginning to blame her. Perhaps the flight had made the child's asthma worse, or the change of home. Perhaps she was allergic to the McBugger's house. Perhaps she was afraid. He began to cry occasionally, thinking of her, thinking of Lala. He cried, shut in the guest room while Martha threw pots and George stood flicking his line across the surf. He cried at the wheel of the car or walking in the untouched forests. He made a sound like forced laughter and did not care that anyone hearing it would think he had lost his mind.

His reason for lingering in America had gone but so had his reason for rebuilding his life in England. The remote beauty of the Californian coast surprised him. After the oppressively artificial community life on the *Paulina*, he was happy to be in a place seemingly without community, where the few inhabitants were strung in pockets of privacy along a wavering coastal line, not bunched unnaturally together. Even allowing for the intrusion of the road (*PCH* as George called it) and the Big Sur campsites and woodland lodges, nature had the upper hand here and man felt like a transitory presence, admitted on sufferance. There were no true locals here. The nearest maternity hospitals and schools were an hour away to the north or south. Everyone had been born and raised somewhere else. Lawrence, however, felt oddly at home. The simple three-colour landscape of red earth, blue Pacific, green-black forests, seemed to claim him as kin and he sensed a deep stirring of recognition as though he had passed time here as a small boy.

'That'll be the sequoias,' Martha said when he mentioned this. 'You must have seen them as a baby in Yosemite. They're the spirits that watched over your birth, if you believe all that stuff. We remember everything from the day we're born, you know, but memories from before we can walk are kinda passive, like pictures in a book that someone has to open for us.'

Maybe she sensed his profound regret at the prospect of leaving, for two days before the end of his stay she interrupted George's planning of how much time they should leave to drive Lawrence the thirty miles to the bus depot up in Carmel.

'There's a job going,' she said, 'if you'd like it.'

'Where?' Lawrence asked.

'Down the coast a few miles. Some friends of Lu– of our daughter run a kind of ranch-stroke-health spa place. Two gay guys, but that needn't bother you none. I met Scott at the stores this morning and got talking about you. They're looking for a new groundsman, someone who can look after trees and deal with the machinery. It's not what you're used to, I expect, but you get to live on the job and it's real pretty there. We'd love to have you join the neighbourhood. Wouldn't we, George?'

The Cliff Ranch was the brainchild of Scott Christie and Jules Lynch, a couple who had made a fortune as LA restaurateurs and decided to seek a quieter life when Jules discovered he was HIV positive. Spread around the site of a derelict farm on towering cliff tops, it was unlike most hotels in that it had only twenty bedrooms and, instead of one large building, was made up of numerous small ones which were designed to disappear into the landscape rather than be seen for miles around. The largest was the restaurant, with wrap-around views of mountains and sea. The twenty rooms were individual structures, some high on stilts among the treetops, some cut down into the cliffs with Hebridean-style turf-covered roofs. Faced in local rock or wood, disguised as trees, stony outcrops or grassy hillocks, they were so harmonious that guests found themselves nose to nose with the local fauna – gophers, racoons, bobcats, coyote, numerous birds and the occasional basking rattle-snake. The rooms were discreetly luxurious, with huge beds, log fires, massage tubs and sound systems, but there was no television or radio to intrude on the anti-urban atmosphere. There was a hot basking pool where vitamin-rich drinks were served, overlooking a dizzying thousand-foot drop to the ocean, a cooler pool for swimming, hidden in a woodland clearing, and a serene health deck where massage and classes in tai chi and yoga were offered. Staff were housed in a no less idyllic cluster of log cabins in the woods and, such was the blissed out ethos of the place, employees came to feel as cherished as the handsomely paying guests they served.

Apart from Alix, the star chef coaxed up from LA by Scott, most of the staff had come into their posts from other careers and were refugees from bad cities, sad marriages, broken homes or thwarted hopes. Scott and Jules made a tidy profit but, since taking up Buddhism, seemed hell bent on ploughing the profit back into the lives of others. Twice yearly they set aside the whole place free of charge for San Franciscans or Angelenos referred to them by the AIDS support networks. Now that he had put down a year's roots in the place, Lawrence could see how seamlessly he fitted in, how he had been hired as much for what he had been through as for any skills he might have with chain saw or pruning hook. At times, wheeling the jeep through the woods or pottering around the orchard, he would see a masseur in a white Mao uniform or a chambermaid in her blue, and imagine himself the inmate of some pioneering psychiatric institution. He freely confessed the irony of he and his murderous father-in-law ending up in such contrasting but equally controlled environments.

He showered off the day's grime in the men's wash house, keeping a weather eye open as usual for creepy-crawlies that skulked out of the water's reach or dangled from the rafters. Quite apart from omnipresent poison oak, an irritant weed Lawrence discovered the uncomfortable way in his first month, the woods teemed with spiders – many of which slung their thick webs horizontally at head height over the lower twigs, hungry for tumbling bugs rather than wing-borne flies. They treated the bleach-free cabins as an extension of their domain. It was Cliff Ranch policy to kill nothing, but several of the local species could deliver nasty bites – as Lawrence's arms and neck could testify – so he washed warily and while he lived at peace with his fellow beasts, the truce was armed. Towel-skirted, he padded back along the grass to his cabin, which lay in a clearing a little beyond the others, and sat out on its rudimentary porch to cool off with a beer.

There was a whistle. He looked up and saw Laurie, one of the masseurs, rolling down from the guest area on her bicycle. Many guests preferred to be treated in the privacy of their rooms rather than pounded on the health deck, so each room's bed concealed a foldaway massage table. She used the bike to transport towels and oils for her work.

'Spare me one of those?' she called out. 'My fridge is dry.'

'Sure. Come on up.'

While he fetched another beer, she slung the bike against a tree and sauntered onto the porch, stretching and flexing her arms. When he handed her the can, she used it to chill her palms then rubbed them across her close-cropped scalp with a sigh.

'Hard day?' he asked.

She grunted assent and pulled up a chair, cracking open the can. She pushed off her sneakers and swung her small bare feet up on the rail before her.

'Some days they're just so needy. Half an hour of back work gets stretched into an hour and half of emotional outpour. Jeez. I should get Scott to pay for me to have some counselling training.'

'Is it people with – you know?'

She grinned at his awkwardness.

'No. No HIV this week. Just the needy rich. There's one woman. God's she's so cute. Ass like a peach and face like Meg Ryan. Guy with her's twice her age. Strong and silent cowpoke type only richer. Anyway, I start to do her. Nice long strokes to begin with, nothing deep, just to get her used to the feel of my hands, and then she just cries. Cries and cries. 'Don't mind me,' she says. 'Don't mind me.' So I keep massaging and she just lies there with tears pouring down onto the towel. It happens a lot – something to do with relaxation. Guys worry they're going to get a hard-on and then they cry instead, which is, like, so much more embarrassing! But she was, Jesus!' Laurie gave him one of her straight, laddish looks, 'She was one of the *saddest* women I've ever seen. And so *cute*! Jesus.' She swigged her beer. 'How about you? Good day?'

'Okay. Grass mowing mainly. And I watered those new trees.'

One of the reasons the job suited Lawrence so well was its lack of human interaction. He had no clients to deal with, no bills to prepare. He had to speak with Scott occasionally, when there was something new – like the tree planting – to be done, otherwise his was a routine maintenance job. He kept the rooms stocked with firewood, he maintained the forest paths, he mowed grass, he watered plants. His wages were paid into an American bank account but he needed little spending money. They bought bargain beers and upstate wine on credit. He rarely went beyond the estate's confines. Generously subsidized meals were provided.

Laurie had sat in front of him on his first night when he was shy and uncertain as a new boy in school, and their neighbour had immediately exclaimed at how alike they looked. It was true, and the identical haircuts they had given one another with her electric trimmers emphasized the effect. She had his rather full, sulky mouth and slightly slanted brown eyes. She was nearly as tall as he was and they even had the same, loose, rangy limbs that seemed always to need propping up, legs on a railing, arms on a chair back. Of course, when he introduced himself and she laughed that they were Laurie and Larry, they became established as unofficial twins.

Their lives were entirely dissimilar. She was San Franciscan, the adopted daughter of a female senator. She was a fourth adoption so, unlike Lawrence, she had grown up with brothers and sisters, but they were alike in that she too had found it increasingly hard to fit in and to be what her parents expected of her. When her father divorced her mother, tired of playing political consort, the family had splintered. She had dropped out of college to pursue an abortive career as a drummer with an all-girl band and had learned massage in night school. Like the others here, she had come to the Cliff Ranch by accident. Hitch-hiking back down the coast from her mother's funeral, she had been picked up by an actress friend of Jules's on her way to visit. The two women had fallen deep in conversation and Laurie found herself with a surprise job interview by nightfall.

She shared Lawrence's love of trees. A natural tomboy, she could climb barefoot like a monkey and had twice bewildered him by nimbly scaling a trunk he would only have braved with a rope and harness. Her love life mystified and fascinated him. She seemed omnivorous. Preferring the bodies of women, if anything, but driven to the company of men, she could radiate an almost conventual purity and seem lithe and genderless as some alien visitor. His interest amused her.

'I'm just an ordinary gal,' she would insist.

He had learned from Bee that it was permissible for a man to befriend a woman without having to want her sexually. Here now was a woman with whom he not only felt instantly at ease but whom he regularly sought out for the simple pleasure of her company. He had never known the mixed blessings of a sibling and had passed through an entire school history without once tasting the ritual pleasure of being someone's declared *best friend*. Laurie, he suspected, represented a teasing combination of the two. He was terrified that she would grow bored of him and pass on so, like devoted brothers since time immemorial, he made a strenuous effort to mask his vulnerability beneath a show of matey indifference. They spent hours sitting on his porch or hers, drinking beers, listening to the night sounds of the woods. Tentatively she asked about his marriage. When he explained how trapped he had felt and then how powerless in the hands of his jealousy, she did not judge him as he feared someone of her dynamism might. She had not a maternal bone in her body so found his bond to Lucy inexplicable, though she respected his grief and edged around it. He told her nothing of Lala. The entire

Lala episode, the cruise indeed, had seemed unreal at the time and hindsight made it more so to the point where he even mistrusted his memories.

'So who else is here besides the one who cries?' he asked her.

'Oh. You know.' Laurie rubbed at the rail absently with her heel. 'The usual second honeymooners. There's a couple in the first cliff studio who haven't emerged since yesterday. Think they must be doing *serious* drugs; no one can be so in love they don't eat. There's a couple of journalists who are really picky about everything and I just know they're not paying a cent for anything. Oh,' she chuckled to herself. 'And there's an incredible woman with a baby.'

'What's so incredible about that?'

'She's on her own with it. That's nothing new, sure, but she's kind of old to be a mother. She has a great body. She had me massage her on her deck this afternoon. But I think she must be one of those biological miracles. Forty-eight. Forty-nine? I assumed the child must be adopted but when I was working on her thighs she moaned about the stretchmarks it had given her. When I came to work on her belly, there they were. She's fun but real self-controlled, you know? Like a saxophone playing quiet. The kid's obviously her all in all. Humphrey Junior. She spends hours just cooing over it. Oh. Sorry. Me and my mouth.'

'That's okay.'

She leaned back on her chair to rub his back apologetically.

'People are still allowed to have babies,' he told her.

'Sure,' she said. 'And shit happens. Jesus your shoulders are stiff! My teacher used to say that the right shoulder harbours your unspoken anger and the left gets all scrunched up by your secret fears. Make of that what you will. Want me to work on them a bit?'

He shook his head.

'You've been doing that all day,' he said. 'Anyway,' he added, hunching forward to hide his hard-on. 'You might make me cry.'

CHAPTER TWENTY-FOUR

The next morning he refreshed the wood piles. The nights were growing cooler and a few guests were starting to light their fires after sundown. There was a small plantation in an inland corner of the estate where the former owners had established swift-growing pine trees for timber and firewood. Part of Lawrence's job was to maintain and occasionally harvest and replace these. However, he was also expected to gather any usable timber that fell elsewhere and to use up the offcuts from any tree surgery he had to perform. There was little of this since the estate was more natural forest than manicured park, but occasionally the wind brought a branch down across a right of way and it was vital the paths be kept clear so that walkers had no excuse for trampling across the forest floor. Scott was ever wary of litigious guests too. The merest chip in a stair tread or hint of slipperiness in a rug had to be dealt with immediately lest it be held responsible for a broken hip or expensively chronic back trouble.

Lawrence made routine checks on all the trees which bordered the paths or balconies, used, from battling with the tougher British climate, to spotting accidents in waiting. On his rounds this morning he heard the tell-tale creaking complaint of straining timber and, after much checking and frustrated waiting for another breath of wind, he found an overhanging branch on a Monterey pine which had begun to split from the trunk under its own weight. It was only ten feet from the ground so he could reach it easily from the back of his truck and bring it down with the chain saw. He painted the large wound – arboreal fungicide was one of the few chemicals he could persuade Jules to let him stock. He had sawed the branch up into fire-worthy logs, discarding needles and twigs among the undergrowth, and was stacking them in the trailer when he saw the mature mother Laurie had so vividly described.

She was tall and dressed like a quiet Englishwoman in calf-length skirt, cream blouse and fawn cardigan. She wore her collar-length grey hair brushed back behind her ears but her face was largely concealed beneath a wide-brimmed straw hat. She carried the baby, which gazed up as she talked softly to it, her face bent over it, careless, apparently, of where she was going.

'Doesn't that smell good, mmm?' she murmured as she drew nearer. 'Fresh pine. Mmm. Good?'

The baby rewarded her with a gassy laugh.

Lawrence rarely encountered the guests. Laurie told him all about them and might occasionally point out a well-known face or some character she had described but, for the most part, they lived in a parallel world. He heard their low, pampered voices over the clink of cocktails in the basking pool when he was delivering wood for the restaurant fireplace or watering the herb garden or trimming the hedges. He saw their expensive cars winding up the drive when he was mowing the grass, and could easily watch them swimming lengths in the pool or practising their yoga *asanas* on the health deck. He never had cause to speak to them, however. Were his placid new life in this surrogate Eden not dependent on their continued patronage, he could have dismissed them as a distant irrelevance. On this occasion, however, even he would have found it churlish to keep silent, so he said,

'I could bring some fresh logs to your room, if you like. Make the whole place smell like a forest for him.'

The woman glanced up as sharply as if he had sworn at her, then turned hastily back the way she had come and began to stride away, cracking twigs beneath her ladylike brogues. Lawrence stared after her from the trailer, his mind reeling at the glimpse he had caught of her haunting face. He said her name softly, almost to himself. She broke into a near run where the trees met the sunshine, but she stopped, as if deflated, and turned to look back at him, waiting.

He jumped from the trailer and ran, irrepressible laughter bursting from him. He wanted to hold her. He tugged off his gloves but his hands still seemed dusty beneath them and her cardiganed shoulders dauntingly spotless so he remained, foot shuffling, before her, hands at his sides, laughter checked.

'I – I don't know what – ' he began.

'Yes,' she said. 'Yes. It's me.'

'Lala!'

'No, dear. She died. Conveniently, but with characteristic panache and a nicely timed flurry of reissued recordings. *My* name is Serena Merle. Madame Merle.'

'Sorry?'

'On account of the lopsided smile, buried origins and unexpected child? *Portrait of a Lady*? Oh I'd forgotten. You don't do that stuff. Well anyway, it's my little literary joke. My proper name is Mrs Humphrey Merle. I'm a widow and my husband was in plastic packaging and died on a Fort Lauderdale golf course. Seventh hole. Excellent handicap. Inherited heart condition. I had it all planned years ago. I never thought I could pull it off quite so neatly. This is Humphrey Junior, by the way.' She jiggled the baby, who was looking cross and sleepy.

'I don't understand.'

'I beg your pardon. I'm probably going too fast for you. This is a bit of a shock for me, too, you know, you popping out of the woodwork like that.'

'*I* didn't die.'

'Well. No. But . . . Can I sit down, dear? The baby's cute but heavy. Is that jeep's cab clean?'

'Sure.'

'You've become American. It suits you.' She grinned and, despite the sober disguise, he caught a shade of Lala.

He led the way to the truck and helped her up.

'Look at us,' she said when he climbed in beside her. 'All we need is a goat in the back and we could be on our way to market. So. Tell.'

'You first. I don't understand. The tiger – '

'Don't. I still dream about that.'

She held the baby closer.

'I found your scarf. It was covered in blood.'

She pulled back the collar of her blouse and he saw she wore it turned up to hide a still livid scar on the back of her neck.

'Claw marks,' she said. 'Bled like hell. I tripped on something, a tree root. I dunno. And it was on me. But it only clawed me once then it just sniffed. I thought this is it. I mean, I just lay there thinking of how a cat plays with a mouse before it finishes it off. I didn't move. But it just sniffed and nosed me. I could feel its breath on my hair – halitosis you would not *believe*. Then you drew it away so heroically, like a mad sweet fool, and it ran off after you. I stood up, found I had nothing broken, and I ran too, down to Nutmeg Bay. I stole a beach towel to wrap around my neck and caught the next ferry across to St Thomas then a little boat to St Croix and the first flight to Miami.'

'Why weren't you traced?'

'Not as Mrs Humphrey Merle. She's had a passport for some time.'

'I don't understand. And whose is this?' He pointed at Humphrey Junior, who was now heavily asleep against her cleavage and looking seraphically content, as well he might with such a pillow.

'Poor darling,' she said, 'I'm rushing you.'

'I thought you couldn't have any – I thought – Everyone thought – '

'That I used to be a guy. Even the obituaries thought. Can you believe that? The *New York Times*! Well I wasn't. I can tell you now because not a soul on earth will believe you. I was born in the Bronx, just like dear Madame Merle, and, like hers, my dad was in the navy. My name was Mary Kopek. Imagine, me a Mary!' She laughed dryly at the thought. 'Anyway, all I wanted to do was be a singer. And I tried, God I tried, but I didn't fit. I was too tall. I sang kinda deep. Then my first agent, bless his darkly cunning soul, had the brainwave of letting people think I wasn't all I seemed. From there it snowballed – all those crazy stories – that I was Algerian, that I was sold as a child tart, that I was found entertaining in some Hungarian clip joint, or Egyptian brothel or Pekinese opium den or whatever. Lies. All lies.'

'So what was the problem?'

She shrugged, stroked the sleeping baby's cheek with a well-manicured but respectably clear-varnished fingertip.

'Mary Kopek was the problem. Tall, funny-looking, deep-voiced, unmarried Mary Kopek, who just ached for one of these. There were fathers aplenty,' she said bitterly. 'No lack of guys got all excited at the thought of screwing a dame who used to have more than a beaver in her panties.' Lawrence felt a pang of remorse at the truth of this. 'But think about it!' she went on. 'My whole career had really taken off by then. I was big. I was making records, cutting deals, touring, but the whole damned thing depended on people thinking I was a sex-change. I had twelve abortions. Twelve. Hard to lose count of a thing like that. I tell you I came close to killing myself a few times. Then along comes you and lucky number thirteen.'

'You mean . . . ?'

'Well I could pretend it was the tiger or some hoary old game fisherman in St Croix but even woodcutters can do maths. Yes, dear. You're a father.'

Lawrence stared in wonder at the baby. His son. Humphrey

Junior. She handed him the sleeping child who stirred and woke with a moan but seemed content to be in Lawrence's arms and stare. She went on, but Lawrence could only look at the baby, searching its face, feeling its weight, its well-fed sleepiness against his dusty hands.

'I missed my period two days out of Miami, and normally I'm as regular as a nun. I couldn't very well get an abortion on the *Paulina* but I figured there was time after the cruise ended. That's why I got so ratty at you. I hated you for what you'd done. I couldn't stand the thought of going through it all again. I was like a caged beast on that boat. I could have thrown myself overboard any number of times. I actually plotted it. I thought about faking a suicide and getting ashore that way.' She laughed. 'That morning in St John I was actually planning on buying myself one of those kid's inflatable dinghies to smuggle back on board. I was a crazy lady.'

'Then the tiger – '

'Then the tiger . . . I had the alias all fixed years before. Changed my name by deed poll from Kopek to Merle. It was always useful for privacy. Dignity too. You can't write Lala on a cheque and expect to be taken seriously. No. Mrs Humphrey Merle, respectable widow, has been tailing my every move like a paid companion for the last twelve years. And now she's taken over and I can't tell you want a delight and a blessed relief she is. Comfy shoes, sensible dresses, no more hair dye. Well. Not much.' She patted a stray silver lock. 'Granted, the child is a tad eccentric as accessories go, but I've hired a real Southern nanny at home and people can believe what they like. I don't care if they think he's my grandson.'

'Where's home?'

She opened her mouth to reply then checked herself.

'Lawrence I – I'm not going to tell you.'

'I wouldn't follow you there or anything,' he assured her.

'I know. I trust you. But all the same . . .'

'I understand. I suppose.'

'You need never have known. I never thought we'd meet.'

'Of course.' He thought a moment, watching the baby who was still watching him, transfixed by his mouth. 'Drive you back?'

She gave him her lopsided smile and patted his knee.

'It's okay, dear. I can walk it. Can't have people talking now, can we?'

She opened the door and slipped down then held out her hands for Humphrey Junior.

'Thanks,' she said softly and bore him away.

Lawrence watched them passing through the dancing shafts of light and pools of green shade.

'Bye,' he said to himself and felt an overwhelming need to curl up on the cab seat and hide, from the world, from the trees, from the reproachful, childish eyes of the untrusting deer.

CHAPTER TWENTY-FIVE

Lying Humphrey Junior briefly on a lounger, Mary slipped her robe off her shoulders then carried the baby gently into the basking pool. She would always think of herself as Mary. Plain, simple, Polish Mary Kopek, never as Lala or Serena Merle. Mary was the face beneath the make-up, the innocent bone beneath the experienced flesh. The secret name lent her power like a magic charm. She had only uttered it once, in the woods that morning, and, as she had said to poor, sweet Lawrence, no one would ever believe him.

Humphrey mewed with pleasure at the warm water. If he peed she would have to swish him about to make it diffuse. Other baskers glanced their way, little frowns qualifying their dutiful smiles. This was not really a place for a baby, but then this was not really a place for Mrs Humphrey Merle either. Honeymooners disliked the presence of a baby. It reminded them of the mixed pleasures that lay ahead. For so many couples a baby was less the reward of love than the karmic penalty for carnal indulgence. Mary's baby had nothing to do with either love or, seemingly, selfishness. It was the late blessing on a life, an undeserved win at the angelic lottery. She sat on the underwater shelf, feeling her back caressed by hot jets, and kissed Humphrey Junior's forehead, which tasted faintly of sunblock. A couple left the pool with clucks of discontent, the man's hairy forearm across the woman's tanned and bony back, as though he were ushering her from something unseemly.

'Screw them,' Mary whispered to the baby. 'We're on honeymoon too.'

Under the conditions of Lala's will, all the earnings from her record and video sales would continue to be paid into the numbered Swiss account from which Mrs Humphrey Merle received her monthly dividends. In the months since her 'death' and her bewildering introduction to motherhood, she had spent a queen's ransom in legal fees. She had sold all her properties and her chattels – auction houses had held grotesque memorabilia sales of Lala's gowns and jewellery. The Swiss account grew ever plumper as her life was exhilaratingly pared down in order that it might begin afresh. She had seen to it that all her friends were remembered. In a touch she thought suitably, disconcertingly Lala, but which she borrowed from Ivy Compton Burnett, she had left each of them a looking-glass from her large collection as if to say,

'Take a long hard look.'

A fitting final stage in the myth, she considered, although she half-hoped that, Elvis-like, she would continue to be subject to reported sightings from time to time. That was the hardest part – both the necessary cruelty to her friends and resisting the temptation to call them up and say guess who. She had been surprised at her coolness, however. She had stepped out of Lala and her address book, as from a discarded skin, and observed that most of the friendships were fundamentally Lala's not Mary's. Still, it was better to be mourned and missed than reassessed and found less interesting.

Running into Lawrence had been more upsetting than any number of catty newspaper tributes from long-faced obituarists. On the boat she had thought him a diversion, nothing more. He was a challenge, exciting in a smouldering, bad-tempered fashion. Had all run smoothly, she would have let him down gently by the end of the cruise then vanished, sending him some trinket to remember her by – some cufflinks from Tiffany or a good watch. He had penetrated her defences, however, reminded her of her father, caused her to fantasize about continuing to see him in another setting, and then, of course, he had made her pregnant. They had no future together, they had even less in common now that she was Madame Merle than when she had been Lala. Only if she could strip the years away and re-emerge as gawky Mary Kopek would they have any common ground and even had that been possible he would probably prefer her glammed up and strutting on his mental pedestal.

She had no qualms about keeping the baby for herself. She had carried it about inside her, she had suffered the morning sickness, stretch marks and episiotomy. She would pay the nanny, shell out the school fees, spoil the boy as she pleased. He was hers to suffer and indulge, as a wealthy man might a penniless younger bride. Lawrence's role had been biological chance. He had no rights in the matter. She would name him as father on the boy's sixteenth birthday, but only if the child showed curiosity. If Lawrence were to pursue them, however, she might consider accommodating him, but he had to make a great effort; he would be granted nothing as his paternal due. There again, she reflected, he had done the domestic thing already, had the painful memories of a wife driven and a child torn from him. He was unlikely to tread that particular path again. If he had settled here in this lovely spot it must be because he had abandoned all thoughts of pursuing the dream family.

She sat back against the hot jets, watched the steady flow of water over the thick glass wall that made up the pool's seaward end, remembered Lawrence's angry hunger for her on the *Paulina*, remembered the total power he had given her over him and thought of him alone and frustrated in the woods.

Humphrey Junior began to fret. He was tired. Roused from her reverie, she stepped from the pool, carefully dried him, and settled him in his carrycot in the shade. From beyond a hedge came the sound of guests assembling for dinner. She was not hungry. She would have something brought to her cliff-top eyrie perhaps. There was just one other guest left in the pool area now, a young woman, painfully thin, sitting stiffly on her lounger, weeping behind her dark glasses while she pretended to read *Architectural Digest*.

'Are you okay?' Mary asked her. 'Well, obviously you're not but, well, is there something I can do?'

The pale young woman shook her head. She was pretty, even with a red nose. She felt in her bag for a tissue, dabbed away her tears.

'Sorry,' she said and Mary heard she was English. 'It's just . . . He's a beautiful baby.'

'Thanks. Isn't he.'

'Is he your grandson?'

'He's mine.'

'Oh I'm sorry. You must think me awfully rude.'

'That's okay. I did have him pretty late.'

'Are you here with your husband?'

'I'm not married,' Mary said, sitting on the neighbouring lounger. 'You?'

'I was. Well. I still am, but we're separated and I'm filing for divorce. That is, I'm going to. It's time I did.'

'I didn't mean to intrude.'

'You're not. I haven't spoken to anyone all day. I was beginning to think my voice had seized up.'

'Are you here alone, then?'

'I came with my . . . my . . . Don't you hate the word boyfriend? He's not a boy, he's a man, and – '

'Your lover.'

They laughed sadly.

'Yes. My lover. He designed this place.'

'Did a good job.'

The girl nodded.

'We came for a holiday but it turns out he had clients to

visit in Monterey so he's left me on my own for a couple of days.'

Mary lay back and looked out at the gaudy sunset that was assembling itself out to sea.

'I can think of worse places to be left. Do you have children?'

'Yes. A little girl. But she's dead.'

'Oh. Oh my God. I'm so – '

'It's so stupid. She died over a year ago now and I still talk of her in the present tense. But I can't say, no, I'm childless, because that would be like denying she'd ever existed. Sorry.'

She reached for another tissue and blew her nose. Mary felt as if a cold breeze had blown down her back. She glanced instinctively towards the carrycot.

'I can't think of anything worse,' she said. 'I used to be so entirely selfish, always looking after number one. And now that there's him, I'd rather die than have anything happen to him. I've gotten like a lioness.'

'Strange isn't it? I was just the same. Till I had Lucy I was such a child.'

'What a lovely name.'

'Everyone thought it was rather old-fashioned.'

'No. It's lovely.'

'What's yours called?'

'Humphrey. Humphrey Junior.' Mary pulled a face. 'Crazy I know but it's after his father. Humph died just after he was born.'

'Oh I'm sorry.'

'Look at the two of us! There's me saying I'm not married because I can't bring myself to feel like an old widowed lady and there's you saying you've got a daughter then having to explain.'

The girl sighed.

'Orphans of the storm,' she murmured. 'My . . . Craig is worried I think of myself as a victim. First my husband, then Lucy.'

'Good God. Did he die too? I thought you said you were filing for divorce.'

'Things got pretty scary before I moved out.'

'Jesus. I'm sorry.'

'No. You mustn't be. If everyone's sorry it makes me feel like I'm a victim. I have to take responsibility. Take control. It's just that feeling hard done by can be like a really deep sofa. You just sink into it then it's impossible to get up again and you think, what the hell, this is nice, everyone feels sorry for me, why move?'

Mary nodded, glad of her dark glasses because her mind was buzzing and she didn't want it to show. She thought of Lawrence in the jeep, briefly being allowed to hold his new baby, his son, and felt compassion well up like heartburn.

'How did your husband take it? The baby dying, I mean.'

'Oh. She wasn't a baby.' The girl threatened to cry again. 'She was five.' She gulped, breathed deeply and carried on. She must have been in therapy a while. She talked as though she were used to having to. 'He wasn't around, of course. He was away. On a cruise. It happened so suddenly. An asthma attack. I don't know how he took it.'

'You didn't *tell* him?'

'I was too afraid. I'm such a coward. And by that stage, after the funeral and everything I was . . . My mother-in-law went with my father. They hoped they could get him to go home with them but he wouldn't. I don't know where he is. It's so strange. Sometimes, on my good days, I feel so lucky. Everything went so badly wrong and now I've been given the chance to start completely afresh, new country, new house, new work, new man.' She broke off, stared out to sea.

'But . . .' Mary prompted.

'Yes. But then I feel there's something holding me back. Like a ship with its sail full of wind but a rope still holding it to the harbour.'

'Are you in love with this new man, dear?'

The girl smiled almost shyly.

'He's wonderful. He's strong and clever and quite impossibly handsome – you know the kind of handsome that makes you feel plain in the mornings?'

'I know, believe me,' said Lala, briefly forgetting to be Mrs Humphrey Merle.

'And he loves me deeply and wants to protect me and make me happy. And, well, I suppose I love him back.'

'But you're not in love.'

'No. Not really. I'm not sure that can happen more than once.'

They sat in silence, the one mourning lost love, the other contemplating just how many times she had thought she would die of heartbreak but lived to fall in love all over again.

'I must just ask,' Mary said at last. 'You'll think I'm a foolish old American trout but do you know a place called Barrowcester. Did I pronounce it right?'

'Yes. Brewster. It's pronounced Brewster,' she added, amazed. 'I grew up there.'

'Never!'

'It's where my father lived before he – And my mother-in-law. Why?'

Mary thought fast, made up a name.

'Do you know the Collie-Wakefields then?'

'Sorry. No.'

'Of course you don't. It's probably a huge place. They're just some people Humph and I met on holiday once. Nice people. He was an attorney. Ah well. I better put the little one to bed properly. Say. Would you like to have dinner with another lone woman?'

'Er. Well. That would be lovely.' The girl hesitated and for a second Mary thought she had gone too far. 'But come to my room. Craig ordered me dinner there as a treat and he always orders too much because he wants to fatten me up.'

'Are you sure?'

'Positive. But don't let me drink or I'll probably cry all over you again.'

'I promise. I can bring the baby alarm with me.'

'Can I see him before you take him off?'

'Well sure.'

Mary held the carrycot up and watched the woman's face as she peered and sighed, and she tried to imagine what mysterious bad chemistry could have brought Lawrence to mistrust her so. She observed the risky openness in her. Perhaps it was just a symptom of the damage done her but she displayed a quivering vulnerability, doomed to inspire either protective Galahadism or intense irritation, never straightforward, reciprocal love.

Mary put Humphrey Junior to bed then showered herself and changed for dinner. She set up the baby monitor, pocketing its radio receiver, kissed the baby then, following the little simplified map from the room's welcome pack, made her way back along the path she had trod that morning down past the cluster of guest studios and into the thickening shade of the trees.

The staff accommodation was a broad, uneven circle of log cabins, built around one end of the service road. She had made no plans for finding him short of making enquiries, but she saw him at once, sitting on the porch of a cabin at the far side, drinking beer from the bottle with the crop-topped girl who had given her such a memorably penetrating massage the previous afternoon. She was startled to see how alike they were, the same hair, skin tone, strong jaws and bony limbs. The girl was merely a softer edition of the same idea, a duplicate drawing whose ink had blurred in a humid atmosphere.

Seeing her, they stirred, respectfully dropping their bare feet from the rail where they had been leaning them. Evidently startled, Lawrence rose to his feet. It was Mary's unvarying experience that if one acted as though strange circumstances were perfectly ordinary, others could be induced to mimic one.

'Hello,' she said brightly. 'Great place to live.'

'Er. Thanks,' said Lawrence.

'We like it,' said Crop Top. 'Care for a Schlitz?'

'No thanks. Lawrence. I wonder if I could have a word?'

'You *know* her?' Crop Top murmured.

'Er. Yeah,' he said. 'Laurie, would you er?'

'I'm already gone.' She jumped off the porch on enviably long legs. 'Nice meeting you,' she called out as she went.

'Bye,' Mary said.

'Sure you won't have a beer?' he asked her when they were alone again. The light had almost gone. She could hear the night sounds of the wood beginning. She had lain awake the previous night listening to them. He was still in his work clothes, hair mussed and dotted with wood chips, hands and forearms thickly dusty.

'Better not,' she said. 'I've dinner with a friend. But thanks.' She joined him on the porch. 'So this is where you live now,' she heard herself begin fatuously. He just nodded. She glanced through the screen door into the cabin's stark interior. A pool of lamplight showed a table and two uncushioned, wooden chairs, a single bed, some magazines and a jumble of discarded clothes. 'Sorry if I was a bit abrupt this morning,' she went on. 'I . . . I was probably as surprised as you were. I thought I'd never see you again.'

'Well I thought you were dead.'

She smiled at the truth of this.

'You win. It's good to see you, Larry. Are you happy here?'

He frowned, leaning against the door jamb.

'It's peaceful,' he said. 'I like the work. Nobody knows me.'

'So you're starting over.'

'Trying to.'

It was on the tip of her tongue to tell him what she knew but she bit the confidence back.

'Did you miss me at all?' she asked.

He smiled sadly.

'What do you think?'

She took a slow step towards him, which was all the sign he needed apparently and he drew her to him between his legs. As he kissed her, she could smell the sweat and sawdust about him and feel how much weight he had lost. He was thin and hard as a man of wood. He was eating off her discreet, widow's lipstick. He was probably leaving great hand prints on the seat of her dress. She pulled back, holding his wrists to control him. She wondered if he had slept with anyone since her. It was getting so dark she could barely read his expression, the light from inside showed her only half a face.

'Someone might see us,' she muttered. 'Your friend with the bone structure . . . did I disturb something there?'

'Laurie's just a mate.'

'Do you want her to be more? She's hot.'

'I don't think she's very interested in men.'

'Ah.' He moved to hold her again but she leaned away, letting him only clasp her arms. 'I have to go,' she said quickly, fighting the urge to linger. 'Come to my room later?'

'When?'

'Late. I have company now. Wait till you see the light go out. It's number eight. Just come straight in. Don't ring or you'll wake the baby.'

She laid a hand on his chest, at once stilling him and indulging herself, then murmured her goodbye and hurried back along the ground-lit path towards the sound of the sea. Something moved in the undergrowth causing her to gasp. She froze. Whatever it was rustled away. She used to be fearless. Tigers and motherhood had left her jumpy.

As she walked on she asked herself for the umpteenth time that evening whether she and the baby and a nanny would be quite a sufficient family, whether a large, protective male of some kind might not be an advisable addition. Perhaps if she settled somewhere with plenty of trees he might prove temptable. Vermont? West Virginia? Kentucky? She went to Bonnie's room via the restaurant so she could effect a speedy repair in the washroom. Combing her hair and repairing the pale lipstick that was still a shock after the extreme crimson Lala had worn, she was assailed by doubt and wondered whether to duck out of dinner, stow baby and baggage and make good her escape.

CHAPTER TWENTY-SIX

Laurie sat on the end of Lawrence's bed watching him dress.

'You didn't tell me you'd had an affair.'

'It never came up,' he said. 'I never thought I'd see her again.'

'She's quite *old*.'

'She's not as old as she seems. She's changed her look. She's *dressing* older.'

'Ohh so that's it . . . Are you the father?'

'No. That was someone after me.'

He turned aside to avoid her gaze and tuck his only clean shirt into his least dirty jeans. He had thought of wearing the linen suit Darius had bought him, which had gone unworn for so long, but decided it was best to appear as himself. Laurie's questioning and his denials were exciting him. He checked his face in the soap-spattered mirror over the sink.

'You going to rekindle the flame?' she teased him laconically.

'She just asked me up for a drink.'

'Uh-huh.'

'I've got to go.'

'If I'd known you were into older women, I'd never have wasted so much time hanging around you.' He fell for it, stopping with a hand on the half-open screen door to look back at her. 'Only kidding,' she said and grinned. 'Just pray that baby isn't colicky or you'll have a *really* unromantic time.'

The night felt immense around him, its velvet blackness only broken by the low-level lights which illuminated the path beside them so that, in the blackest parts, it seemed like a walkway floating in a void. Then, emerging from the woods, he saw a canopy of stars and a few guests' windows still lit up. Room Eight was one of the studios designed to blend into the trees. It was tall and circular and clad in what looked like redwood bark but was actually a cunning synthesis of wood fibres and resin. One third of the circle was balcony, facing out over the Pacific. It was known to be the best room, the one Laurie claimed was always taken by post-detox film stars or discreetly philandering senators. Lala might have died but Mrs Humphrey Merle had evidently inherited some of her influence and all of her money.

From the path, all Lawrence could see was the long, narrow window set at a curious angle high in the sloping roof so that guests could stargaze from bed. It was still alight and he prepared himself for a frustrating wait. As he drew closer, however, he heard the door open and Lala's deep voice saying,

'Good night, dear,' as she might to a woman.

There followed the sound of footsteps as someone walked briskly down the stairs and away along the path to their room. The main lights were turned off soon after that and the only thing visible was a flickering pattern cast by the burning logs in the grate. He could make out the thin trail of smoke from the chimney, grey against the purple-black sky. He climbed the stairs, made to ring the bell then remembered her saying to come straight in rather than risk waking the baby. He pushed open the door and stepped in.

The room was far wider and higher than one would have judged from outside. By the light of the glassed-in fire, he made out smoothly curving plaster walls, a granite bar, a huge sofa, an even bigger bed. He noticed the bed linen was turned back. There was no sign of the baby. Perhaps he was sleeping in the room downstairs, away from the noise of dinner. He noticed the light was on in the bathroom and could hear the bath filling. He felt a familiar hunger, like something uncoiling in his belly.

'Hello?' he said softly, his mouth so dry all of a sudden that his voice croaked. 'I waited till the lights were off. Are we alone now?'

There was a sudden rush of bare feet on polished floor-boards and something struck him a staggering blow on the back of his head. He fell to his knees and just registered the separate pain this caused him before the room was swallowed in blackness.

'Lawrence? Lawrence? Bloody hell. Lawrence! Oh Christ. Can you hear me? Wake up. Lawrence!' Someone was patting his cheek, cradling his head in their hands, his head which felt like a block in a vice. He opened his eyes, winced at the brightness of electric light, saw Bonnie and opened his eyes rather wider. Their gaze met for an instant before she jumped up, letting his head crack on the floor, causing the vice to tighten by several rapid degrees. 'What the hell are you doing here?'

He lay with his eyes closed, mentally cursing Lala, until the pain lessened a fraction. He tried to sit up but it was beyond him.

'I work here,' he said quietly. 'I thought you were some-one else. Lal – She said this was her room. You almost fractured my skull.'

'You almost gave me a heart attack. I'd just got into the bath. I thought you were – Is it very bad?'

'It's quite bad.'

'Here. Try this.' He felt her hands raise his head again to slide a cushion beneath it. 'How's that?'

'Better.' As he opened his eyes again, she stepped back abruptly as though in fear. She was naked and very thin. 'You've got very thin,' he said. She swore and ran to the bathroom to re-emerge knotting a bathrobe about her.

'It's the stress,' she said. 'You're not exactly plump yourself.'

'I don't drink like I used to. The beer's like fizzy water and the wine's – well the good wine's alright but I can only afford the bad stuff. I've given up meat too. The staff canteen's vegetarian so it's eat beans or starve.' Watching him warily, she sat at one end of the sofa, dislodging a poker which fell heavily onto the rug. 'Is that what you . . . ?' he began. 'You could have brained me.' Opening his eyes wide caused his head to throb all the more painfully. There was a time when she would have apologized, instinctively appeasing him. Instead she only continued to stare, inquisitive rather than nervous now.

He remembered Craig and tensed himself defensively. He was younger than the American, fitter too, probably, yet he found he feared him. He dreaded him as one dreaded retribution. It could be argued that Craig had stolen his wife, which gave Lawrence the moral high ground, but now that husband and spouse were reunited, Lawrence could look in her eyes and know it had been rescue, not theft.

'Where's . . . ?' he began, trying to lift his head from the cushion. 'Are you alone?'

'I'd hardly be prowling round the place with a poker if I wasn't,' she said wryly. 'He's driven up the coast to visit some clients near Monterey.' He saw the way she pulled a cushion to her as she spoke, seeking warmth by proxy. 'They want him to build them a house. He built this place, you know. Well. Designed it.'

'I hadn't realized. He did a great job.'

'Thank you.'

'Fuck it, Bonnie!' he swore suddenly, incensed that they were reduced to courtesy. She flinched, as though his exclamation had stung her cheek.

'Please don't shout.' She clutched at a second cushion as she said this; it was protection she sought, not warmth.

Ignoring the dizziness in his skull, he sat up, supporting himself on the granite coffee table.

'We're making small talk here,' he shouted. 'I don't want this.'

'So go away.'

'I want to hear about your father. Jesus! What was all that about? And – '

She cut him short, holding up a white hand as if trying to halt traffic. One of her cushions fell to the floor.

'Please,' she gasped and looked down, unable to return his gaze. 'Sorry. Please. Listen. I'm just not really ready to *deal* with that right now.'

Lawrence stared at her incredulously.

'Are you on pills? Has that bastard put you on pills to stop you – '

Again the hand went up. Her voice was tight, her anger barely controlled.

'*No*. Damn you. I'm just not . . . I took some stuff for a while. Just Prozac.'

'I knew it.'

'But I stopped. It was stopping me feeling.' She snorted bitterly. 'Which I suppose is the general idea.'

Now it was he who reached for a cushion and the relative security of mere conversation.

'So,' he said with something like brightness. 'You're living in Chicago now.'

'Yes. Craig wants us to marry. And you're working here, of all places?'

She snatched at the fleeting chance for conversation too. For a few desperate seconds they exchanged rapid, safe information. They clicked the words into place as an ineffectual screen to block out the truth neither would confront. New lives, new homes, new addresses piled up like bright building blocks between them and the undiscussable.

'Yes,' he told her. 'I – some people on the cruise were friends of Scott and Jules. They hired me as a kind of forester.'

'You've got a work permit?'

'I have dual nationality. I was born here, remember.'

'I forgot. Do you like it here?'

'It's quiet out of season. It's healthy. I think a lot.'

'What do you think about?' she asked.

She had broken the rules of the fragile game by asking the wrong question. It brought the building blocks clattering down and for a hideous moment she remembered, and he imagined, their daughter's corpse. Then each began to talk at once but they were doomed now, building on swamp mud.

'No sorry.'

'After you.'

'You first,' he said. 'Christ!'

'Does your head hurt?'

'Stupid question. You crowned me with a fucking poker.'

'You crowned me with your fist.'

'Don't lie. I pushed you. You fell. You hit your head.'

'So?' she snarled. 'You didn't punch me. I hit my head. But you left me on the kitchen floor. You left me for dead. She found me lying there covered in blood. She had heard us shouting then she found me. She drew her own conclusions.'

'I was so scared,' he said, mentally retreating. 'I remember. I – ' He was going to apologize but that now seemed crassly pointless. They each fell silent and, as the wooziness from the concussion was driven aside by the clear pain of the lump swelling on his scalp, his senses sharpened and he became aware of Lucy standing to one side, watching them both, her small eyes glittering with accusation in the firelight. He shut his eyes to make her leave.

'I should have come to Miami,' she began, her voice high with the effort of holding back tears. 'I should have come to tell you myself. I'm sorry about that. I thought I'd find the strength and then I didn't. Then we lost track of you. We all did. Then there was – you know – the trial. I didn't go to that either. I thought you'd go back to Barrowcester and I could maybe visit you there to . . . It was too late and we lost you.'

'*Craig* could have hired a private dick.'

'You don't have to spit his name out like that.'

'You should be surprised I can bring myself to say his name at all.'

'He loves me, Lawrence. I love him.'

'So? Did she? Did she love him?'

'She was starting to.' She faltered, gulped back grief. 'He loved her. He made her very happy.'

'And I didn't?'

'No. Yes. Well of *course* you did but . . . You can't just sit there, and – ' she spluttered then lost words for her anger.

'Tell me how she died,' he asked quietly.

She sighed, ran a hand through her hair then pulled her cushion tight against her.

'You know how. Dora told you.'

'No but *how*? How exactly? Was it at his – his house or in hospital? What was her last meal, her last words? Was it day or night? Did she suffer? Did you bury or cremate her? Where the hell *is* she?'

'Lawrence, I *can't*!' she sobbed. He was relentless, however. He had to be now.

'Did she suffer?' he insisted.

'Of course.'

'And – '

'What?'

'I need details. Facts.' He defied the pain in his head, lurching over to lean on the sofa near her feet. 'Don't you see I need to know to make it real.'

'She's dead. Lucy is dead.'

'Please, Bonnie. Just – ' He flinched at a stab of pain, breathed in sharply. 'Please tell me. Then I'll go. You'll never see me again.'

She told him everything then. She sat on the sofa, hugging

her legs, curled in on herself about the cushion. She was good. She understood what he needed and missed out nothing. She described her new home in detail, even telling him which district in Chicago it was in, which he heard now without interest. She described how she and Lucy could wave to one another from their beds. Hesitantly at first, then with more assurance when she saw how calmly he was taking it, she described how she began sleeping with the architect and how the child was dead when she found her.

Watching her talk he found himself seeing her afresh, as a stranger might, and being entirely uninterested in her. She was attractive, but in a way that touched him not at all. It was inexplicable that they could ever have been married. Madness. He supposed she was feeling the same about him.

She did not spare herself. Tears bathing her cheeks, she said that Lucy had not used her inhaler, which was to hand with the drugs at the bedside.

'I thought she was happy there, with her new nursery and new friends and the house and Craig, but now I think she was protecting me, mothering me, the way I mothered Dad. I think she needed me and saw I wasn't there or she saw . . . Actually *saw* me in bed with him.'

'No,' he said, appalled. 'Don't do this to yourself.'

'It's possible. It was a bad attack but she could have stopped it. She'd had bad ones before. That Easter she nearly had to be hospitalized, remember?'

''Course I do,' he said, remembering his blind panic at Lucy's heaving shoulders and colourless lips and his daughter's amazing fortitude, amounting to a kind of poise in the face of annihilation.

Bonnie's voice dropped to a dull near-whisper.

'I think she killed herself. I think she woke in the night, needing me, had a bad dream or something, and looked across the courtyard and saw my bed was empty. Oh God.

Maybe she even left her bed and came across to look! And then I think she looked the other way and saw me in bed with him. Not just in bed. Making love. We made love very late that night. I remember. He came to bed late and couldn't sleep and woke me. We'd had a bit to drink. We made quite a lot of noise.'

'This is crazy, Bonnie.'

'No, no. It's not.' She pulled her hands away from his, which were seeking them in comfort, and let out a harsh, choked laugh. 'I see it now. I haven't told anyone this. Not Dr Marcus. Not Craig. Nobody. But I see it now. We were making love and I think she saw us and I think she was shocked and afraid and probably felt utterly alone and rejected and she started to have an attack. She had a good supply of drugs at her bedside and the inhaler was there. I checked. She killed herself.'

'No.'

'She *decided* not to use her inhaler, Lawrence. Lucy killed herself.' She laughed again only now it was closer to a sob. 'I should have stayed in my room. I should have stayed in England. I should never ever have –'

'Stop it. Listen!' Lawrence seized her hands in his, seized them hard so she had to snap out of the dangerous curve she was sliding down and focus on him. 'You were *right* to leave,' he said. 'I was bad for you, which means I would have ended by being bad for her. And if he loved you and if he loved her, you were *right* to sleep with him. You're not a monster. If anything, you're too obsessed with not hurting her. I've seen –' he broke off abruptly, stumbling on the cruelly erroneous tense. 'I used to see you snatch food from her hands to read the ingredients on the packet. I used to see how closely you watched whatever she was watching on TV in case it was *bad* for her.'

'You noticed that?'

''Course I did. I know the kind of mother you were. I know you won't have gone to bed with him on a whim. I bet you havered, and worried, and weighed up the pros and the cons and even thought about asking her *permission* before you so much as kissed him. You say she loved him. She was *starting* to love him?' Bonnie nodded, biting her lip.

'She'd started to run to meet him when he came back to the house. She'd started to hang around his neck burbling on about things. He made her very confident. I think – ' She stopped, then continued judiciously. 'I think she liked him for the effect he had on me.'

'Then this blaming yourself is stupid. It's self-centred. She had an asthma attack worse than anything she'd had before. It killed her before she could get her inhaler. Nothing to do with you.'

'But she was sitting up.'

'Maybe she was sitting up when the attack started. Maybe she couldn't sleep.'

'She'd heard us making love. She woke up and she saw.'

'Listen.' He squeezed her hands between his now, his hold gentler than it had been. 'If she had started to love him, she'd have been happy at what she saw. She might have laughed at how silly you looked but it wouldn't have scared her or – You can't blame yourself. You can't. I'm as much to blame as you are.'

'No.'

'I drove you away. Maybe the flying affected her. Maybe the new house or the new water. There are so many maybes. Follow them back far enough and we end up not having her to start with.'

'I know.' Now she was holding his hands, gravely touching their scarred surfaces. 'It's just – I miss her so much.'

'I know.'

'And all this time, in Craig's house, in Dr Marcus's office, driving around the place, trying to get back into some kind of life, I knew that you were the only one who could understand because you were – '

'I know.'

He saw her surprise as he began to cry. She had never seen this. *He* had never seen this. He had meant to comfort her, to steady her mad, self-lacerating thinking but now he staggered back, sat on the coffee table and wailed. It was a terrifying noise, beyond his control. It was as if all the pains and frustrations and dark nights of anger and grey hours of remorse he had ever experienced were now dragged from him in a single, concentrated agony. It had begun as a lament for Lucy but it became a cry for himself, for his childhood, his marriage, his mother, his failure to connect, truly connect, so that chances for real happiness slid from him. Lala and her baby, Laurie on the porch, even sweet, determined Bee grasping joy with both hands on her island. It seemed to him now that he was tasting undiluted despair like black bile and that it lay in his having no future, merely an unvarying, loveless, denatured present.

Perhaps the concussion had disoriented him, but he found he was hearing the sounds coming from him as though they were not of his own making and he was beside himself as a man possessed. Similarly he found that a part of him could register Bonnie's consternation. She was like someone with a malfunctioning car alarm on a quiet suburban street. She tried to shush him and glanced about her anxiously. She even closed the sliding door onto the balcony as though fearful his noise would draw the attention of neighbours. Finally she sank to her knees on the floor beside him, touched his shoulder gingerly, then, weeping too by now, took him in her arms and held him tight against her toughly bony chest.

Her touch soothed him, his howl became a low moan then merely jagged breathing as he leaned into her neck and smelled the soapy, almond scent of her skin that he remembered. She stroked his back, held the nape of his neck and rocked him slightly, wetting his hair with her tears. At last she scrabbled for a box of tissues and blew her nose heavily. He sat back to do the same. At the sight of one another's tear-blurred faces they snorted with wretched laughter and held each other again, each hiding from the shocking mirror of the other's grief.

'When does he get back?' he murmured over her shoulder, adenoidal with swallowed tears.

'Tomorrow,' she said.

'Do you want to marry him?'

'I don't know. Maybe. Anyway, you don't want me back,' she said. 'You just want me to forgive you.'

'I . . . Do I?'

'I think we could both use a little absolution.' She pulled back, smiled sadly and pushed her fingers through his hair. 'For what it's worth, I think I do. Forgive you I mean. I think I have to. If only for my own sake. So I can push off from the shore.'

'What?'

'Nothing.' She yawned delicately. 'Just thinking of a conversation I had with an extraordinary woman earlier.'

She suddenly felt exhausted. She crossed the room and slipped decisively into bed effectively declaring the dialogue at an end. There was nothing childish about her but, spreading a blanket over her quilt to keep out the chill and sitting on the edge of her mattress, he could not help remembering the countless times he had similarly seen Lucy off to sleep. He turned out the lights so the room was once more lit only by the flames of the dying fire.

'Shall I give you our address in Chicago?' she asked.

'Do you want to?' he replied.

She thought a moment.

'Do you mind if I don't? I think maybe . . .'

He squeezed her hand to reassure her.

'As for the other thing,' he muttered. 'I mean if . . . If he wants to marry you and you – I mean. Well. Tell your lawyers there's no problem.'

She nodded. He took her sad smile as thanks. They did not kiss.

Outside, bemused in the darkness, he wandered up and down for a while, trying to discern which might actually be Lala's room. There were no tell-tale baby's cries however, and the occasional, still-lit window gave nothing away.

Back in the staff village, he saw that a light still burned in Laurie's cabin. He knocked. After a moment or two she glanced out of the window clutching a torch, then opened the door a little. She was in striped man's pyjamas. He noticed she had done the jacket up wrongly so the buttons were out of step with the holes. She smelled of toothpaste.

'Oh. Hi,' she said, scowling sleepily. 'No dice then?'

'I told you. It was just a drink. We sat and talked.'

'Oh.'

'Laurie, I – I meant to ask you.'

'Evidently.'

'Sorry. Were you asleep?'

'Not quite. What?'

'Well.' He leaned on her porch rail. 'Tell me to bugger off if you want but I wondered if, on your next free night – '

'My every night is free here.'

'Well, whatever. I wondered if you'd like to drive somewhere with me. Go out for a meal for once. Maybe to a cinema. Find some meat to eat.'

'You're asking me on a date,' she said, half as flat statement, half tentative enquiry.

'No no. Nothing like that. Just asking you out. As a friend.'

'Brother and sister sort of thing?'

He nodded.

'If you like.'

She stared at him speculatively for a few seconds.

'I like to sit really near the front,' she said, 'so the picture's really big and you have to move your head like at a tennis match.'

'That's alright.'

'And you have to let me drive.'

'Fine.'

'And choose the film.'

'Fine too.'

'Well I guess that's fine then. Only not tomorrow. I have to stay in and wash my hair. Only kidding.'

Striding over to his table just as he was finishing breakfast the next morning, Laurie threw herself into a chair in a foul mood. She had argued with Jules about her pay. Lawrence was astonished. Money was something they never discussed, yet it transpired she had been dissatisfied with her income for months and wanted a raise. Jules would not allow it and now she had impulsively handed in her notice and would be moving on in a couple of weeks.

'Where?' he asked, stunned.

'I dunno.' She shrugged, dipping a piece of bread roll in the honey and butter which remained on his plate. 'East? Somewhere they have a Fall? Come too. We could sign up with a car courier firm, drive someone's car across country for them. Go to New York or Boston. Or Vermont. Lots of trees in Vermont.'

Going about his work, he found that her restlessness had transformed his pure idyll into an ambivalently enchanted limbo. Should he go? *Could* he go? He was mowing the grass along the main drive, thinking of his mother and Darius and Barrowcester and Wumpett Woods, daring for the first time in a year to entertain the possibility of returning to them, when a car pulled up beside him and he saw Lala at the wheel. Serena, rather. Whoever she was.

'Hi,' she said, and wrinkled her nose in mock apology. 'About last night ... Do I apologize?'

255

He cut the mower's engine and walked over to lean on the car roof, unable to resist glancing past her at Humphrey Junior in the strap-on baby seat. Humphrey dutifully stared back.

'It was a shock,' he said. 'And she almost brained me with a poker.'

Lala whistled softly.

'But thank you,' he went on. 'It helped. Are you – ?'

'We're off. We've got a long drive.'

'To Wherever.'

'Uh-huh.

He could not read her expression through her dark glasses.

'Are you okay?' she asked. 'You seem, well, down.'

'I'm fine. I was just thinking. Laurie – the masseuse you met yesterday.'

'She looks like you.'

'Yeah. Well anyway, she's handed in her notice. She's moving on. So, well . . .' He shrugged. 'I'm just thinking.'

'But you're happy here, right? You're peaceful. You like the work.'

'Of course. Yes.' He nodded. Swallowed. 'I love it. I'd better get on.'

'Sure you had. Well. Bye, Lawrence. Stay well, soldier.'

'You too.'

She pressed a button that sent the window purring up, raised a hand in a mock salute and slid off down the drive. He stood watching her go then turned wearily back to the lawnmower. He thought of Bonnie waking alone and restored in her room, enjoying breakfast on her balcony over the Pacific and waiting eagerly for Craig's reliable return. He thought of Laurie pummelling someone's back and allowing her anger to be dispelled by tentative excitement at the thought of pastures new. He thought of himself and pictured a desolate blank.

He had started the lawnmower's engine again when he

heard the moan of a car in recklessly fast reverse, glanced up and saw Lala speeding back up the drive towards him, window winding down as she came.

CHAPTER TWENTY-SEVEN

It was high summer. The wisteria's heavy, blue-grey tassels of blossom swayed from the foliage that framed the open windows, and filled Dora's bedroom with their nostalgic scent. As she rose from touching up her lipstick and tidying her hair, she could see Darius and Reuben sitting in deck chairs by the pond. They were talking. It amazed her that they never ran out of things to discuss just as it amazed her, still, that her brother had at last acquired such a loving partner in debate.

Watched by the dogs, she scrutinized her appearance in the full-length looking-glass with a little pout. Dark blue suit, highish black heels, hemline on the knee. It was what Tennessee Williams called a 'neat, tailored outfit'. She tried it with the hat. Tried looking at it sideways on.

'I look like the bride's mother,' she thought.

She discarded the hat, replaced the pearls with Charlie's garnets and undid a button on her blouse. She sprayed a puff of scent into the air and walked through it in the way her grandmother had taught her. Megan sneezed and Dora laughed at her.

Until very recently, it had seemed that her days were full of yawning voids. She missed Lawrence more keenly than she dared admit, especially now that Darius was otherwise engaged. She felt the lack of Bonnie almost as a twin bereavement to the lack of Lucy. Bonnie had written ecstatically to announce that she was pregnant again. Happy for her, Dora was hurt that she should have written rather than telephoned and thereby risked a motherly inquisition. She was shocked too at the rapidity with which Bonnie was adjusting. Less than two years on, the advent of the new child could only seem the first block in a new wall between them. The new child, Craig's child, had none of Dora's blood in it and could never claim her as Lucy had. Most disturbingly, Bonnie went on to admit that Lucy was not the first baby she could have had with Lawrence. There was another apparently, aborted by her in secret when she felt she was too young to cope or commit. Of course, if she had not aborted it, Dora would still have a grandchild, Lawrence a family.

Inspired by this evidently therapeutic truth-telling and by a joint encounter on a trip they had made to an Eve Arnold exhibition, with a sequence of photographs of a birth in progress, she had confessed to a startled Hecate that Lawrence was not *her* only child.

'I had twins,' she admitted. 'There was a boy and a girl. My mother made me give one up for adoption. I had to choose. I never forgave her. I hope it haunted her dreams and speeded her to a painful death.'

Lucy's death was thus bound up in her mind in a complex of thorny loss with the effectual death of her own daughter and what now seemed the casual, profligate discarding of Lucy's unknown sibling. There was no social structure to support the bereavement of grandmothers. She felt the bleak absence as a spiritual wound, as deep as if the child had been her own, and yet nobody wrote her notes of condolence or sent her flowers or thought to ring her on hearing the news, to ask how she was coping. Certainly no one thought to remember the black anniversary. Even Darius, usually so adept in anticipating her reactions, underestimated her suffering, perhaps because he was rendered insensitive by new love, perhaps because he had barely known Lucy and therefore registered her death so little himself. Charlie, of course, had mourned alongside her for the few weeks before his arrest, but he was squeamish, unable to discuss his pain or hers. Hecate sent flowers and a note then rang or called around every day for a fortnight, and so unwittingly raised herself in Dora's esteem above any of her acquaintance. Hecate had remembered the anniversary and organized the Eve Arnold excursion as a kind diversion. Theirs was a friendship forged in death.

Sad in a useless way which apparently had no issue because it had no progression, Dora could not help feeling demoralized as Lawrence, Bonnie and Darius started new lives and left her marooned in her old one. Then she received the letter.

Dora,

My Dora. I'm sorry but I'm too used to calling you that to go back to Mrs Frost. First I want to thank you for what you did. Obviously we couldn't talk in court so I'm thanking you now. I was desperate after what I did but somehow I couldn't just give myself up and coming to love you and share all we had ahead of us made it even harder. I know you didn't know it was me you were helping to incriminate but you probably saved my life. I know you will have helped Bonnie by organizing the house sale, so thank you for that too. I gather the dogs are with you now. That's good. I was really glad to hear about the new baby on the way. She doesn't write but Craig sent me a letter which was kind of him. Poor Lucy. I still dream about her you know. Maybe that's how people live on. In our dreams, Dora, I know you may not want to. I'll understand, honestly. But would you visit me? Just the once. I'd refund your travelling expenses. It would mean a lot. They're not a bad bunch here. My cell-mate used to be a merchant seaman so he has many stories to tell but I have no one to talk to. Not properly. Still yours. Charlie.

He had been placed in Barrowcester Prison during and immediately after his trial but had now been moved to a place on the bleak outskirts of a town nearer Birmingham. When Dora rashly showed her the letter, Hecate needed barely a minute's contemplation before she decided,

'Of course you *must* go to see him.'

'But I wasn't that keen on him even before.'

'Why not?'

'He . . .' Dora wondered just how much Hecate understood. She continued to improvise wildly. 'He was always trying to get me to go out with him, as if we were two lonely, widowed people, made for one another.'

'He's not very handsome, it's true.'

'That has nothing to do with it,' she snapped, instinctively touching the garnets in the opening of her blouse. 'Keep your eyes on the road.'

'Sorry.'

'Anyway, what does it matter what I thought then? Now I know he would have seen Lawrence in prison for . . . He's a bloody murderer, for God's sake!'

'You visit other murderers.'

'Not ones I know socially.'

'Jesus was crucified with malefactors. He made one his first friend in Paradise.'

'Leave your pal Jesus out of this.'

'I think you should see him if only to tell him how angry you feel. Go for your sake, not for his. We could pray if you like, for guidance.'

'No.'

'Why not? It helps.'

'I'll go. I'll go! Just keep your hands on the wheel.'

So she wrote back to him, as dryly as she could, throwing away several drafts that she judged too confused or emotional. She agreed to come and see him at his convenience.

At the first visit, he asked for her forgiveness and she raged at him, lips tight with anger, fingers clutching at the desk between them. How could he? How could he have watched what Lawrence had to go through? Granted the boy was no angel, granted he had hurt Bonnie, they all knew that, but did he deserve *that*? Wasn't the death of his marriage punishment enough? And what about Carla Rushton? Everyone knew about her, she sneered, they had known for ages. About his little tart he wouldn't marry for the sake of his precious reputation and the honour of his dead wife. So she died to no purpose.

The venom of her words astonished Charlie but he took it all equably without a murmur in his own defence. When she had done, he merely asked if she would come again and to her surprise she said yes, of course and how about next Tuesday. She told Darius nothing of the letter nor of her visit and, having not told him at first, it grew harder and harder to tell him as the year went on. The secret compensated her, in a petty way, for his having found Reuben.

On her second visit, they began to speak of all the things they had not discussed during their affair, preoccupied as they had been with lovemaking, tongue-tied by mature desire. Charlie said he was sorry that Lawrence's arrest had exposed the fact of her never having married. He knew how hard she must have taken that. She suspected he was mocking her and parried the thrust by asking him about his wife.

'I was so young, I hardly knew what love was, much less marriage. I had to marry her if I wanted her to sleep with me. We hardly knew each other.' He laughed at the memory, tapping his cigarette on the tin foil ashtray. 'I had to get engaged just to be left alone with her.'

'Did she look like Bonnie?'

He smiled sadly.

'Yes. I suppose she did.'

Dora liked him better like this – without house, or money, or position. He had – how did Hecate put it – nothing to 'put over' her. She also found she desired him more fiercely. Biting the inside of her lip, she made him tell her about Carla Rushton.

'I was involved with her longer than I was with my wife,' he said. 'We met in a pub.'

'Which?'

'The Tracer's Arms. She was on the game, then. Very discreetly. But I still put a stop to it.'

'How?'

'I took out a lease on a flat for her, gave her housekeeping, paid her bills.'

'Was she so special? Did you love her?'

'No,' he said. 'But by Christ I wanted her. I wanted her all the time. I'd be looking round some site or talking to my accountant and I'd remember her and feel all, well, you know the sort of thing. I kept a pair of – Sorry. You don't want to hear this.'

'Yes I do.'

He looked down at his big hands on the desk and manoeuvred his wedding ring.

'Panties,' he said gruffly. 'I kept a pair in my trouser pocket. Just to feel. You know. During the day.'

'Why didn't you marry her?'

'I wanted to but – '

'I thought she did – '

'That was later. She thought it would make her a laughing stock at first. You know what a tight little place Barrowcester is. No. She preferred it the way it was.'

'I suppose she had most of the things women marry for.'

'She thought she did. Then she started talking to her friends. She learned about wills and alimony and next of kin. She worried about the lease. She wanted more security.'

'But by then you had all the things men marry for.'

'Not quite.' He grinned fleetingly. 'But most, I grant you.'

'I don't understand why you killed her. People kill for love or money and you – '

'I didn't mean to. I . . . I only hit her the once, with my fist, but she moved and I got her on the side of the neck.

It must have done something to her windpipe or a blood vessel. She just collapsed like a sack of potatoes. She was a big woman. There was a fireplace with a little brass fender. You know the sort of thing? She hit her head.'

'Then you panicked.'

'Yes.'

He nodded, tears in his eyes now.

'I tried resuscitating her. Mouth to mouth. Everything. I should have called an ambulance but her heart had stopped for so long and I thought by the time they came . . .'

Dora watched him cry, watched the blinded, clumsy way he reached for a handkerchief to mop his eyes, watched the action of his profound shame and was disconcerted to perceive that it would not be out of the question to forgive him. Forgiveness after all would be like their love affair; a private matter. It required no public declarations or speeches of defence. When he had controlled himself again, she laid a hand on his.

'Charlie,' she said, quietly.

'It's good of you to come, Dora. I never thought you would.'

'Neither did I. How we've both surprised ourselves.'

'Why didn't you marry when you first came back to England?' he asked. 'You're an attractive woman.'

She smiled to herself.

'So I've heard,' she said then she sighed. 'But even lovesick men used to think twice about taking on another man's son, legitimate or no.'

'So you made do with married blokes?'

'I'm sure I don't know what you mean.'

'Bonnie dropped a hint or two.'

'The little cow.' Dora unclicked and closed her handbag clasp. 'And I thought I was so discreet.'

'I'd have had you like a flash years ago.'

'Ssh!'

'You know I would.'

'Yes but there was Carla Rushton.'

'She paled beside you.'

'Nonsense. I'm sure she was . . .'

'Marry me, Dora.'

'No.'

'Please.'

'Now you're being ridiculous.'

'No one need know.'

'Why? What possible – ?'

'Bonnie won't have anything more to do with me now, I know that. Before the baby's born she'll divorce Lawrence and marry Craig. I'd see you well provided for. I've no use for the money. Not now.'

'I'm very comfortable, thank you.'

'Yes but – I'd just like to know that you were there.'

'Well I am here.'

'You know what I mean. We could do it here. The chaplain could marry us. It happens more often than you think.'

'Then you get out in twenty-five years' in time to join me in some tasteful sheltered housing development of Darius's. No thanks.'

'Please.'

'No, Charlie. Let's talk about – '

'I love you, Dora.'

'You can't do. Not really.'

'I love you. You're all I think about. I lie in my bunk at night and stare at the moon through that tiny window.'

'Spare me.'

'And I think of you.'

'You're becoming fixated. Stop it.'

This was one of those rare occasions when she felt keenly the lack of a mother. Dora smiled at the thought of how mortified hers would have been by what she was about to do. Hearing tyres on the gravel, she snatched up her bag and hurried down with the dogs at her heels, keen to avoid a meeting between Darius, Reuben and Hecate Murray. She had given her strict instructions to dress as though this were simply another afternoon of prison visiting but, knowing Hecate, she would have splashed out on some ill-judged finery that would give the game away and incur an inquisition.

Dora flung open the front door and waved to Hecate who, as she had feared, was wearing a corsage and a pink hat with netting on it.

'Hang on,' she barked, meaning 'stay in the car,' then walked briskly round to the pond to say goodbye to Darius and Reuben and ask them to keep Rex and Megan with them so Rex didn't chase the car into the lane.

'You look smart,' said Reuben sleepily, rubbing Megan's ears.

'Why are you so dressed up?' Darius asked.

'This old thing? I just wanted something a little fresh. They see so few nicely dressed women, poor things. You don't think it's too much?'

'I think it's a treat for them,' Darius assured her. 'Where's St Joan?'

'In the car. Leave her alone. Bye, darlings. I'll be back by six.'

'I'm cooking,' Reuben said. 'So you don't have a thing to do.'

'How sweet of you. Help yourselves to tea and gin and things. Bye.'

Hecate leaned across to open the passenger door for her. When Dora fastened her seat belt, Hecate kissed her on the cheek in the solemn way she had that made Dora feel they were initiates in some secret society.

It was a rather charming ceremony in the tiny prison chapel. Charlie had arranged for flowers to be delivered – sprays of lilies, mock orange blossom and pink roses. Hecate was matron of honour and the other witness was Jeff, the merchant navy cell-mate, a gentle, tattooed giant with sad eyes who shook Dora's hand as though it were made of snow and smiled at Hecate so warmly she blushed to her roots. They were married in the eyes of church and state, using the wedding ring Dora had worn fraudulently for years. Charlie gave her one, deep, startling, pepperminty kiss before the warders stepped forward to lead him and Jeff away. Dora had to sit down a moment to recover her composure while Hecate prayed stoutly beside her. Then the chaplain led them both back to the bald sunlight of the outside world. At Hecate's request, he assured them he would see that at least one of the floral arrangements found its way up to the bridegroom's cell.

'An honest woman at last,' said Dora in the car park, as she opened the half-bottle of champagne Hecate had kindly brought in a chiller bag. 'Cheers.'

'Praise His name!'

'Phooey.'

'Will you tell Bonnie?'

'I'm not telling a soul and neither are you.'

'Cross my heart. It does seem sad, though. I mean, no reception, no presents, no honeymoon.'

'All three greatly overrated. No more of this for you or you'll wrap us round a tree on the way home.'

Darius was alone in the kitchen when she came in. He was diligently peeling and slicing potatoes. Apparently Reuben had received a telephone call from his agent with a commission to write the authorized biography of the singer who had died so shockingly on the cruise.

'He's rushed into town to hunt for her recordings in the music shop to get him in the mood. It's quite a coup. She died with a huge following. Just the career boost he needs.'

'Good.'

She pecked his cheek, hoping he would not smell champagne on her breath. She had sucked fruit pastilles all the way home till her tongue was sore.

'So he's left me to make a start on dinner. It's rather rich. A creamy, mustardy, lamb thing. Do you mind?'

'Sounds lovely.'

'You know his book will have to mention Lawrence in the last chapter?'

'Of course. He was with her when she disappeared.'

'And they were, well, involved rather by then.'

'I didn't realize. But I'm sure Reuben will do it all as tastefully as possible.'

'Yes.'

'I'm very glad, you know.'

'Are you?'

'He's a dear. I don't know why it took you so long.'

'Me neither. Perhaps it's our early mistakes that help define the rightness of our later choices. Drink?'

'Not just yet.'

'There was some more post after you went. It's in the hall. There's . . . There's a letter from America.'

'From Bonnie?'

'Actually I think it must be from Lawrence.'

In the hall, Dora brushed the other letters aside and picked up the airmail one. It was from Lawrence and this time he gave a return address. In Kentucky. Stunned, she opened the garden door and walked outside to enjoy it in privacy. The cathedral bells were ringing in the distance, presumably after someone's wedding, and the still afternoon air was criss-crossed by swifts which swooped across the pond after newly hatched flies. On the far side of the lawn, the bantams ran loud, ungainly races after beetles on the floor of their run.

Dear Ma, he wrote, *Sorry to take so long to reply. You must have thought I had died. You know me and writing. Never my strong point. But there is always the telephone so there's been no real excuse except sadness and fear and general uselessness. The longer I left it the more difficult the idea of hearing your voice down the line seemed to be. Almost – sorry! – like talking to someone in Heaven. Also I didn't know what to think about Charlie. I still don't. And that stopped me writing or whatever for a bit. It all seems so far away from here, almost as if it belongs to the past and is no longer important. Thanks for all those newspaper cuttings, by the way, and for dealing with the salerooms over my stuff.*

Another reason I never wrote was because I was never sure how long I would be staying. I kept thinking I might move on, might come home, no point in writing now etc etc. And now so much has happened and so much time has passed. But that's enough apologizing or you'll run out of patience and I'll run out of paper!

I've had two jobs, working for someone else this time. For a year, nearly, I was the forester – actually a glorified groundsman – in an amazing hotel called Cliff Ranch, at Big Sur. It was very quiet and remote and beautiful. I think Lucy would have liked it. Like all the staff, I had my own cabin in the woods. I think most of us were there because we were escaping from something or getting over something but no one said that aloud. I felt at home there right away.

I saw Bonnie. Quite by chance. Here some word beginning with M was crossed out. *Craig had designed the place and brought her there on a visit. I didn't see him. Just her. Don't worry. I behaved myself. We had a long talk. She tries to blame herself for Lucy. I told her not to but I doubt it did any good. If she wants a divorce, she can have it, but she hasn't asked yet.*

Now I've moved to the other side of the country. A guest at Cliff Ranch, an amazing woman, very rich, called Serena Merle, actually headhunted me to run her estate in Kentucky. There's her and her little boy, Humphrey, and Willa the nanny (who's local and can tell fortunes with coffee grounds) and Laurie and me. We're like family together. We all live in the same house and eat at the same table. We get to ride the horses as well as care for them. Humphrey is great. Rather serious but very sweet. Reminds me of Lucy sometimes. I miss her so much you know. She haunts my dreams. Poor Ma. I bet you miss her just as badly. No one ever talks about bereaved grandparents but of course they suffer too.

'Bless you for that,' thought Dora.

I should have explained: Laurie worked at the Cliff Ranch too. Laurie Petersen. I know this sounds strange coming from me but she's my Best Friend – just like people were meant to have in school. Don't get excited. She's not my girlfriend or anything like that. We just clicked straight away. Like missing parts of the same jigsaw. If Serena hadn't come along, Laurie and I would be travelling around together like a pair of hobos. She reminds me of you – don't be cross – not so much to look at but when she's impatient with me . . .

Dora cursed the disorderly thinness of his narrative, desperate for details.

She's the one in the pictures. Looks like me, I think you'll agree, so people tease us about being long-lost twins. Of course she's not my twin, she's very American. But she was born in central California, like me, before her parents adopted her and took her to San Francisco. And she climbs trees barefoot better than I ever could!

Dora stopped reading to pull out the handful of photographs still in the envelope. There was a cabin beneath massive trees and a view of a sunset with an indistinct figure, possibly Lawrence, waving. The third caused her to sit heavily on the tree seat. It showed Lawrence and a woman, arms round one another's shoulders, sitting on a white painted fence with some beautiful horses behind them. The first shock was that Lawrence was tanned, had cut his hair very short and was smiling as he had scarcely done since he was a little boy. The second was the woman. She was his height and build exactly, slim-hipped, small-breasted, her hair cropped like his, a silver star on a leather thong about her neck, vivid against her honeyed skin. Hair and jodhpurs aside, she was the very image of Dora at that age, Dora picnicking with Darius in the sand dunes at Studland Bay with a wildly happy little boy between them.

It was her daughter. She had no doubt of it. The un-named girl baby she had barely held and kissed before the midwife placed Lawrence in her arms and took his sister off to another room and another life. With another, better pre-pared, married and certainly older mother. In their first weeks at the Ahwahnee, the doctor had made an inspection and confirmed it would be twins. Dora had panicked at the thought. How would she ever cope? They would wear her out! Leave her penniless! She half hoped the prospect of such a burden on their cast-off daughter might cause her parents to relent. Her mother had agreed with her. Twins were too great a burden. She had not relented however. If they both lived, she must give one up at birth, the girl if there was one. She wrote to a discreet adoption agency on Dora's behalf to arrange matters in advance. She wrote on hotel notepaper, naturally, using an assumed name lifted from a suitably sordid novel in the hotel library.

Dora turned back to the photograph, staring at it so closely that her eyes ached and began to water. Hecate would have praised her friend Jesus. Dora merely sat back on the bench, her head against the rough bark of the walnut tree, and closed her eyes as she squeezed the letter and photographs against her empty belly. Should she tell him, she wondered. Should she raise spectres and secrets and demand blood tests and ugly proofs? Surely all that mattered was that Laurie – so strangely named in harmony with her brother – was alive and happy and reunited with her other half? She determined to say nothing to Darius but to raise the matter with Hecate when they next spent time together.

Already the mute repository of one great secret, her friend could easily accommodate a second.

She read the last few sentences in a daze, having to reread phrases her eyes had scanned but her mind had not taken in.

I think you'd like Serena. She's calm, like her name, and dry and rather sexy (!). Would you be very disturbed if I took up with an older woman? I think maybe that's what I've needed all these years. Men grow up so much later than women and some of us, Serena is always pointing out, never catch up with them at all. She says to ask you to visit. (She's sitting nearby with Humphrey as I write. In fact me writing at last was her idea.) Would you like that? Come in the autumn to see the trees turn colour. Do write soon. And come and stay. I mean that. Then he signed off, as he never had before, *Much love, and to Darius, from Larry.* There were two kisses.*

Feverishly, she shook another photograph from the envelope. It was taken on a blue verandah with wicker seats and bushes in pots. Laurie and Lawrence sat on either side of a skinny black woman who held a toddler on her lap. All were laughing except for the toddler, who looked furious. Looking closer, Dora made out the reflection in the window behind them of a fourth adult, the elusive Serena surely, taking the photograph. She was tall, wore a dark dress and had a straw hat on. Dora could see little of her face but the figure intrigued her, the strength in its arms, the solidity of its pose. It was so typically maddening of him to trail a clue to something desperately interesting right at the end of a letter then to break off as though he had simply lost concentration and wandered out of the room.

She re-read the letter, scanning for clues. Lawrence had set up house with three women; a smokescreen worthy of her own ingenuity over the years. If he had indeed taken up with a rich, older woman, she found that she, who had just married a known murderer, could embrace the situation with benign equanimity, such was her welling relief at his happiness. She liked the sound of this Serena – even if the witch *had* seduced her blundering son. She had always liked the sound of Kentucky, too; more Irish than American. She would talk to Darius about her finances. Perhaps she could afford an autumn trip and even take an internal flight to call in on Craig and Bonnie. For fairness' sake. If they'd have her. She could picture herself with the mysteriously potent Serena on the blue verandah, drinking afternoon Manhattans and watching Lawrence and Laurie exercising horses in a paddock in the golden autumn light.

She heard a car swing up the drive, then Reuben's light voice greeting Darius, and hastily stuffed the photographs back into the envelope. These were revelations and possibilities she wanted to cherish alone at her leisure. A few minutes later, the young man emerged from the house, his jaunty walk expressing as always his extraordinary confidence. He carried a small shrub in a pot.

'It's a white lilac,' he said. 'I remembered you saying how much you'd like one in the corner by the bench there. It's not very big, I know, but they grow quite fast apparently.'

'How sweet of you.' Deeply touched at this small but significant gesture, unconsciously so well timed, she stood to kiss his cheek. 'An unbirthday present. Let's take it over there now. I might even dig it in before supper so it has a nice cool night for settling its roots in. It's going to be boiling tomorrow.'

She took the plant from him and they followed the path around to where an old stone bench stood diagonally across the corner where the evening sun warmed the old walls.

'Perfect,' she said. 'If I plant it right there, behind the bench, it can form a lovely scented canopy.'

'Your bower.'

'Exactly,' she said, and laughed, squeezing his hand.

He left her so that he might stop Darius spoiling the lamb. She took off her elegant heels and stepped into the battered gardening shoes she kept in the greenhouse, then dug a hole. She forked in compost and a little dried blood and bonemeal and poured a bucket of water into the packed cavity. Waiting for it to soak in, she looked about her and noticed how heavily the fruit trees had brought forth after the brutal pruning Lawrence had meted out. Laxtons. Worcester Pearmains. Conference pears. Victoria plums. She would have enough to leave boxes of windfalls outside the gate for passers-by. She thought of Charlie in his cell with the heady scent of lily and smelled again the rose she had held back from the bouquet to place in her button hole. She thought of Bonnie with Craig and beautiful Laurie with Lawrence – or Larry as he now was – with mystic Willa, wealthy Serena and the sweet, solemn baby. She heard laughter from the kitchen and pictured Reuben leaning his chin on Darius's shoulder. Sixteen months ago she believed her small, fragile family damaged beyond repair and now, though further flung, it was twice the size and encompassing her with a more secure shelter than it ever had. She prised the lilac free of its plastic pot, teased out its roots and rested it into the moist, nutritious hole.

'Burial brings new life,' she thought, pressing the soil back about it with her ungloved hands. 'How do we manage to go so awry, break so utterly apart and still find the strength to continue?'

AUTHOR'S NOTE

Heartfelt thanks to Susan Boyd and Glenda Bailey for the country and western cruise,

to Charlotte Windsor and Philip Gwyn Jones for bearing with me,

to Armistead Maupin, Terry Anderson, Peter Gadol and Stephen Gutwillig for showing me California,

to all those patient bridge partners,

and to my mother, whose cuttings and counsel helped me start a garden of my own.

Cornwall, 18 September 1996

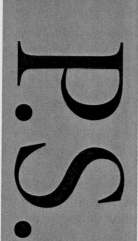

p.s.

Ideas,
interviews
& features . . .

Q & A with Patrick Gale

What inspired you to start writing?
Reading, undoubtedly. I was blessed in coming from the sort of family where everyone read at meals and nobody ever told you off for preferring reading to being sociable. Writing emerged quite naturally from all the reading when I was still quite small, and again I was lucky in that I was encouraged but not too much so that I didn't get self-conscious about it. I never thought it would become a career, though. I was trying to become an actor and writing was just something I did, a sort of itch to self-express . . .

When and where do you write?
I'm a daylight writer and tend to keep the same writing hours as my husband does farming ones. We get up early and, if I've a book on the go, I'll start writing as soon as I've walked the dogs. In good weather the dog walk often becomes the writing session as I like writing outside and we have a lot of inspiring corners where I can settle, looking out to sea or hunkered in the long grass. We have very patient dogs . . .

Your novels are often set in places you know very well. What significance does the setting have for you in this novel?
What matters with a landscape in fiction is what it draws from the characters. One of the delightful ironies in life is that we take ourselves off to different places thinking it will help us and, hey presto, all the same

problems – only probably more so – in a prettier setting! I'm dreadfully lazy geographically; I write about places on my doorstep. *Tree Surgery for Beginners* begins and ends in Winchester, which I disguised as Barrowcester, but emotionally, if not geographically, I was describing my boyhood home. When I wrote it I was unhappy, spending a lot of time away from home and restlessly travelling which possibly expressed itself in both the almost ceaseless motion of the story and the palpable relief in its rooted, pastoral ending.

There are many dramatic – often traumatic – twists and turns throughout this novel. Have you experienced life-changing events which have led you to write fiction with such intensity?
My life hasn't been without its traumas but I think it's more that I'm drawn to trauma in plots because I like the way it peels back the layers on a character. Whether my plots are serious or comic I suspect they all involve the central characters in being tested or tried to some extent. I think there's something fundamental about the experience of reading fiction that makes the vicarious enduring of a trial and an eventual sense of healing resolution deeply satisfying. But yes, I confess I have a weakness for old film melodramas and they have a way of influencing some of my plot twists, consciously so in *Tree Surgery for Beginners*. ▶

6 I think there's something fundamental about the experience of reading fiction that makes the vicarious enduring of a trial and an eventual sense of healing resolution deeply satisfying 9

Q & A with Patrick Gale *(continued)*

◄ **And yet the books almost always end happily. Do you feel pulled towards writing a happy ending?**
I don't think endings need to be happy so much as right and satisfying. In a curious way I experience in writing a novel all the things I hope my reader will experience in reading it. I usually begin with a problem or a trauma and a clutch of characters and the plot that grows from those characters will usually involve a working out and a resolution that may or may not be happy but will often feel healing. Reader and writer together need to feel they've emerged on the other side of the novel's events with a broader sympathy or a better understanding. Without that a book just doesn't feel like a full meal . . .

Would you categorise yourself as a romantic novelist?
If I hesitate to it's only because romance fiction isn't a genre where my work comfortably sits. But I am an incurable romantic, if that means believing in the power of love to heal and transform, and my novels are, repeatedly, about love and its effects, and love-gone-wrong and the effects of that. Perhaps I'm a love novelist? I think romantic novelists tend to focus on the getting of love – following the Austen pattern of plots that end in marriage – whereas I'm just as interested in the losing of love and in its rediscovery, late in marriage, in unromantic middle age or whatever.

Your characters often suffer from depression and mental illness, and in many

cases we see the huge impact of their childhood on them and particularly their relationship with their parents. What is your view of psychotherapy and do you see fiction as a form of therapy – for the writer and for the reader?

Psychotherapy and its processes fascinate me and I often cite psychotherapist as the job I'd like if I had to stop writing. But I'd never dare undergo it myself in case it cured me of my hunger to write fiction. On one level my characters are like patients and my task is to help them find their own way out of their dilemmas. I think the best kind of novels are the ones that take the reader on an emotional journey similar to the psychotherapeutic one. We learn about ourselves through empathy with fictitious characters. I certainly know myself a lot better through my years of writing, almost too well sometimes . . .

How important is your sexuality to you as a novelist?

It was very important initially as it convinced me, in the arrogance of youth, that I had a unique insight on love and marriage, which in turn gave me the confidence to keep writing. I'm rather more realistic these days and I'm so very settled that I'd have to go and do some serious research if I was to write with any precision about contemporary gay life. I don't think gay people are automatically blessed with such insights, for all the claims made in various shamanistic faiths about true vision only existing outside the circles of reproduction. I do think, though, that being gay and having had a childhood ▶

6 We learn about ourselves through empathy with fictitious characters. I certainly know myself a lot better through my years of writing, almost too well sometimes . . . 9

5

Q & A with Patrick Gale *(continued)*

◄ where I felt neither flesh nor fowl for several years really freed up my ability to try on the different genders for size. I've never felt like a woman in a man's body, but relating to men sexually certainly gives me an area in which I can be confident of conveying something of the female experience. I've always had close women friends and I come from a family of strong women – those two things have probably helped my writing as much as my sexuality, but perhaps they're all linked.

Do you have a character with whom you empathise most strongly in this novel?
Time and again in my books there seem to be characters, often old, often female, who stand outside the novel's central circuit of sexual or familial relationships. And I suspect these are my way of projecting myself into the narratives like a sort of chorus, albeit one with dubious wisdom. In *Tree Surgery for Beginners*, it's Dora's relentlessly well-meaning Christian friend Hecate.

Your exploration of family relationships – between parents and children and between siblings – is at the heart of all your novels. How often do you fictionalise your own experiences?
I think I do this all the time, and probably never more so than when I convince myself that I'm making something up. It would be impossible to write about relationships – not just familial ones – without using the relationships I have or have had as my points of comparison. I may make my plots up, but

the relationships I portray have to be based fairly closely on what I know (and know intimately) to be the case.

Even though you often present unusual family set-ups in your novels, and show the power of overwhelming sexual desire, you seem to uphold marriage and commitment too. Do you have a strong conventional side?
Oh heavens yes. Like a lot of keen gardeners, I suspect that I'm a spiritual Tory, for all that I've read the *Guardian* all my life. I come from an immensely rooted and conventional background. My father's family lived in the house they built for five centuries. The three generations ending in his father were priests and my father could so nearly have been one too. Both my parents were deeply, privately Christian and had a daunting sense of duty. I rebelled against all this for all of five years in my late teens and early twenties but deep down all I ever wanted to do was move to the country, marry a good upstanding chap and create a garden . . .

Can you talk a bit about the importance of music in your life?
I so nearly became a musician. I was a very musical child and sent to schools that specialised in it, to the point where I couldn't conceive of doing anything else when I grew up. First acting and then writing blew that idea aside, thank God, but music remains my magnetic north. I work to music. Every book tends to be written to a cluster of pieces which haunt my car's CD player or live on my laptop and I find this a really useful ▶

Author photograph © Graeme Craig-Smith

LIFE *at a Glance*

Patrick Gale in 1997 when *Tree Surgery for Beginners* was first published.

BORN
Isle of Wight, 1962

EDUCATED
Winchester College; New College, Oxford

CAREER TO DATE
After brief periods as a singing waiter, a typist and an encyclopedia ghostwriter, among other jobs, Gale published his first two novels, *Ease* and *The Aerodynamics of Pork*, simultaneously in 1986. He has since written twelve novels, including *The Whole Day Through* and *Notes from an Exhibition*; *Caesar's Wife*, a novella; and *Dangerous Pleasures*, a book of short stories.

LIVES
Cornwall

7

Q & A with Patrick Gale *(continued)*

◄ emotional shorthand for helping me resume work on a novel if I've had to break off from it for a week or two. I have music going round in my head whenever I'm walking or cooking or gardening to the point where I really don't see the point of getting an MP3 player.

The importance of nature is a recurrent theme in your novels. Do you enjoy being outdoors? If you weren't a writer, what job would you do?
I'm very outdoorsy and never cease to be thankful that I was able to marry a farmer and end up surrounded by fields and sky and cliff-top walks and wonderfully dramatic beaches. I owe my parents for the outdoorsiness as they made us take long walks with them throughout my childhood and the habit has stuck. Not just walking, though. I'm really keen on botany and insects and birds and regularly drive the dogs crazy with boredom on walks because I keep stopping to look things up in guide-books. If I weren't a novelist and couldn't be a psychotherapist, I can imagine being very happy as a jobbing gardener. Nothing fancy, just mowing lawns and pruning rose bushes. Farmer's spouse is a pretty wonderful position too, though. We have a herd of beef cattle and I love working with them. ■

Top Eleven Books

1. *Persuasion*
   Jane Austen

2. *Middlemarch*
   George Eliot

3. *Tales of the City*
   Armistead Maupin

4. *The Bell*
   Iris Murdoch

5. *Collected Stories*
   Mavis Gallant

6. *The Wings of the Dove*
   Henry James

7. *Dinner at the Homesick Restaurant*
   Anne Tyler

8. *Remembrance of Things Past*
   Marcel Proust

9. *The Flint Anchor*
   Sylvia Townsend Warner

10. *The Woman in White*
    Wilkie Collins

11. *Collected Stories*
    Saki

The Writing of *Tree Surgery for Beginners*

by Patrick Gale

IT'S SAFE TO say that *Tree Surgery for Beginners* baffled my publishers. My previous novel, *The Facts of Life*, had been a big, fat thing covering three generations of a family's tormented lives and loves. A thoroughly serious book, for all its moments of gaiety, which seemed designed to stop me being marketed ever again as a comic novelist. And instead of delivering more of the same, I handed over a sort of picaresque fairy tale, mixing light and dark in equal shares, which began for all the world like a detective story and ended bathed in pastoral sunshine and unexpected blessings.

I was not a very happy animal at the time of writing. I had lost my way emotionally and, because *The Facts of Life* had never found a publisher in America, was feeling professionally nervous too. The only delights in my life were the acquisition of an impossibly subversive deerhound cross called Fingal and being taught bridge, to which I became briefly addicted.

Two things besides bridge fed directly into the subject matter of the novel, one unhappy and one surreal. The unhappy one was the breakdown of my brother's marriage after twenty years and all the distressing fall-out that entailed. The surreal one was my being invited by *Marie Claire*, the magazine whose generous commissions to write scurrilous life stories of dead filmstars had been paying my mortgage for a while, to fly out to Miami and join a country and western cruise around the Caribbean. My brief was to find out what country and western meant to women. My way of surviving the ordeal was to hide in the library with my short-tempered companion night after night and play bridge with two Scandinavian ladies who had not been able to book the bridge cruise so had booked the country and western one on the off chance they would not be the only refugees . . .

Time and again I find that, when I think I'm writing a story to amuse others, I'm unconsciously writing it to comfort myself or to work through some unspoken conflict. I didn't exactly write this one on automatic pilot but I consciously avoided plotting it out in advance the way I usually do but simply started writing and let the characters take me where they would. What emerged had elements of fairy tale – dark secrets in woods, the contemporary equivalent of a woodcutter and a princess and even, arguably, an enchantress – and echoes of *A Winter's Tale* and Shakespeare's 'problem' plots in the harsh lessons Lawrence and his wife must undergo. Looking at it again after all these years I think I was probably angry with my brother and set out to put his fictional surrogate through the emotional mill but ended up feeling amused by and then sorry for him. Those three linked impulses caused his sections of the novel ▶

The Writing of *Tree* ... *(continued)*

◄ to fall into three separate 'acts'. *A Winter's Tale* is a play about a man's murderous jealousy and its lingering punishment and forgiveness, but it's also a play where the women's voices, baffled and maddened by male behaviour, are peculiarly direct and I think I hoped to echo something of this by interleaving Lawrence's sections of the book with the thoughts of the arguably far more interesting women at whose hands he receives his education in love. ■

Have You Read?

Other titles by Patrick Gale

The Whole Day Through

When forty-something Laura Lewis is obliged
to abandon a life of stylish independence in
Paris to care for her elderly mother in
Winchester, it seems all romantic
opportunities have gone up in smoke. Then
she runs into Ben, the great love of her
student days and, as she only now dares
admit, her emotional yardstick by which she
has judged every man since.

Are they brave enough to take this
second chance at the lasting happiness
which fate has offered them? Or will they be
defeated by the need, instilled in childhood,
to do the right thing?

Notes from an Exhibition

Gifted artist Rachel Kelly is a whirlwind of
creative highs and anguished, crippling lows.
She's also something of an enigma to her
husband and four children. So when she is
found dead in her Penzance studio, leaving
behind some extraordinary new paintings,
there's a painful need for answers. Her Quaker
husband appeals for information on the internet.
The fragments of a shattered life slowly come
to light, and it becomes clear that bohemian
Rachel has left her children not only a gift for
art, but also her haunting demons.

'Thought-provoking, sensitive, humane . . .
by the end I had laughed and cried and
put all his other books on my wish list'
Daily Telegraph ▶

Have You Read? *(continued)*

Rough Music

As a small boy, Julian is taken on what seems to be the perfect Cornish summer holiday. It is only when he becomes a man – seemingly at ease with love, with his sexuality, with his ghosts – that the traumatic effects of that distant summer rise up to challenge his defiant assertion that he is happy and always has been.

'Hugely compelling. *Rough Music* is an astute, sensitive and at times tragically uncomfortable meditation on sex, lies and family . . . a fabulously unnerving book'
Independent on Sunday

The Facts of Life

A young composer exiled from Germany during World War II finds love and safety in rural East Anglia only for tragedy to erupt into his life. In prosperous and esteemed old age, he must then watch as his wilful grandchildren fall in love with the same enigmatic and perhaps dangerous young man – and learn life's harder lessons in their turn.

'Gale is both a shameless romantic and hip enough to get away with it. His moralised narrative has as its counterpart a rigorous underpinning of craft' *New Statesman*

A Sweet Obscurity

At nine years old, Dido has never known what it is like to be part of a proper family. Eliza, the clever but hopeless aunt who has brought her up, can't give her the normal childhood she craves. Eliza's ex, Giles, wants Dido back in his life, but his girlfriend has other ideas. Then an unexpected new love interest for Eliza causes all four to re-evaluate everything and sets in motion a chain of events which threatens to change all their lives.

'Gale's most questioning, ambitious work. It amuses and startles. *A Sweet Obscurity* is worth every minute of your time'   *Independent*

....

The Cat Sanctuary

Torn apart by a traumatic childhood, sisters Deborah and Judith are thrown back together again when Deborah's diplomat husband is accidentally assassinated. Judith's lover Joanna, the instigator of this awkward reunion, finds that as the sisters' murky past is raked up, so too is her own, and the three women become embroiled in a tangle of passion and recrimination.

'*The Cat Sanctuary* is a book with claws. It has a soft surface – a story set in sloping Cornish countryside, touching on love, families and forgiveness, delivered in a gentle, straightforward prose – but from time to time it catches you unawares. Scratch the surface, suggests Gale, and you draw blood'
                                        The Times ■

If You Loved This,
You Might Like ...

Other novels about men who have lost their way, suggested by Patrick Gale:

The Good Apprentice
Iris Murdoch
Blaming himself for the shocking death
of his best friend, Edward embarks on a
haunting quest for forgiveness and
enlightenment. One of the novels to mark
Murdoch's late second flowering in the
1980s, this is a funny spiritual thriller, if
such a thing is possible.

The Easy Way Out
Stephen McCauley
One of several delightfully acerbic comedies
by McCauley, this has a gay man, phobic
about committing to domestic bliss, coming
to the rescue of his straight kid brother and
so stumbling on the answers to his own
quandaries.

Larry's Party
Carol Shields
Like Anne Tyler, Shields was always
especially good at writing hopeless men
and few come as inadequate as Larry Weller,
the maze-designer at the heart of this funny,
tender and brilliantly structured portrayal of
late-twentieth-century maleness.

The Wig My Father Wore
Anne Enright
Enright's debut novel is a deliciously quirky
comedy in which TV producer Grace finds
her life falling apart when she falls in love,
and indeed lust, with a Canadian angel who
turns up on her doorstep.

By Chance
Martin Corrick
An entrancing modern-dress fairy tale in
which a shy engineer-turned-technical-writer
loses his exquisite wife and must spend time
in a remote island hotel in order to face up
to the terrible deed he may or may not have
committed. ■

Find Out More

www.galewarning.org

Patrick Gale's own website in which you can find out about his other books, read review coverage, post your own reviews, leave messages and contact other readers. There are also diary listings to alert you to Patrick's broadcasts or appearances and a mailing list you can join. ∎

What's next?

Tell us the name of an author you love

| Patrick Gale | Go ▶ |

and we'll find your next great book.

book army

www.bookarmy.com